Chelsea

From Waverly Fitzgerald

Fiction
St. John's Wood
Chelsea
Mayfair
Grover Square

As Waverly Curtis
co-authored with Curt Colbert
Dial C for Chihuahua
Chihuahua Confidential
The Big Chihuahua
The Chihuahua Always Sniffs Twice
A Chihuahua in Every Stocking

Nonfiction
Slow Time: Recovering the Natural Rhythm of Life

Chelsea

Waverly Fitzgerald

Genesta Press

First published in hardcover in 1979
by Doubleday & Company, Inc.

First published in paperback in 1980
by Fawcett Coventry Books

This edition published in 2017 by Genesta Press

Genesta Press
1211 E Denny Way #187
Seattle WA U.S.A. 98122

For ELLEN,
whose advice is invaluable,
whose friendship is priceless,
and because
she deserves a dedication of her own

Special thanks to my family,
who made this book practically possible
and Sharon Carter, my editor,
for her wise suggestions

Contents

Chelsea

Chapter One

Introducing Wellington Willet, Gentleman's Gentleman,
and His Views on Art

IT WAS JANUARY. The waning sun shone feebly through the ice-grimed window panes, admitting a watery, weak light into the narrow attic hallway. It was late afternoon. The shadows clustered in straggling ranks along the grey walls, almost obscuring the stooped figure crouching near the one door in the otherwise Spartan corridor. It was very cold. Willet's breath emerged in a small white cloud as he pressed his large ear more closely to the door jamb and rubbed his gnarled, reddened hands together fitfully to keep them warm. From within the room he discerned the angry tones of a quarrel, and he breathed a sigh of pure pleasure, a sigh which hovered about his head as a broad white mist for a moment before dispersing. There was nothing which Willet loved so much as a quarrel.

Particularly a quarrel between his employer, Mr. Devin Sheridan, the well-known portrait painter, and Miss Flo, latest in a long string of artist's models who had become involved with Mr. Sheridan on a more than professional basis.

There was no love lost between Willet and Miss Flo. She had once, shortly after her entry into the household several months past, attempted to oust Willet, afraid perhaps of the power wielded by

1

the little valet, annoyed perhaps by the self-righteous indignation with which he treated her whenever he was forced by circumstance to deal directly with her. Her brave manoeuvre had ended in total defeat. It was, of course, impossible for a Sheridan to dismiss a Willet, for the Sheridans and Willets had been indissolubly linked since the first Sheridan had come to England with the Conqueror, a Willet in his retinue. Willet himself had served Mr. Sheridan's father, Sir Eric Sheridan, for twenty years until that gentleman died at the untimely age of forty-two years whereupon Willet immediately and solemnly transferred his attentions to the then twenty-one-year-old son, the only scion of that noble house. No black-haired avaricious daughter of a laundress from Lambeth was going to sever a union sanctified through centuries of service. To the contrary, Willet intended to see that Miss Flo should get the boot, and it was only a matter of time before this wish was realized, for whatever a Willet decided, a Sheridan must do. The Willets were the captains of the ship on which the great name of Sheridan was written, and the Sheridans, powerless to direct their course, were at the mercy of the Willet at the helm.

It seemed that Willet had not long to wait. The voices from within the artist's studio grew shriller and more discordant. Willet could pick out random words and phrases—

"What do you mean you—"

"—temper—"

"—don't understand how you can say that!"

"Let's not blow this out of proportion. You—"

"Some painted doxy—"

"—a jealous minx."

"Why, you inconsiderate, selfish boor. I—"

"Now, then."

Tucking his large hands under his armpits to keep them warm, Willet snuggled closer to the doorframe and was rewarded by at last being able to distinguish complete sentences.

"Just try to introduce another female into this here household. Go on and try. I won't stand for it. I warn you. She'll not last a day. I don't permit other females to trifle with what's rightfully mine."

"Nonsense, Flo! We're talking about a strictly commercial concern. I will merely be employing another model beside yourself."

"Hah! I know perfectly well what you mean when you say commercial concern. Didn't I begin as a model? Strictly commercial! Faugh!"

"Well, if you must, I don't recall being the one to change the terms of that original agreement. As I remember distinctly, you—"

To Willet's chagrin the remainder of this sentence was muffled by a series of scuffling noises, punctuated with occasional grunts and exclamations of pain and at length terminated with a crash of broken china.

"Now see here, Flo, don't touch that T'ang dynasty camel," shouted Mr. Sheridan, "or I'll break every bone in your body!" His threat was interrupted by the clatter of splintering china.

Sensing a precipitate climax to the argument, Willet prudently stepped aside, just in time to avoid being bowled over by Miss Flo who came hurtling through the door and bounded down the narrow, attic stairs, evidently under the impression that Mr. Sheridan was close behind her with murderous intent.

There was, however, no sound from the field of battle. Willet hopped from one foot to the other for a few minutes, simulating the energy required to run up to the attic floor. Considering himself sufficiently red in the face and short of breath, he presented himself in the open doorway, inquiring politely,

"Is there something amiss, sir?"

Devin Sheridan stood in the midst of the large, stark grey room, his hands thrust into the pockets of his velvet smoking jacket, his under lip thrust forward in the pout he had acquired in childhood. He kicked at some shards of pottery with one foot.

"Why, sir!" exclaimed Willet in assumed amazement. "That isn't—no, it can't be—is that the T'ang dynasty camel?"

Devin stared at him curiously.

"I had no idea you knew which piece was which, Willet," he commented peevishly.

"I thought, sir," Willet replied with great dignity, "that it behoved me as butler of this establishment to be aware of the factors which contribute to the unique value of the various art objects you collect. Now it is my understanding that T'ang dynasty figurines are usually found in excavations of the tombs and are admired for their use of coloured glazes, particularly when applied in a dappled pattern. Is that not so, sir?"

"And figurines of the Bactrian camel are much appreciated for the spirit of the poses, but that is neither here nor there now, is it, Willet?" swore the artist, stepping on a shard of porcelain with a savage scowl.

"Quite," was the succinct reply.

A few minutes of silence intervened.

"May I ask how it occurred, sir?" Willet ventured.

"That vicious, scheming, little, green-eyed—" Mr. Sheridan said through clenched teeth.

"Miss Flo, I presume, sir," put in Willet smoothly. "A regrettable accident, but surely we mustn't blame her for clumsiness, a certain gaucherie which one might, I venture to guess, expect in a girl of her class."

"It was no accident," muttered Mr. Sheridan, stepping over to the nearest window and attempting to gaze out through the frost and mist to the Thames which usually lay beyond. This evening the streaming surface of the river was indistinguishable in the gathering gloom. "She did it deliberately."

"Surely not, sir? Why, what would occasion such an immoderate response?"

"I merely informed her of my decision to use a new model for the picture I intend to submit to this year's Royal Academy exhibit."

Willet lifted an eyebrow.

"Hard to believe, isn't it?" snorted Devin derisively. "She flew off the handle, began clawing at me, calling me names. Absolutely extraordinary display of temper." He shook his head in wonderment.

"Very odd, sir," Willet replied. "Most peculiar. Perhaps she objected to the person you selected to be your new model."

"But that's just it," said the artist, turning away from the window and taking out a cigarette from the silver case within his jacket pocket. Willet stepped forward with a quivering flame, which Mr. Sheridan applied to the end of his cigarette before extinguishing it with a quick and practised exhalation of fragrant smoke. "I haven't chosen a model yet. I know exactly what I require, have had it in

4

mind for months now, but I can't find the girl. I've been round to all the agencies. I've interviewed at least two dozen likely prospects. I've got Algernon out looking for me. I must drop by every studio in London twice a week on the off chance that some young lass will have just arrived looking for work, but nothing! I'm beginning to despair of ever finding her."

"Perhaps you will discover that Miss Flo will do as well," put in Willet primly as he stooped to collect the shards of broken china.

Mr. Sheridan's lips compressed and his dark eyes grew darker. "Willet, are you an artist?" he inquired in ominous tones.

"Indeed not, sir."

"And do you intend to submit an entry in this year's Royal Academy show?"

"I should say not, sir."

"Then permit me to observe, Willet," Devin said cynically, "that I must know more about my requirements in a model than you."

"You make your point quite clear, sir."

"Not that I don't thank you for the suggestion," the artist added jovially, having made his point. "But it would never do. Flo doesn't have the proper manner for the picture I envision. She did fine for all of those medieval costume things, she had the pallor, the sort of dreamy absence that one wanted. But now I demand vitality, a sort of fresh, country quality, the sort of face which goes with a big, courageous heart and, most importantly, red hair—thick, waving, glorious red hair."

"Red hair?" Willet's eyebrows dipped in slightly towards the bridge of his large and prominent nose.

"Don't eye me like that, damn it, Willet!" snapped the artist, tossing his half-smoked cigarette into the fire on the hearth. "When I say red hair—thick, waving, glorious red hair—I mean precisely that. No one but another artist would understand how significant such a detail can be. The hair is the main design element of the picture. If it lacks the warmth, if it lacks the body, if the face does not carry out the promise of the hair, or vice versa, the entire project might as well be abandoned."

"If you say so, sir," was the nearly toneless reply.

"Well, I do, and it may—have to be abandoned, that is," said Mr. Sheridan gazing down gloomily on his empty canvas sitting upon an easel near the windows.

"I trust such discouragement is merely temporary, Mr. Sheridan, sir," Willet observed quietly, withdrawing towards the door. "There must be a hundred girls who fill that description in London alone."

"A simple statement for you to make," was the bitter rejoinder. "It's always easier to make a general remark, than to produce a specific result."

"I cannot agree, sir, with your insistence on the rarity of this sort of female. Why, I know a young lady who must be exactly the sort of person you have in mind."

"Who is she, Willet?"

"A young friend of the family. Now, sir, I trust you recollect that Lady Holly will be here within the hour to discuss your doing a portrait of her daughter."

"What's her name?"

"Lady Holly's daughter? Why, Constance, I believe."

"No, no, you stubborn old ox. The young friend of the family. The girl I need for my picture."

Willet shook his large head slightly. "Oh, she wouldn't do. Not at all. She's not a model, quite the opposite, she's a nursery governess."

"Let me be the judge of that."

"But, if you will permit me to differ, sir, you cannot be the judge of that. It's an established fact, not a matter of judgement. She's employed by a family in Bayswater as a nursery governess, two little girls, five years old and three years old, and another on the way, though of course I've phrased that poorly as there's no way of knowing whether the new one will be a girl or not. Even Mrs. Davenport can have no way of knowing that, not at this point."

"Goddamn the man! Willet, I've never known anyone who can be so direct when he wants something of you and so indirect when you want something of him. What's the girl's name?"

"Sir, you couldn't do Miss Cecily any good. Harm is much more likely. She has a hard enough life, as it is. It takes a girl of rare courage to endure as much as she does in that household. It speaks highly for Mrs. Polyander's training."

"Mrs. Polyander, now who is she?"

"My aunt on my mother's side, sir. You must remember, I told you that she runs a little school for training of domestic assistants down on the old Brompton Road. Cecily, Miss Hawthorne, attended it. Now, would you prefer the black coat or the—ahem!—amber velvet jacket for the Hollys' visit, sir?"

"Willet, how many times must I remind you that I am an artist and therefore must dress the part, not like a blasted banker or M.P.! The velvet by all means, and the address of the Davenports."

"Sir," Willet nodded stiffly, "I must earnestly protest—"

"Now, now, Willet, I merely wish to observe this girl. You tell me that there are at least a hundred girls in London who would be suitable for my picture, and then you refuse to tell me how I can find just one of them. Probably there is no such person as Miss Cecily Hawthorne."

Honesty was a strong point with Willet. He bristled at the mention of mendacity.

"Very well, sir. She is employed at Number Eleven Prokington Terrace, Bayswater, but I warn you, her mistress is a hard woman and doubtless won't permit her any visitors. Why, I was turned away myself the last time I wished to go inquire after her health," Willet's voice quivered with indignation. "The woman had the audacity to suggest that I was coming to—well, that I was not, did not harbour the paternal affections for Miss Hawthorne that I professed. A beastly, abominable woman! Which reminds me, sir. Lady Holly will certainly require some refreshments. Shall I have Cook make the teacakes special, or go out to the pastry cook's for something?"

"Number Eleven Prokington Terrace," murmured the artist thoughtfully. "Oh, by all means the pastry cook's, Willet. Lady Holly devours far more than Chlorrie could produce. Thank God, her daughter shows some restraint." He picked up a paintbrush and poked at his canvas tentatively. "Number Eleven Prokington Terrace," he muttered again.

Chapter Two

In Which Cecily Is Accosted by a Madman

IT WAS VIRTUALLY INDISTINGUISHABLE from its neighbours up and down the grimy, narrow street. Mr. Sheridan shuddered slightly as he proceeded up the front steps of Number Eleven Prokington Terrace for his aesthetic sensibility was offended by the smeared name plate over the door which read "Wee Bideaway" and the violent purple colour of the curtains which could be glimpsed through the spattered front windows. A grubby, little maid answered his knock.

Taken aback by the sight of the slim, elegant gentleman swathed in a fur-collared greatcoat who lounged upon the steps, the girl forgot her habitual greetings.

Devin took the initiative. "I'd like to have a word with Miss Cecily," he said.

The maid's eyes narrowed. "She ain't allowed to have gentleman visitors," she said sullenly, "and if she was, they'd 'ave to use the side entrance." She put her hands on her hips, and surveyed him thoroughly. "Who might you be? One of Miss Cecily's cousins?" She winked broadly. It was a particularly unpleasant grimace, twisting up her spotted sallow face into a gargoyle-like mask.

"See here, young woman. I am Devin Sheridan, the well-known portrait painter and—"

"And I'm the Queen of England," she smirked, pinching some folds of her stuff gown between her two fingers and waving them back and forth in an affected manner.

"Hannah! Stop this foolishness immediately!" came a sharp, punched voice from within the dark hallway. Its owner, a tall, pale woman with a nose as sharp and pinched as her voice and a swollen belly that loomed before her, emerged from the shadows. Her fingers fastened upon the back of Hannah's neck, and she shook the hapless girl back and forth like a terrier worrying a rat. "I thought it was only that flighty piece who calls herself a nursery governess that I had to concern myself with, but now I see that even such an ugly, spotted creature as yourself thinks to entertain a follower on the very steps of my home."

Devin hastened to correct this unfortunate connexion. "I am calling, Ma'am," he put in politely, with a slight bow and a wave of his hat, "to speak with Miss Cecily."

Hannah, seeing a chance to escape while her mistress absorbed this information, broke free and scurried off down the hall.

"Another one," declared Mrs. Davenport in tones of such disgust that she might have been looking at a dead sparrow dragged in by a cat. "I shall really have to look for another person. That girl does nothing but make assignations. First, poor Mr. Thrush, an otherwise sober and steady young man, and then," she shuddered, "an older gentleman, he appeared to be a butler of some sort. Really quite revolting. The difference in their ages. But I'm told that certain females don't mind in the least, having an old monster pawing at them and chucking them under the chin and slobbering over them. Why, he tried to pass himself off as a friend of her family's though the girl's an orphan. I made quite sure of that when I hired her. I won't have relations hanging about the place, begging for handouts and employment and such. Now, I suppose you're going to say you're a relative also?"

"A brother, Ma'am," Devin lied solemnly. "Also an orphan. I was separated from my sister upon the death of our mother and was only recently informed of her existence."

"Rubbish!" declared Mrs. Davenport. "Remove yourself from my doorstep immediately or I shall be compelled to call out my servants to eject you forcibly."

"Ah, but Ma'am, you surely wouldn't come between a brother and sister who have no one but each other in the world, a brother and—"

But the rest of his sentence was lost as the door was slammed in his face. Devin chuckled. He kicked at the door with his foot. Then, he backed up until he could see the windows in the upper story and, cupping his hands around his mouth, shouted out, "Cecily! Cecily!"

A white curtain in the neighbouring attic window fluttered down. The drawing room drapery of Number Eleven Prokington Terrace was pulled aside, revealing the haggard countenance of Mrs. Davenport. She knocked at the pane with a set of bony knuckles.

"Cecily! Cecily!" Devin continued to shout out, his rich baritone echoing in the crisp, winter air. A dog in a nearby kennel began to howl. Mrs. Davenport emerged from the front door brandishing an umbrella.

Considering that he could not penetrate the inner sanctum of the Davenport household nor coax the captive damozel from her imprisonment within, Devin shrewdly withdrew. He set off through the chill January afternoon, contemplating with increasing rage and chagrin the unsuccessful outcome of this errand. Ignoring the puzzled stares of passers-by and the scowls of bystanders, he slashed out at the tops of the bare hedges with his ivory-tipped cane as he walked along. Flocks of broken twig ends flew in a cloud about him.

It was a satisfying outlet for his irritation, and Devin became so absorbed in it, that he didn't notice the young woman who approached with her two young charges. There was not much to distinguish her even if he had noticed her. She was muffled in a drab brown coat several sizes too large for her and her face was dwarfed beneath the brim of an unfashionably bulky brown silk bonnet. Unfortunately, the bonnet itself was not fastened; it had been one of Mrs. Davenport's castaways and was missing both ribbons.

In one of Mr. Sheridan's vicious passes at the top of the hedge, the momentum of his swing brought the end of his cane into sudden and violent contact with the bonnet which promptly flew off the young lady's head, permitting her hair to tumble down in long, rich, thick, rippling waves of red. Devin stood transfixed. The two little girls, who were bundled up so snugly they resembled bulky packages, began to titter and shriek.

"Pandora!" uttered Devin hoarsely.

Cecily had once been told by her mother that the best way to stop a vicious dog from attacking was to stare directly into his eyes, operating on the principle that whoever looked down first was the weaker. She was not certain whether or not this theory applied to escaped lunatics, but she couldn't think of anything else to do. So, she stood on the London pavement, bareheaded, trembling a little with the chill and uncertainty, keeping her eyes fixed on the sinister stranger who bad just knocked her bonnet from her head.

"Pandora!" he uttered again in a harsh voice, stepping forward as he spoke.

Cecily did not flinch. Instead, she regarded the man carefully, hoping to discern some weakness by which she might elude him. He did not appear to be an escaped maniac for he was well-dressed, though with some eccentricity. His coat of grey felt trimmed with dark fur was well cut and obviously costly. His longish and luxuriant dark hair and his unusually slender cane with a peculiar caryatid carved in ivory at the tip were evidences of a certain degree of affectation, but his soft, yellow kid gloves, his highly polished boots and his meticulously brushed grey top hat were all in impeccable taste. His eyes, however, disturbed her the most. So dark brown in colour as to be almost black, they were glittering with a strange and fervid intensity.

"Pandora!" Although the stranger's voice had become lower and softer, Cecily started at the third repetition of this name.

"I fear you are mistaken, sir," she said distinctly. "You must have some other person in mind for that is not my name." She turned her head and bent to pick up her bonnet.

It was just as her mother had warned her. As soon as she had looked away from him, he attacked. With one swift movement he had stepped forward, taken her arm and pulled her close to him, pinning her with his hypnotic eyes.

At the same time, one of the two little girls at her side deliberately jumped upon the disregarded hat, squashing it into the dirty slush which lay in the gutter.

Cecily broke loose from her attacker's grip and struck out at Flossie, with a sound box to the ear. The child began to bellow. She had an ear-deafening cry, the achievement of five years of constant practice.

"I'll tell my mama," she declared between howls. "I'll tell her that you meet strange gentlemen on the street, and take down your hair for them, and hug them where everyone can see! I'll tell her you threw away that bonnet and called it an ugly old thing! You wait and see if I don't, Miss Hawthorne."

"Why, Flossie, you spiteful little beast," declared Cecily, giving her a brisk shake. "You'll do no such thing." She attempted to drag her truculent charge along with one hand, fumbling to do up her hair with the other.

"If you will allow me to help—" suggested Devin.

"Really," said Cecily, turning on him, her eyes flashing. "I think you've done enough damage as it is. You've frightened me half out of my wits, you've exposed me to Heaven knows what sort of ridicule and comment on a public thoroughfare, and you're likely to cost me my position, for all I know. If you can think of some other humiliation to which you can subject me, pray save it for another time." She tugged at the string which fastened the smaller child's coat, and propelling Flossie with a firm grip on her shoulder proceeded up the street.

"No, wait!" called out Devin. "Miss Cecily, I must talk to you."

The use of her real name sent a shiver down Cecily's back. It confirmed her suspicions that the man was some sort of lunatic and that her life was in great danger. Her pace became brisker.

"Stop! Please hear me out, Miss Cecily!" called the artist desperately. "You mustn't worry about your position. I came to offer you employment, employment—well—with room and board, we can work it out—excellent pay. I'll double what you're earning now."

Cecily was almost running as she rounded the corner toward Prokington Terrace, pushing Flossie before her and dragging Sarah behind, her hair flying loosely about her face.

"You'll be the toast of London. I'm an artist. I want you to sit for me. I—damn it! What's wrong with you, girl? Why are you ignoring me? I know! I have it! Willet! Yes, Wellington Willet. Do you know him? Do you remember him? Deuce take it, you must remember him!"

Cecily paused and looked back over her shoulder. "Mr. Willet," she repeated softly. "Yes, he was Mrs. Polyander's nephew. He's a valet to a—to a—well, to an artist."

"Mr. Devin Sheridan of Number Seven Swan Walk, Chelsea, very pleased to make your acquaintance, Miss," said the artist with a hurried bow.

Flossie slipped from her governess's grasp and went scampering up the pavement toward Number Eleven.

"Flossie! Come back here this instant!" shouted Cecily. The little girl, slipping on the icy pavement in her haste, went rolling into a bank of muddy snow, and then, scrambling to her feet, scurried up the front walk.

Cecily sighed. "They never mind," she said, whereupon Sarah, whom she was holding firmly by the coat-strings, bit her upon the hand. With a yowl of pain, Cecily released her, and Sarah went bowling up the walkway following her sister. Cecily glumly sucked her bloodied knuckles.

"I'd be glad to find a new position," she admitted frankly, favouring Mr. Sheridan for the first time with her warm and open hazel gaze, "but I'm a nursery governess. What could I do for an artist? Give Mr. Willet my regards."

The two little girls had managed to rouse the household with their yells and poundings upon the door, and now it opened to reveal the grubby little maid.

"Coo! Are you going to catch it, Cecily," she called out. "Mrs. Davenport! Mrs. Davenport!"

"I'm quite serious," put in the artist quickly. "I want you to model for me. I'm doing a portrait entitled 'Pandora' for this year's Royal Academy show. I'd like you to be the model. I can provide you with room and board, a good salary, you've no need to stay here."

"I assure you, Mr. Sheridan," began Cecily, but was interrupted by the angry exclamations of Mrs. Davenport whose peaked face and misshapen stomach had appeared in the doorway.

"Come in at once, Miss Hawthorne. That man is some sort of lunatic. Something has badly frightened the children, and I expect you to explain it to me, and, oh my gracious goodness! What have you done to your hair, you wanton creature?"

"There's the end to my ever seeing a day off," declared Cecily, with a little moan. "I can explain everything, Mrs. Davenport," she called out.

"Well, I should certainly hope so," snapped Mrs. Davenport. "I've a good mind to find someone to replace you if it wasn't just as likely I'd get another thieving, sinning, lying snippet like you. All servants are a bad lot these days."

"Thank you for your kind offer, Mr. Sheridan," said Cecily, putting out her mittened hand to shake his. "I'll think of it with gratitude and hope someday to see some of your works. I'm very fond of Art."

As their hands clasped, she allowed herself for one moment to consider seriously the prospect of escaping from the drudgery and misery of life at the Davenports. An end to lying awake nights shivering in the unheated attic bedroom she shared with the loathsome Hannah, who alternated between snoring and grinding her teeth. No more sharp pinches delivered by her harsh mistress, no more sarcastic lectures on her duties, nor vicious innuendos about her personal life.

Freedom from the fumbling and ardent advances of Mr. Davenport who lay in wait for her at the foot of dark stairs with hot breath and moist palms, whose rolling eyes remorselessly followed her as she went about her tasks. And blessed relief from the torments devised by Flossie and Sarah, whose intelligence Cecily would have questioned were it not for the cunning and perspicacity with which they designed and engineered various traps for their governess.

"Miss Hawthorne, I am warning you," Mrs. Davenport announced in a voice shrill with rage. Her daughters had joined her at the door and were jumping up and down in gleeful anticipation of Miss Cecily's imminent castigation. "My patience is wearing very thin."

"I don't understand how you endure it," put in Devin sympathetically. "Why don't you turn around and walk away with me now?"

"I'll have that maniac prosecuted to the full extent of the law," screamed Mrs. Davenport, locating the umbrella she had wielded earlier and venturing out to reclaim her nursery governess.

"I wish that I had the courage to do so," Cecily murmured ruefully, before Mrs. Davenport gained upon them and, fastening her bony fingers about Cecily's wrist, began to beat Mr. Sheridan about the head and shoulders with her umbrella.

Chapter Three

A Hasty Retreat and an Unexpected Guest

IT WAS A BLEAK, GREY, DEMORALIZING MORNING, and yet Wellington Willet, valet extraordinaire, buzzed about the corridors of Number Seven Swan Walk with a merry tune emanating somewhat creakily from his throat. Rain had been falling steadily upon the London streets and the London rooftops for the past twelve hours, and despite the fact that he would have to slop through the mud and water in a waterproof and galoshes (a costume which ordinarily insulted his dignity) in order to walk Mr. Sheridan's terriers (a task which customarily he resented as a waste of his talents), Willet was actually smiling as he ascended the stairs.

It was past noon, the Countess of Throttle was due at one for a sitting, and Mr. Sheridan had not yet rung his bell for his morning coffee. Nonetheless, Willet, who was under strict orders never to wake his master without being summoned, rapped briskly on the door of the bedchamber and trotted into the room without awaiting a reply, saying as he did so:

"What a lovely day, sir. A trifle humid, one must admit, but then the vegetation appears more handsome by contrast. A wonderful day and a wonderful opportunity to capture on canvas the agreeable countenance of Lady Throttle, who is your first sitter today."

The man upon the bed, who was not readily identifiable since he had the bedclothes drawn up over his head and a pillow pressed against his ears, groaned, a muffled groan but a groan nevertheless.

"I beg your pardon, Mr. Sheridan?" Willet said politely, bustling about the room fetching stockings from the drawer, setting out a tie, draping the trousers over the chair and, in general, performing the complete morning ritual preparatory to shaving and dressing his employer.

Again the groan, this time unmistakably more violent, and the upheavals of the pillow and bedclothes confirmed this impression.

"I cannot distinguish your words, Mr. Sheridan," Willet said jovially, inspecting the nap of a jacket which he was brushing thoroughly.

A rumbling was heard, similar to the sort of rumbling heard before the eruption of a volcano. Bedclothes, pillows, garments began to fly through the air in every direction. The shaking of the sheets became more extreme until at last a figure, ghastly in its aspect, rose up from the middle of the bed and, like a fiend portrayed in some lurid horror tale, poised as if to fall upon the hapless valet.

Willet did not seem at all perturbed.

"Good morning, sir," he chirped brightly.

"Goddamn it, Willet," roared his employer, who now seemed ready to rend his valet into tiny pieces. "Why have you woken me? Did I not hire you with the distinct instructions that you were never to enter my bedchamber in the morning until I rang?"

"One does not hire a Willet," the valet replied, unperturbed. "One inherits him. I do believe that you made such a request, sir, at the time of my engagement."

"Then why the devil have you ignored it?"

"No Willet ever ignores a reasonable request, sir," Willet responded equably. He faced Mr. Sheridan and added blandly, "You rang, sir. Have you forgotten?"

Devin Sheridan sank down upon the bed with a moan, burying his face in his hands. "I cannot believe it," he muttered tonelessly. "Why don't I remember it? What happened? Why do I feel as if I have been run over by a train?"

"A very telling description, sir," Willet said primly.

Mr. Sheridan staggered from the bed, supporting himself against one of the elaborately carved bedposts.

"What did I have to drink last night, Willet?" he asked cautiously.

"You had me bring up the specially bottled Chateau Lafite, sir. That was after the brandy and...ahem...the champagne."

"Good Gad! After the price I paid for it, I was particularly saving it for a memorable occasion"

"I fancy the other gentlemen will long remember both the wine and the occasion, sir. I believe the white pique waistcoat is the most appropriate for Lady Throttle, if that's agreeable with you, sir?"

"The orange silk," Devin muttered mechanically, "How often must I remind you Willet that—"

"That you are an artist and not a banker or M.P. Very well, sir."

"What gentlemen?" inquired Devin, massaging his temples with caution.

"Gentlemen, sir?"

"The gentlemen you mentioned. The ones who were... ahem... attended my little, well, gathering last night."

"Oh, those gentlemen. Merely a few of your colleagues. Mr. Alma-Tadema, Sir Frederick Leighton, Mr. Millais, Mr. Poynter, I believe that was the lot, oh, Mr. Lawson."

"Lord, I didn't realize my invitations were so well received. And what did we discuss?"

"To be sure, I couldn't say, sir. Pardon me, I believe that's Betty with the coffee." Willet marched briskly to the door and opened it a crack, just wide enough to permit the silver tray to slide through but not so wide that the maid could see Mr. Sheridan wrapped in the embroidered burnous that served him as a *robe de chambre*. Not that Betty would have made such a mistake anyway; she kept her eyes discreetly upon the carpet. Willet, nodding his head with approval (for he had been responsible for hiring and training her), sent the maid off with a mumbled "thank you" and placed the contents of the tray upon a small inlaid table which he drew up before the armchair.

"Hem," said Devin reflectively, as he settled down before this feast, taking a sip of the coffee and then biting into a warm, crumbling croissant. He had acquired a taste for the latter during his student days in Paris, and now there was nothing for it but Chlorrie, the cook, must learn to make croissants for his breakfast. Remarkably, she had a real talent for producing the buttery pastries, and they were the featured attraction at Mr. Sheridan's notable Sunday breakfasts (which he held in friendly rivalry with Mr. Whistler's.)

"You know, I don't believe you, Willet," the artist mumbled through a mouthful of his breakfast. "I've never known you to be unaware of one word spoken in this house, whether or not you were in the vicinity of the speaker."

The valet, who was absorbed in straightening a recalcitrant collar, paused and stared off into the space between the molding and the ceiling. At length, he said quietly, "I do seem to recall a great deal of conversation relevant to the upcoming Royal Academy show. Mr. Poynter told an especially amusing tale about certain differences which developed between his various models."

"I don't suppose I had much to offer on that point," put in the artist glumly.

Willet twisted the ends of the collar with skill and care. "To the contrary, sir. You described your model in detail, sir, and I might say, rather frank detail. You informed the company that her name was Cecily Hawthorne, and she was currently employed as a nursery governess in Bayswater."

"Good Lord!" groaned Devin.

"You called for a toast to her beauty, sir," Willet went on relentlessly, "and you promised that all of London would be able to talk of nothing but her after they had seen her portrait. You waxed eloquent, sir. One might even say you rhapsodized."

"This is dreadful."

"That was when Miss Flo broke the Nanking vase over your head."

"Not the T'ang Hsi vase with the dragon on it?" cried Mr. Sheridan in horror. "Why she wouldn't dare to touch that. She knows how much I value it. And she knows what I would do to her if she even threatened it."

"You did, sir," replied Willet mournfully. "You did."

"I did what?"

"You slapped her, sir."

"I slapped her? Before all of the guests?"

"Indeed, sir. Though it was rash, I dare say the guests thought it not so unreasonable when they saw what she did next."

"What did she do next?" inquired Devin with growing apprehension.

"She kicked you, sir, with amazing accuracy and vigour, in a rather delicate spot, sir, which I fancy might account partially for your sensation of having been struck by a locomotive, which you forbore like a gentleman, sir, with great dignity and admirable silence, except, of course, for your groans."

Devin groaned.

"Quite by contrast, Miss Flo was most vocal and revealed her questionable ancestry and breeding in the sort of epithets she hurled at you."

"Epithets?"

"Merely comments upon your artistic ability, revelations regarding your financial affairs, and aspersions about your manliness, sir."

"That's the end of it," Devin shouted leaping up and pacing back and forth across the room. "I won't put up with her sulking and her fits of temper and her destructive rages any longer. I rescued her from the clutches of that lecher, Griot. I saved her from a life as a laundress. I made her famous with 'The Girl in the Red Cloak,' only to have her smash my possessions and assail my character. No, it's too much. I don't ever wish to lay eyes on her again. You go, Willet, and inform her—"

"That won't be necessary, sir," Willet interrupted.

"Not necessary?"

"No, she has left already, sir." Willet could not repress a smile of triumph. "I can only surmise that she was afraid to face you this morning, sir, after her conduct the previous night."

The second half of his sentence went unheard for his employer, with a briskness contradicting his former languor, had rushed out the door and raced up the stairs to the chamber Flo had occupied. He could see at a glance that everything Willet related was true. Flo's customarily cluttered room was devoid of all signs of life. There were no scent bottles, no ribbons, no fringes of curls, only crumbs on the dressing table, and the pictures which had lined the mirror, mostly sketches of Flo done in pencil by Devin, were gone.

"I might add, sir," put in Willet sharply, appearing at the door, "that she got none of the silver or plate" (these were the items under Willet's care) "though she did depart with some of the linen and many little household ornaments. She tried to take the picture you did of her as 'The Ballet-Dancer in Repose,' but I wrested it away from her, sir, upon the threshold."

Devin noted the absence of the delicately coloured Copeland candlesticks which had adorned the bedside table. Also missing were the pretty marble French clock from the mantel and the twin pierced-silver lanterns which Devin had purchased in Venice. Across the bed, which had been stripped of everything—linens, the counter pane, even the pillows—lay a celandine-green silk Japanese robe, gorgeously embroidered with golden chrysanthemums. It had been a recent gift from Mr. Sheridan, presented on Christmas and worn only once. Flo complained that it did not suit her; the colour tinged her pale complexion with a greenish cast and the style was outlandish. Now with the contempt born of parting, she had savagely torn it in two, flinging the severed halves upon the bed in a gesture that cut Mr. Sheridan to the heart.

He drew out a cigarette from a silver box he carried in his pocket and lit it with a slightly shaking hand. Inhaling heavily, he gazed out of the rain-streaked window at the jumbled roofs and chimney pots of his neighbours and out to the Thames, sleeping in a shroud of fog. From far below came the sound of a knock.

"That is doubtless Lady Throttle, sir," said Willet, in a voice which was faint, as if far away. "It is past time for the sitting. If we could get on with the morning toilet, sir?"

"One moment, Willet," came the remote reply. The smoke of the cigarette curled up and brushed against the frosted windowpane as if attempting to escape and join its larger brother, the fog, beyond. Willet tapped his foot upon the ground. It made a faint but distinctly irritating sound. Still the man at the window did not stir.

"You wish to be alone, sir, which I can certainly understand. Permit me to withdraw and see to your guest," Willet said, attempting a new approach and expecting a quick refutation. None was forthcoming. Willet's bluff had been called and there was little he could do but retreat down the stairs (after clearing his throat several times and saying, "Very well, sir," twice), thinking as he went, with a certain superiority which was not one of his nicer traits, that his employer certainly was a jellyfish where women were concerned.

Betty was coming out of the drawing room as Willet gained the front of the house and he inquired pleasantly as to whether or not she had offered Lady Throttle any refreshments.

"But it isn't Lady Throttle, Mr. Willet, sir," declared Betty, wide-eyed. "'Hit's a strange young person and she says she's here to see you or Mr. Sheridan. I don't know what to do with her, sir. She's dripping rainwater all over me clean carpets."

Willet frowned, an expression which brought his bushy eyebrows in close to the jutting arch of his large nose and which terrified Betty so much that she scurried into the kitchen after a hasty bob. Deciding that his frown must be highly effective and thus might be used to great advantage to quell the intruder in the drawing room, Willet stalked, countenance unmoving, to the drawing room door and flung it open.

The inhabitant of the chamber was indeed as wet as Betty's description had suggested. Water was still streaming from her dark cloak and dripping off the brim of her unattractive brown bonnet. A large parcel, done up in brown paper and string, sat in a puddle beside the hearth.

"What, may I ask, is your purpose in coming here?" inquired Willet in his most stentorian tones, drawing himself up to his full height which was some four inches shorter than the young lady who stood before him. She removed her bonnet revealing a gleam of red hair, two clear hazel eyes, an upturned nose, a delicate mouth.

"Mr. Willet, don't you remember me?" she asked softly. "It's Miss Cecily Hawthorne. I've come to stay."

Chapter Four

Sets Forth the Schemes of an Unscrupulous Woman

"NOW, CONSTANCE, MY PET. This is no time to give way to qualms. We've discussed it time and again, and there is simply no other prospect. You must get a declaration from Mr. Sheridan."

"But, Mama. He doesn't show the slightest signs of interest in me."

"Rubbish, my child," declared Lady Holly in her large booming voice. She was an immense woman in every way and she had decided long ago to throw he weight around as effectively as possible. Having inherited the build of a dray-man, she proceeded to graft upon it every possible pound of flesh produced by unbridled eating and drinking, and then swathed herself in heavily ornamented costumes, feathered headdresses and bulky wraps, like the ermine capelet which lay across her broad shoulders on this crisp January morning, the mummified noses of the little rodents pressing into her capacious double chin. There was so very much of Lady Holly that the livery stable owner who had rented her the equipage which she and her daughter presently occupied, had expressed some concern about the durability of the carriage and the well-being of his horses. Constance herself, anxiously awaited the end of their journey, what with her fears about the humiliation if the carriage should break down and her discomfort at being squashed—she herself was not a thin wisp of a woman—into a corner no larger than a bedpost.

"Rubbish!" reiterated Lady Holly. "Mr. Sheridan is quite smitten with your charms. Why, upon our very first visit, he vowed that he was honoured at the opportunity to paint you—"

"Surely he was honoured at the opportunity to earn the handsome commission you offered him, Mama," Constance gasped. A shift in Lady Holly's position in the carriage had jeopardized her daughter's respiration.

"He took particular notice of your appearance, my dear on our next visit," went on Lady Holly irrepressibly and inattentively. "You must recall it was a rainy day and Mr. Sheridan was behaving in a most peculiar manner, very gloomy, very remote, yet he took the time to comment on the colour of your dress—"

"He asked me to choose a blue gown instead."

"And he admired your bonnet—"

"He requested that I remove it for the sitting," Constance put in with a small voice. "Mama, you are making a mountain out of a molehill. He treated me with the respect and courtesy with which he treats, I presume, all of his female sitters. Not only is he not romantically interested in me, but I don't believe he has the slightest desire to be married. He's still a young man and—"

"Ah, but there's the rub, as the immortal Bard so cleverly phrased it. Hamlet, my dear. You must cultivate a few allusions and some *bon mots*, a snatch of poetry here and there, if you're to move in artistic circles. 'She walked in beauty like the night—' Ah!" Lady Holly uttered a hearty sigh and clutched her large beringed hand to her fur-covered bosom. "Dear, wicked Byron. I do so love the man."

"You were saying, Mama."

"Oh, yes, thank you, my dear. Trust my sweet, solemn Constance to muster my arguments for me. You are no longer a young woman, my dove. Thirty-two years old. I am afraid you are, what we used to say in my maiden days, nearly upon the shelf. And your poor sisters. So many of them."

Lady Holly sighed. There were six Holly daughters and only one son. The family curse, it was called. The son, the present Lord Holly, had married a quiet country parson's daughter, and thus he and his wife were of no assistance in presenting the unmarried sisters to eligible parties. This challenging and incessant task (for the sisters had little beauty and less fortune) devolved upon their mother, who was fond of declaring that this project would be the death of her, while it was quite clear, for the most part, that there was nothing that so stimulated her as the development of the intricate schemes which she found necessary to secure suitable bridegrooms. Lady Holly had decided, since it made her labours all the more difficult for Alva had already won the heart of a young soldier and Olivia was the object of the affections of an elderly scholar, that none of the younger girls should marry until their eldest sister, Constance, was safely embarked upon the matrimonial path, and the heaviness of this responsibility oppressed Constance.

"I'm well aware of the burden I am upon you and my sisters, Mama," she said miserably, "and I do wish to be married. But I feel certain that Mr. Sheridan would prefer another sort of female altogether, someone with more presence of mind and more self-assurance—"

"Now, now, Constance," snapped her mother, careening to the left as the carriage swerved around a corner. "I will not accept your continual self-disparagement. There is nothing wrong with you that a little attention and application won't cure. Sometimes I think you are determined to die an old maid. And have your sisters follow in your footsteps too, alas. There's the tragedy."

"No, Mama, truly I don't wish that at all," Constance said plaintively. "It's just that I find it difficult to make conversation with gentlemen, and I don't—well I'm not, bewitching."

"Well," snorted Lady Holly, with a rear of her head which caused the peacock feathers in her coiffure to tremble violently, "if you mean 'sylph like' or 'diminutive' my dear, then no! None of the Hollys will ever be sylph-like or diminutive, more's the blessing! We're all of us solid, buxom, substantial, not to be bowled over by a stiff wind. And there's many a gentleman who admires that in a woman, your dear departed papa was certainly one." Constance repressed a smile, thinking of her father who had seemed to shrivel up as his wife ballooned out. "You must make the most of what you have and not regret the things you lack," Lady Holly continued.

"Your eyes are very fine, the sort men enthuse over, dark and soft—you must use them more effectively, my dear. Perhaps a little intrigue, like so—"

Lady Holly batted her eyes feverishly and then tilted her head to one side, favouring her daughter with an arch and girlish gaze. Constance observed this manoeuvre gravely.

"Now you try!" commanded Lady Holly.

"Oh, Mama, I can't. No, I really can't. I'd feel so silly. Oh, very well." The dutiful daughter blinked her eyes once, darted a timid and terrified look at her mother, and subsided into confusion, regarding her blue-silk skirt with fixed intent.

Lady Holly moaned.

"Well, if that's hopeless, at least we can improve upon your conversation, my dear," said the patient mother. "Now Mr. Sheridan is an artist, a rather modern artist, and his taste in conversation is bound to be modern also. You must say profound things and yet treat them as if they were mere whims, for instance, 'Ah, the weather's abject, but then that really never matters, does it?' Do you think you could manage that? Really, you don't even have to be original. I'll invent the phrases for you before every occasion."

"But, Mama," wailed Constance, "the weather isn't abject. It's bitter cold, but the sun is shining and the clouds are gone."

Lady Holly threw up her hands in a gesture expressive of exasperation. "Constance, Constance, you haven't heard a word I've been saying. It doesn't matter what it means, it must sound profound, that's all. I promise you that if you say the weather's abject when it's not, you'll be even more fascinating. Now let me reflect for a moment and I'll produce several other witty sayings for you to use this morning, but oh dear! Here it is. We've arrived. '*Veni, vidi, vici,*' as Caesar said. Now remember, you must comment about the weather. Will you do that for me?"

"Yes, Mama," Constance murmured dutifully as she was handed out of the carriage by the coachman and waited for the extrication of her mother. This took time for Lady Holly refused to jeopardize her peacock feathers, and her bulk made it difficult to remove her from the vehicle in any ordinary fashion. At length, she was removed, in somewhat the same manner a troublesome cork is pried loose from a bottle. After rigging her ermine sails and hoisting her peacock-feathered flags, Lady Holly launched herself up the walk, butting up against the front door with her usual imperious knock, Constance bobbing in her wake like a tentative tugboat.

Willet did not seem his usual, imperturbable, efficient self when he flung open the door to discover the Hollys on the doorstep. He fidgeted, he hemmed and hawed, he bit his lip, and eventually stammered out, "Oh, good day, Lady Holly, and, er… Miss Holly. We…ahem…weren't expecting you for your sitting for yet another hour. It's only ten o'clock."

"Ah, time is the chattel of fools and monarchs only," declared Lady Holly, sweeping by him, and nearly bowling him over. "Any opportunity to be in the company of a man of genius cannot be neglected, no matter how fleeting. Is that not so, Constance?"

"Yes, Mama," replied Miss Holly dutifully.

"The truth is, Madam," Willet hurried after Lady Holly, who had stopped to finger a bronze statuette which stood upon the hall table, "that Mr. Sheridan, not anticipating your early arrival, is still at breakfast. If you would care to—"

"To join him? We would adore it, wouldn't we, Constance?"

"I don't believe that was what Mr. Willet intended to say, Mama," put in Constance nervously.

"Your daughter is correct, Madam," Willet said smoothly. "Mr. Sheridan's fare is rather humble, and the amount meagre. And perhaps you would not care for the company present—"

"Well, the wretch dines with others but sees fit to exclude us. That will never do! Merely because we are not artists, but only mortals who grow weak and humbled in the presence of beautiful things, is no reason to deprive us of every opportunity to improve our aesthetic sensibilities. You don't have to show me the breakfast room, Mr. Willet. I recall its location from the day on which Mr. Sheridan gave us a tour of his very precious home. It's this dear little door down the passage here. Come along, Constance."

It was done in a moment, before Willet could intervene, before Constance could break away from her mother. The door was thrust open, Lady Holly had burst into the room, and the intimate mood of a companionable breakfast was shattered.

Devin Sheridan had been used to take his breakfasts in his bed-chamber until the advent of his new model, whereupon he had begun inviting her to join him for the meal in the cosy little downstairs room with the bay window overlooking the Thames. On this chilly morning, a blazing fire had been lit on the hearth and the panes were steamed over from the warmth within the room. A glass bowl containing two large and lively goldfish stood in the centre of the gleaming wooden, table, and a fluffy terrier slept on the window seat. Cecily had just finished describing a typical nursery breakfast at the Davenports, and both she and Mr. Sheridan were laughing. She was in the act of pouring herself another cup of tea from the polished brass teapot (not having yet acquired the artist's taste for coffee) and he was holding out to her a croissant dripping with butter, when Lady Holly came flying into the room.

Cecily, seeing the expression on Lady Holly's face, felt as if she were back under the baleful eye of Mrs. Davenport, felt the old feelings of doubt and misgivings and smallness surface again, along with their companion sentiment—resentment.

During the week since her arrival at Number Seven Swan Walk, she had managed to erase many unpleasant memories from her mind. Recollections of Mrs. Davenport's intolerance, the stinginess of the servants and the hostility of the little girls, all had been swept away with the generous approval of the artist and his household. She had been welcomed enthusiastically (perhaps a bit too enthusiastically, for Mr. Sheridan had engulfed her in a bear hug until she wiggled free). Willet ushered her up to a private room, tucked in the corner of a stairway, and Cecily was overwhelmed by the prospect of her own fireplace (which she found was always lit) and her own little window looking out over the Thames.

Reminders of the grim economy and shabby fittings of Prokington Terrace, a poverty both economic and aesthetic which had dampened Cecily's spirit, soon faded with her enjoyment of luxury and beauty which imbued Mr. Sheridan's home. Cecily savoured the opulence of the medieval library, decorated by one of the artist's friends named William Morris—the embroidered draperies, the intricate design of the Persian carpet, the elaborately carved Gothic writing desk, and the jewelled tones of the leather-bound books which lined the floor-to-ceiling shelves. She delighted in the simple elegance of the drawing room, which was called the "Whistler Room" both because of the Japanese inspiration for the decor (pale grey walls with pink-satin draperies, straw mattings on the floor, ebony furniture and a flight of fans mounted above the mantel) and for the creator of the striking portrait (a young woman with an unfurled parasol, wearing a pink Japanese robe) which hung in the place of honour. She relished the clutter of the studio, crowded with portfolios, plaster busts, discarded paintings and Chinese porcelains. In truth, every part of the house pleased her from the upstairs hallway, which sported caricatures of Mr. Sheridan drawn by various artistic friends, to Willet's snug pantry, where Cecily was a welcome guest and occasional assistant.

The most repugnant and irreversible memories remaining from her sojourn in Bayswater were those of the restrictions upon her time. The invisible chains of habit still bound Cecily to her days of servitude. She awoke before dawn each morning, expecting a grim summons and a tasteless breakfast, and it was some time before she became accustomed to the fashionable late hours observed at Swan Walk. Though she would have been willing to sit for the artist twelve hours a day, so inured was she to hard work, Mr. Sheridan could only set aside two or three hours a day to work on his pet project, the portrait entitled "Pandora." The rest of his time was given over to commissioned portraits of society ladies and social calls. Cecily was expected to amuse herself during these hours. At first, she helped Willet polish the silver and assisted Betty in her chores, only gradually realizing that she was free to do things she had only dreamed of for years—reading books, taking walks, venturing out to the Park and then to the Museum.

Despite the gradual supersession of her bad memories with delightful new experiences, there was a memory that haunted her. Yet it was not a memory from her past, but rather a memory from Mr. Sheridan's past. The spectre of Flo.

Cecily knew very little about her ousted predecessor, but she had assembled a fairly accurate understanding of Flo, her role and her character from the few clues available—the torn Japanese robe, the paintings which littered the studio, the scraps of conversation between Chlorrie and Betty which they suppressed in Cecily's presence. She even knew, though she never confirmed her guess, that the room she now occupied had once belonged to the evicted mistress.

The image of Flo she had pieced together served as a warning to Cecily of all the things she must not become. After a long chat with Willet in the pantry, Cecily reaffirmed her desire to be a nursery governess and agreed with him that her position at Swan Walk could be only temporary. She ought, Willet cautioned, to enjoy this sybaritic life while she could, keeping an eye out for openings in amenable families and, Cecily added to herself, keeping an eye out for Mr. Sheridan who was often overly warm in his greetings and exceedingly friendly with his gifts of flowers and books. She had managed to keep a fair amount of distance between them for seven days, refusing his invitations to dine and his offer to escort her to a play, only to succumb to his cajoling to join him at breakfast, the breakfast which Lady Holly invaded with her indignant eye. All of Cecily's doubts surfaced again, as well as her easily ignited temper.

"Mr. Sheridan, what a charming repast!" Lady Holly was saying. After a contemptuous glance at Cecily, she had turned her attention upon the artist. "You must permit Constance and me to join you. It is so much more amenable to the digestive processes when one dines with agreeable companions who share one's own, well, discernment and tastes. Constance, weren't you going to remark about the weather?"

"Yes, Mama," Constance said miserably. "When the weather is abject, it makes one realize it doesn't matter in the slightest."

"Indeed," said Devin with some surprise. "Allow me to introduce—"

"Oh, here's your man. Do bring in some chairs, immediately," called out Lady Holly to Willet. "Constance, observe, my little pigeon—we all call her that at home, Mr. Sheridan, because she is so sweet and mild—observe Mr. Sheridan's table. Ah, an artist's table, not like the crude accompaniments of the meal of a Philistine. No, all is conducive to the eye and harmonious to the stomach, quiet, restful—"

"Excuse me, I must leave," said Cecily, rising abruptly and flinging down her napkin. Her voice was defiant despite the sinking feeling in her heart that the position in which she found herself was a compromising one.

"Oh, no, don't leave on my account," said Constance hastily. "Why, I don't need a chair. We've already breakfasted. Really there is no need for you to leave, Miss."

Lady Holly stared directly through Cecily. "Well, I for one, would be glad of a chair," she declared, pressing her hand to her furry bosom. "That wretched butler of yours, my dear Mr. Sheridan, seems to have become completely unhinged at my simple request, and I really feel rather weak. My sensitive heart, you know." She edged around the table and plumped herself down into Cecily's abandoned seat. "There now, a freshly poured cup of hot tea is just what I require."

"Oh, I'm so sorry," breathed Constance to Cecily who was trying to leave. "We never—I never realized that Devin—Mr. Sheridan— would be, well—engaged so early in the morning. But then—oh!— I suppose I shouldn't say that," she subsided in mortification just as Willet arrived, struggling to maintain his dignity while sandwiched in between two green rush-bottomed chairs.

"Let me return the second chair, Mr. Willet," said Cecily firmly, taking hold of it with knuckles that were clenched white. "There is no need for it, and I'm sure that's fortunate for I don't know if it could have supported the weight it would have been required to hold." With a snap of her head and a flick of her sage-green skirts, she had vanished.

"I wonder what's gotten into her," mused Devin, biting into the croissant.

Chapter Five

An Aesthetic Rivalry

"AND THEN, MY DEAR MRS. FLUSTER, the wretched girl brazened her way out of the room as if nothing at all was amiss," declared Lady Holly, reaching out for the last of the nougats in a fluted dish.

Mrs. Fluster narrowed her eyes and clenched her fan tightly, though it was difficult to determine whether this was due to her guest's revelations or to the fact that within five minutes Lady Holly had consumed all of the viands which had been displayed for her delectation. "He tried to explain her away," Lady Holly rattled on, "as a model he was painting, claimed he had found her walking in the Park. Ah! Sweet Deceit, the favourite of Artists, those mendacious villains. What a farrago of nonsense they expect us to believe. Do you have any more of those delicious jam tarts? Don't bring them out just on my account, I pray."

Mrs. Fluster smiled, revealing two rows of even, faultlessly white teeth. "I wouldn't dream of it, my dear," she replied in her soft, dulcet tones as perfect as her teeth. "I do think it's the duty of the hostess to provide what is right for her guests, regardless of their wishes. Why, when Mrs. Tremblechin dined here I had the waiters serve her beef without the sauce—you know she is utterly devastated by rich sauces and our cook simply indulges in them—and I refused to allow the butler to take in another bottle of brandy to Lord Smotling who *tout le monde* knows suffers intensely with the gout." She unfolded a cerulean blue fan which matched her gown and tapped the mole alongside one nostril with it. "They both thanked me most fervently afterwards, though, as I recall, it was nearly two years before I received the little note from Mrs. Tremblechin, after she gave up eating meat altogether, and Lord Smotling, alas, never availed himself of our hospitality again. Not, I hasten to assure you because of the little contretemps with the brandy—for the poor befuddled old dear protested vigorously at the deprivation he felt—but, unfortunately, he passed away the subsequent week, falling down in the throes of a fit on Bond Street. Can you imagine?"

Lady Holly's strident voice cut across the stream of Mrs. Fluster's reminiscences. "I, for one, will not thank you for superintending my diet, a task at which I am extremely capable. If you have no more of the jam tarts, the sweet macaroni pudding will do as well. When one lives on the elevated plane of existence upon which I dwell, one requires an extraordinary amount of nourishment merely to keep up one's heart. What an absolutely extraordinary decoration that is, my dear. Would it be terribly banal of me to ask what it is intended to represent?"

This seemingly innocent question would have been impossible without a long-standing familiarity with the Fluster household for there were not many objects in the room which were not absolutely extraordinary. Mrs. Fluster was receiving her callers in a chamber which she designated as the "Early Italian Drawing Room" though by what merits it was considered Early Italian had never been made clear.

Every fashionable colour for interiors had been employed in its decoration. A high dado marched around the room in alternate bands of mauve and drab surmounted by walls of dark drab and topped with a frieze of maroon leather. Curtains of dark bluish green divided the room from the corridor; they were bossed with pale yellow and black velvet bands, with circular peacock-feather devices appearing at intervals. The pelmet was of olive-green fringed with gold, and the Indian-design rug was citrine with puce figures.

Within this motley enclosure, an equally motley collection of furnishings was grouped: a high-backed settle painted green, three satin-covered sofas; two carved oak chests, a pair of burnished brass griffins, a harpsichord and all around on various small tables of black-dyed deal pieces of willow-pattern blue china, copper vases full of peacock feathers and sunflowers in hawthorn-pattern ginger jars.

Lady Holly was pointing at a banner which hung limply from a brass rod above the entrance. It featured a pinkish-white creature, resembling a pig, though dignified with wings, rising from what could be a boulder or a mushroom, the whole design emblazoned across with the word "FLUSTER" in red Gothic lettering.

Mrs. Fluster bowed her head slightly. "My latest art work," she said with pride, "and I'm utterly delighted that you would notice it so quickly, though Pemberton told me that no one could ignore it, the concept being so ultra-original and the execution so, well, bold, the notion being, of course, that this is the Fluster family coat of arms. That is, a creative interpretation of what would be our coat of arms if we had one, though, Heaven knows; we probably do, but Mr. Fluster would forget his head if it weren't attached, so there is little chance of his recalling the coat of arms. Alas! It is lost in the murky depths of history."

Lady Holly was, for once, stricken silent and merely sat fixing her eyes upon the hanging with a glazed look. Her hostess, Mrs. Fluster, taking this as a sign that she had once again regained the lead in the heated battle of Culture which raged between the two ladies, permitted herself another satisfied smile.

In appearance the two matrons were a study in opposites. Mrs. Fluster, small and fine-boned, with skin the translucent, waxy colour of water lilies, seemed a china doll before the bulk of Lady Holly. Her waist was as small as it had been when she was seventeen, her eyes were as wide open and as startling a blue as they had been when she was a blushing bride, and her simple, Grecian-style gown of cerulean blue (to set off her eyes and her fair hair) revealed a pair of plump, white shoulders as breath-taking as the shoulders which had coaxed a declaration from Mr. Fluster some twenty-seven years previously. For despite the girlish appearance of Sophronia Fluster, an appearance whose percentage of artifice and naturalness was known only to Mrs. Fluster and her lady's maid, Spinks, she was very nearly the same age as her arch-rival.

To the great satisfaction of both, they moved in entirely different circles in London society, and seldom had to endure the direct animosity which infused the present occasion. Careful tallying of the other's artistic achievements was maintained through a network of spies, first-hand accounts and rumours, so that when news of Mrs. Fluster's purchase of a harpsichord had reached Lady Holly's ears, she came armed with information regarding her daughter's romance with Mr. Sheridan to vanquish her High Cultural adversary.

"I thought your Joconda would be here," Lady Holly declared loudly. "Constance was so looking forward to seeing her. She has such wonderful tidings to share."

"Oh, Mama, you can't be thinking of—" protested Constance, at the same time as Mrs. Fluster turned to the gentleman at her side and asked sharply, "Pemberton, where is Joconda?"

For though they had been silent, there were two other occupants of the Early Italian Drawing Room, the eldest Miss Holly, and Mr. Pemberton Fogwell, and both had been diverting themselves by eyeing each other with speculative interest. He was most appreciative of the curve of her neck as it plunged beneath the lace-trimmed edge of her collar and the ample swell of bosom evident beneath the oriental cashmere basque. Constance, in her turn, thought him one of the most handsome men she had ever seen, Mr. Sheridan notwithstanding. She admired his elegant, quiet dress, his shining black hair and his snapping black eyes immensely. But she was uncertain in her mind as to his position in the household. Had he come to call upon Mrs. Fluster? Surely not, for he was too young. Then perhaps he was a friend of Mrs. Fluster's son? But no again, for Cedric was barely out of his teens, and this gentleman was nearly thirty. Was he possibly some brand of superior servant, for he had been handing round the sweetmeats and pouring the lemonade? Impossible, for his coat was of the finest cloth, his fingers were covered with rings, and he now spoke, in tones of utter clarity, with the intimacy of a long-time confidant.

"My dear Sophronia, how can you have forgotten Joconda's insistence that without her expert intervention the soup *à la reine* for tonight's dinner would not be *comme il faut?*"

"Oh, my daughter!" sighed Mrs. Fluster, tapping herself on the head as if in castigation. "When I was young, I pored over poetry, I gazed with rapture upon fine Art, I waltzed to the music of the finest orchestras and thrilled to the Philharmonic concerts, finding what little pleasure exists in this inexpressibly woe-filled caravan through Life, in the products of the spirit, the tortured outbursts of sensitive souls, only to be afflicted with a child whose sole delight (second to the annoyance of her mother) is to putter about in the kitchen with the cooks and scullery maids, that is, when she's not mixing up some cleaning paste for the housemaid or demonstrating the proper method of turning over a bed."

"Joconda excels in the Domestic Arts, you might say," observed Mr. Fogwell, with a slight bow toward his hostess, "and you in other Arts, my dear."

Mrs. Fluster squealed with delight and tapped him playfully with her fan. "Oh, do tell, what Arts?" she asked.

"Shall we say the Romantic Arts?" he drawled.

"Why, you wicked—" Mrs. Fluster was beginning, when Lady Holly put an end to a further exchange of pretty sentiments by announcing, "Constance is going to marry Mr. Sheridan."

Mrs. Fluster's mouth dropped open for a moment and all of her perfect white teeth shone out at them. "No!" she gasped, while her mind raced over schemes to match Joconda with certain prominent artists.

"Mama!" wailed Constance in gentle anguish. She faced Mrs. Fluster and Mr. Fogwell, putting her gloved hands together in a pretty gesture of supplication, her brown eyes wide with pleading. "It isn't so. A misunderstanding. Nothing of the sort."

"Surely Mr. Sheridan must find your very presence an inspiration to him," said Mr. Fogwell politely. "Women have only to do what is most natural to them—be beautiful—and they give meaning to the world, while we frail male creatures must struggle to carve out a niche in which to huddle for protection."

"You speak like a poet, Mr. Fogwell," Constance said, forgetting her usual shyness, "for you have a very ready store of metaphors and philosophies."

He seemed startled and Mrs. Fluster frowned, though only briefly, for frowns produce wrinkles. "I am afraid I must disillusion you, Miss Holly," he replied. "I live upon my wits and my phrases, but my vocation is not poetry."

"Then what—" began Constance, only to find that her mother was poking her in the side with a steely finger. At that moment, a commotion taking place in the hall diverted attention somewhat, and Lady Holly availed herself of the opportunity to hiss into her daughter's ear, "You utterly stupid child. You can't be as naive as you pretend!"

These sharp words were muffled by the altercation in the hall which ended with the abrupt appearance of a peculiar-looking young woman who burst through the curtains.

She was a short, plain girl of eighteen or nineteen with freckled cheeks, a stubby nose, and an engaging, broad grin. Her homely countenance was at odds with her coat—a large satin pelisse trimmed with fur—and her bonnet, a fantastic concoction of velvet and quail feathers:

"Oh, there you are, Mrs. Fluster," she called out in a clear, confident voice, storming into the centre of the room. "I'm looking for Cedric. Where is he?"

A tall footman, dressed in the outlandish livery which Mrs. Fluster considered "aesthetic," looked around the curtain.

"Please excuse me, Ma'am," he said, his blue eyes twinkling, "but she wouldn't wait in the hall to be announced."

"Good heavens, Alfred!" declared the young woman. "You know I don't hold with all that nonsense. It isn't his fault, Mrs. Fluster, it's just that I'm a bit impatient this morning. Well, here are two people I don't know," she studied the Hollys with her warm hazel eyes. "I'm Veracity Flutterby, Vera for short." She peeled off her glove and presented her hand to Lady Holly who reared back indignantly at the thought of shaking hands with a social unknown.

"Vera is the daughter, the only child, of the well-known American banker, Mr. Frederick Flutterby, of New York, who is gracing our fortunate city with his presence and that of his charming wife and delightful daughter for an unspecified period of time," Mrs. Fluster said quickly. "Our Cedric has developed quite an interest in Miss Flutterby—"

"Call me Vera," she said.

"Vera," Mrs. Fluster smiled, her calm, perfect smile that narrowed her eyes as it exposed the full expanse of gleaming teeth. "They make quite an attractive couple. Mr. Fluster and I are quite pleased, and they are found at all the parties together, whispering in corners and carrying on in all those little ways that I, a matron now, have completely forgotten—"

"Not so," interposed Mr. Fogwell.

"But which I may relive when I see the pleasure my dear son derives from his association with this very remarkable and quite, quite refreshing young woman."

"Where is your mother, young woman?" inquired Lady Holly with a majestic scowl threatening to obliterate her nose.

"Why, my mother's at the hotel," the American girl replied. "Where should she be, I'd like to know?"

"Why, with you, of course," insisted Lady Holly. "You don't mean to tell me you're here without an escort of any kind, and calling upon a young gentleman also?"

"Everything is so different in America, my dear," Mrs. Fluster interjected, tapping her fan briskly upon the gilt table beside her. "It may be difficult for someone of your advanced years to adapt to such an unusual and novel practice, but I assure you, I am quite accustomed to dear Vera's delightful honesty and independence, and I find myself improved for it, I know I do, don't you, Pem?" He inclined his head "And I feel that probably there is a lesson here for all of us. Perhaps even the Fiji Islanders could teach us many things."

"Indeed!" interjected Miss Flutterby. "The Fiji Islanders could provide us with excellent examples. Nothing is so ludicrous as the preoccupation of modern, so-called civilised man with the compulsive concealment of the human body; a Temple of the Spirit, behind layers of hideous and nonfunctional clothing. Now if we adopted the customs of the Fiji Islanders—"

Lady Holly sniffed audibly.

"Miss Flutterby is ever so knowledgeable about every subject you can imagine," interrupted Mrs. Fluster quickly. "The education of young women in America is most original. They attend lectures and concerts rather than parties and balls. It seems a most judicious system, is that not so, Pem?"

"Remarkable women, American women," he drawled.

"Oh, bother," said Miss Flutterby, bending over and inspecting the lower portion of one of her legs. "I've torn my stocking. It must have been that hedge two streets back. That's the problem with these silk stockings. As flimsy as spider webs and as precious as gold"

"Good Heavens, you don't mean that you walked here," questioned Lady Holly. "Without any sort of chaperone?"

"Walking is excellent exercise," the American girl explained candidly. "I would recommend it to you; you might benefit by it. It restores the circulation and calms the temper. A more excellent remedy for every ill it would be hard to find." She proceeded as she spoke towards the round marble-topped table on which the refreshments had been laid and wrinkled her nose at the sight of the empty plates.

"Why, you've eaten all the refreshments," she said with annoyance, "and you haven't replaced them!"

"Oh, but we were just doing so, my dear Vera," Mrs. Fluster put in rapidly, "isn't that so, Pem? We were just ordering some of that sweet macaroni pudding you admired so much last week, weren't we, Pem?" She poked at him with her fan. "And the lemon custards and gooseberry tarts Joconda prepared yesterday." Lady Holly, who had been considering withdrawing, beamed with pleasure. "And, oh, Pem!" called out Mrs. Fluster, as he arose to ring for the maid. "Do ask the domestic attendant—" her pretty way of saying servant "—to furnish us with more negus. I know Miss Flutterby would enjoy some after her arduous walk, and the Hollys have quite finished with theirs."

This was a surprise to both Constance and her mother who had been previously drinking lemonade, but neither objected as the thought of the hot, sweetened wine was appealing when facing their inevitable departure into the brisk January weather.

Miss Flutterby said happily, "Well then, I'll settle down and have a bite to eat before I look for Cedric," shrugging out of her coat to reveal a dress of mandarin yellow silk festooned with Egyptian red tasselling. Lady Holly clasped her large hands together, contemplating the promised feast with pleasure, and Constance studied Mr. Fogwell, with a puzzlement clearly discernible on her face, as he held aside the curtain for the very pretty housemaid who was transporting a silver tray of refreshments.

The tray sparkled. The food promised immediate gastronomic satisfaction. A coal fire burned hot on the hearth. The young maid smiled an enchanting smile. For a moment, the scene represented the pinnacle of comforts available in a prosperous London household.

At the next moment, the tray had been upended, the jam tarts were on the carpet, the macaroni splattered over the satin sofas, and the maid was swearing at a very young child who had darted around Mr. Fogwell, become entangled in the housemaid's skirt, crashed into a table of ginger jars, and was presently clinging to Mrs. Fluster's knees crying, "Mama! Mama! Mama!"

"How the devil did you get loose, you little monster?" shouted the housemaid, dabbing at the stains on her dress at the same time as she attempted to pry the child away from her mother. "I swear to you, Missus Fluster, I had her tied up by her leading strings, just as you told me. She must have wriggled loose somehow. She's such a handful. Here, you little beast!" She slapped at the baby's hands half-heartedly.

"Mama! Mama!" wailed the little girl, who was a miniature replica of her parent, from the fair curls to the big blue eyes, the flawless pale complexion to the diminutive build.

"I paid one hundred pounds for that vase!" gasped Mrs. Fluster who sat frozen, her eyes wide with horror, looking at the shards of porcelain on the floor, completely heedless of the demands of her offspring. "Alas! Alas! Oh, Pemberton, do tell me, is there a chance, no matter how slim to salvage it?"

Mr. Fogwell was kneeling beside the shattered object, skilfully inspecting the pieces.

"I am afraid not, Sophronia," he said, shaking his head. "A horrible mishap! A dreadful blunder!"

"Mama! Mama!" whimpered the infant.

"Oh, do go away, Baby, and leave me alone," snapped her concerned parent. "Nessie, take this child away. I don't know why you couldn't watch her as you're supposed to."

"Ma'am," replied the pretty housemaid with dignity, cocking her head to one side. "I am paid to be a housemaid. I do light dusting, some cleaning, polishing. I told you when I was hired, and I tell you again, I don't answer the door, I don't make beds, and I don't wait on table. And I do not watch babies. That's the duty of a nursemaid. This child has driven me half-crazy already, with all her fussing and fretting. I cannot take it a day longer. Either you hire a nursemaid, or I gives my notice." With a toss of her head, which set all the ribbons in her hair fluttering, she pranced out of the room.

Lady Holly, who was not one to allow such an opportunity for malicious speculation to pass neglected, found her tongue. "My dear, Mrs. Fluster," she boomed in her heartiest voice, "I had no idea felicitations were in order upon the blessed addition of another little Fluster to your family. So it was your interesting condition, you artful creature, which prevented you from accepting the presidency of the Ladies Society for the Relief of Starving Artists last winter. Yet you've kept up such a busy round of engagements since then. One can hardly believe, well, perhaps there are a few tell-tale signs here and there, that you are the mother of three children, and the last at your age! A miracle surely!"

"Well, I must confess," said Mrs. Fluster with a pout, uncurling the little fingers which clutched her silk skirt, "I didn't expect such a—well, such a, well—a—rather surprising increase to our domestic bliss, and what with the Ladies Society and the subscription concert series and the box at the Opera and my promises to work at the Charity Bazaar, well I've found it a little bit annoying and awkward even, though I make the best of it. And then Mr. Fluster, he was of course, overjoyed, his Christmas child he calls her—she was born just before Christmas and a more awkward time to be confined I cannot think of—and is able to take a great hand in her rearing now that he no longer goes to the Firm, as he realizes how utterly meaningful my artistic endeavours are and how completely unsuited I am to the grosser, more mundane tasks of motherhood." As she spoke, she handed the child, still fretting, to Mr. Fogwell, who, obviously not a father himself and lacking any instinct regarding children, tucked the baby under his arm like a parcel and carried her out of the room.

Mrs. Fluster sighed and fanned herself rapidly. "I wonder how I survived the rigours of motherhood with the first two," she said languidly. "It is too difficult to be concerned with teething and whooping-cough and all the operations of rearing by hand — well, to think of it, makes me weary. Once the spirit is used to the higher realms of existence, one finds oneself unable to bear the oppression of these fleshly concerns."

"But you need a nursemaid, my dear," declared Lady Holly brightly. "What is this about your not having one?"

Mrs. Fluster darted a concerned look at Miss Flutterby, who was chewing her fingernails in lieu of the tarts and pudding, before replying with a set smile, "Oh, we just lost one. The silly girl gave no notice, merely walked away. You know the domestic situation these days. Impossible, *n'est-ce pas?*"

"Well, I shall make it a little project of mine, no, no, don't protest! I would be only too delighted to locate a suitable person for you," Lady Holly savoured the thought of a servant of her choosing in the enemy territory. "It will be a matter of a few days. I must make certain to choose the proper young person, one with the right credentials and experience, but don't disturb yourself, my dear Mrs. Fluster, I shall find this paragon of the nursery within a fortnight. There will be time enough then to thank me." She waved away Mrs. Fluster's protests. "And now I do believe," she swept her eye contemptuously over the remains of the proposed feast, "that Constance was about to remind me that we have another call to make this morning, wasn't that so, Constance?"

"Yes, Mama," replied the daughter arising dutifully. "Farewell, Mrs. Fluster. Thank you for the delicious refreshments. Good day, Miss Flutterby. Give my regards to Mr. Fogwell. Goodbye."

Chapter Six

The Main Character of Which Is a Wombat

DEVIN SHERIDAN WAS NOT the solitary sort of artist, who finds his inspiration in isolation, his subject matter in seclusion. He did not lock himself in his studio for hours at a time, refusing food and water, snarling at visitors, while working feverishly on a compelling idea. He was not an abstruse alchemist of paints, dabbling away at new mixtures in an ivory tower at midnight, nor was he an aesthetic hermit, cloistered in a barren cell, communing only with the products of his imagination.

Rather, the chaotic condition of his studio represented his preference for working in the centre of a hurricane of activity, clutter and companions. Half–finished portraits which had been promised and paid for months before were neglected while he, hot in the pursuit of a new fancy, scribbled over endless tablets of drawing paper. In order to find a place to perch while she posed, Cecily had to pick her way through heaps of discarded costumes, broken frames, rejected canvases and plaster studies of various portions of human anatomy. In addition to these obvious accoutrements of artistic endeavour, the studio contained such inexplicable items as several broken pillars, a tree stump, an old wooden sign from "The Swan and Bush," a Neo-Classic pediment, bulbous apothecary jars filled with coloured water, several wrought-iron fence railings, and an enormous cat, with rusty black fur and gold eyes, who was seldom seen in any other room of the house but would jump out at Cecily unexpectedly whenever she had settled down for a sitting.

Cecily was the only stationary individual in the realm of Mr. Sheridan's occupation. He leapt about like a porpoise, bounding up to Cecily to rearrange the lines of her gown, rummaging through the debris searching for a particular item, darting back and forth to the table which Willet kept loaded with sandwiches, coffee and brandy and soda water, or welcoming his friends and followers, all of whom possessed open invitations to drop by at any time.

Cecily had, at first, been self-conscious in the presence of these visitors, many of them well known in London for their eccentric political views, their opinions on Art or their literary accomplishments. Gradually, she relaxed as she saw they paid little more attention to her than they did to the cat or the plaster replica of a Greek athlete, jokingly called "Tommy Traddles," though she sometimes resented this inattention and frequently blushed at the liberties they took with their conversation.

Mr. Whistler could still, however, make her wince. A running feud existed between him and Mr. Sheridan, much like that between Lady Holly and Mrs. Fluster, though conducted with better humour and little spite. Cecily enjoyed the fusillade of stinging remarks which were bantered back and forth when he appeared, enjoyed seeing Mr. Sheridan, usually so self-possessed, cringe a little at a particularly telling remark, and enjoyed the snippets of gossip which Mr. Whistler was fond of recounting. But she quailed whenever he turned his bright eyes in her direction, inspecting her thoroughly with his monocle in one eye, and then whispering to Mr. Sheridan, gesturing in Cecily's direction with his cane and abruptly walking off with his strident, "Ha, ha!" still ringing in her ears.

On the other hand, she felt only sympathy and concern for Mr. Swinburne, a gangly red-haired poet, ever since the afternoon he reeled and staggered up the stairs, shrieking for Devin to come and help him wrestle his hat away from a cabman who had apparently taken custody of it in partial recompense for the fare Mr. Swinburne had refused to pay.

On a bleak, winter day, more than three weeks since Cecily's arrival at Number Seven Swan Walk, Mr. Swinburne burst into the studio again, dragging behind him a portly, long-haired stranger in a bottle-green coat.

"Sheridan! Sheridan!" he shouted, waving his arms like a windmill. "I must make you known to my friend here, Mr. Oscar Wilde. Devilishly clever fellow, Oscar is."

"And what does Oscar do?" queried Devin, taking in the newcomer's peculiar coat, which was trimmed with braiding, gold frogs, and some unusual, wild sort of fur. The young man's face was moon-shaped and pale, his hair lank and his eyes intense. In fact, he was Cecily's image of a poet.

"He's a poet! He's a poet!" Algernon Swinburne announced with a grandiloquent gesture as if beseeching the heavens to bear him witness. Cecily beamed. In a milder tone, he added, "He also writes reviews."

"My vocation is Poetry," said Mr. Wilde, in a slow musical voice, throwing off his greatcoat to reveal a dark velveteen jacket over dark knee-breeches, a frilled white shirt and a daffodil for a buttonhole. "But my occupation is Criticism."

"So, you comment upon Art, do you, Mr. Wilde?" Devin asked.

"No, I comment upon Life," was the other's reply. He studied Devin's work in progress with his head tilted to one side and a finger pressed thoughtfully to his lips. Then he turned to Cecily, enthroned upon a dusty sofa, in the amber velvet gown which was required for the picture. It set off the rich colour of her loosened hair so that Cecily, and not the small fire in the brazier, seemed the focus of warmth and brightness in the grey room. "Ah, what have we here?" asked Mr. Wilde, favouring her with his alert gaze. "An excellent likeness! Very well done!"

"You refer to the portrait?" Devin inquired, a bit confused.

"Rather to the young lady's portrayal of the subject matter of your painting. A hint of stubborn determination, a touch of innocent fear, the suggestion of a smouldering passion and, of course, the overriding curiosity one expects in a Pandora—I assume your subject matter is Pandora?"

"It is," the artist acknowledged. "Do I understand you to be implying that Cecily...er... Miss Hawthorne—is posing as something other than her natural character?"

"Ah, naturalness is merely a pose, and the most irritating pose I know," drawled Mr. Wilde in response. "One is never more true to oneself than when one is wearing a mask."

"Ha, ha! Excellent, Oscar! Capital!" exclaimed Mr. Swinburne, who bounced up and down with joy and rubbed his hands together with relish. Mr. Wilde favoured him with a slight bow.

"And the painting?" Devin asked with interest.

"At least, you don't suffer from the modern obsession with being true to Nature," Mr. Wilde said in the manner of a pronouncement. "If one wants realism, one should go to a photographer, not a painter. From an artist we require distinction, charm and imaginative power, and I see all three in this work."

"And what do you require from a model, Mr. Wilde?" asked Cecily in a cool voice.

"Merely that a model be quiet and look beautiful," suggested Mr. Sheridan.

"Ah, no, a subject that is beautiful in itself offers no suggestion to the artist," Oscar Wilde contradicted. "In truth, we require nothing from the model, for if the model affected us in some way, either for pain or for pleasure, or appealed very strongly to our sympathies, she would be outside of the sphere of Art. To Art's subject matter we should be more or less indifferent. We should at any rate have no preferences, no prejudices, no partisan feelings of any kind."

"Then you would have the model be merely decorative?" Cecily inquired.

"One should either be a work of art or wear a work of art." He inclined his large head.

"It seems to me that such an individual as you describe would be quite shallow," Cecily protested.

"Ah, but only the shallow know themselves," Mr. Wilde replied, the solemn tone of his words denied by the twinkle in his eye.

"Mr. Wilde," Cecily said, with a smile hovering about her lips, "I don't believe that you're sincere."

"Sincere!" he cried in mock dismay, pretending to stumble back in horror. "No! I am never sincere. In all things it is style, not sincerity that is important. A little sincerity is a dangerous thing, and a great deal of it is absolutely fatal."

"Ha, ha!" shrieked Swinburne, doubling up with laughter. "Sincerity! Fatal! Ha, ha!"

"I would say Mr. Wilde follows his own edicts," put in Devin, "for he fulfils his own criteria for a work of art—charm, distinction and imaginative power—and he is certainly wearing one."

"I knew you'd find him amusing, Sheridan," declared Swinburne. "What do you say? Shall I bring him to your next Sunday breakfast?"

"Indeed," replied the artist. "You're both most welcome. I only hope you are not disappointed in my table. The menu is quite simple."

"Ah, Mr. Sheridan," Mr. Wilde replied with an elegant wave of one of his pale hands. "I have the simplest tastes. I am always satisfied with the best."

"Oh, ha, ha! Simple tastes! The best!" Swinburne howled. "Oh, I say, Oscar, that is rich. Ha, ha!" and off he went on a round of convulsive mirth.

"Ah, a mere nothing," his friend answered. "Just my endeavour to stave off the frightful ennui of modern existence."

With a yawn illustrative of this last remark, he went on, "I see it is time to be going if we're to present dear old Rossetti with his wombat today."

"A wombat?" Cecily queried.

"Well, the poor chap's been so morose lately," Mr. Swinburne explained, "that we thought a wombat might lift his spirits. The last one died you know." He nodded his head gloomily. "Starved to death in a cigar box. It crawled in during a party—you remember those parties, Devin—and was found months later, dead, after having consumed all of the cigars." He sighed. "A frightful way to die, isn't it?"

"Especially as Rossetti has dreadful taste in cigars," Devin agreed.

"May we see this wombat?" asked Cecily eagerly, eyeing a small carpetbag which Mr. Swinburne had set down by the door.

"To be sure," the poet replied, holding out to her this bag partially opened to reveal a dark-coloured rodent who immediately leaped out of his bondage and settled down in Cecily's velvety lap, providing her with the opportunity to stroke his long, brush-like fur and admire his soft, dark eyes.

"Oh, what a lovely little animal!" she said softly, bending over the beast so that her hair obscured her face. "How I should love to have one for a pet!"

Mr. Swinburne hopped up and down on one foot nervously, glanced at Mr. Wilde who shrugged his shoulders, appealed to Mr. Sheridan who nodded, and, at length, proclaimed in a squeaky voice.

"You may consider him your own, Miss...er... Flo, isn't it?"

"No, it is not Flo," snapped Cecily, briskly rising and handing back the animal, who emitted tiny cries of protest, to the startled Mr. Swinburne. "My name is Miss Hawthorne, Miss Cecily Hawthorne, and if Mr. Rossetti is expecting a wombat, then I think he should be given one." With which words she exited peremptorily from the room. "Good Heavens, Devin, old man," she heard Swinburne saying as she left, "I hope I haven't caused any trouble. I just cannot keep your female friends straight, there's so many of them."

This last remark was not likely to extinguish the blaze which raged in Cecily's heart, rather it fanned the flames. Her violent temper was Cecily's greatest cross to bear, and the good Mrs. Polyander had told her time and time again, "Now, Cecily, whenever you feel you simply must explode, go find a quiet place where you can be alone, without interruption, and spend some time contemplating the problem, until you feel calm enough to deal with the cause of your distress without spiteful words or rash actions."

Accordingly Cecily stormed into the sanctuary of the library, settled down in a huff on the wooden, high-backed settee near the door and fastened her gaze upon the stained-glass window opposite, which depicted long-necked, angelic figures making their way up a stairway, presumably to Heaven. She endeavoured to fancy herself as part of this ethereal scene, hoping thereby to achieve some degree of composure, but to no avail. Next, she got up and roamed about the room, imagining a scene in which she would tell Mr. Sheridan exactly what she thought of him and his amorous pursuits, when there was a hasty knock upon the door, followed by the entrance of Willet, who said calmly, "A guest to see Miss Hawthorne." Cecily scowled and would have motioned him away but he continued, "A Mr. Chester Thrush."

Cecily's eyes widened and one hand flew to her mouth to stifle a started exclamation.

"Oh, my Lord! How did he find me?" she gulped.

Mr. Thrush was a senior clerk in the employ of Mr. Davenport. He had become enamoured of the nursery governess after glimpsing her in a hallway at his employer's home. That one glimpse had been enough to convince him that Miss Hawthorne was the woman with whom he wished to share the rest of his life, and he had haunted Number Eleven Prokington Terrace, burdened with gifts of flowers and declarations of undying devotion. Freedom from Mr. Thrush's unwelcome attentions had been one of the major attractions of her new position, and Cecily undoubtedly would have instructed Willet to send him away had she not been piqued with Mr. Sheridan.

"Very well, Willet" she said curtly. "I'll receive him here. Can you have Cook send in a tea tray?"

"As you wish, Miss Cecily," Willet replied in his usual agreeable manner, obeying her commands so quickly that she barely had time to turn around before Mr. Thrush was framed in the doorway, staring at Cecily goggle-eyed through gold-rimmed spectacles.

Chester Thrush was a gangly, awkward individual with large bony hands, a prominent Adam's apple and protruding ears. Afflicted by a score of nervous habits and mannerisms, his presence unfailingly made Cecily jumpy and irritable, and it was no different now, especially as he continued to gaze at her abjectly. "Good day, Mr. Thrush," she said briskly, observing his apparent inability to speak.

Chester swallowed convulsively several times and at last blurted out, "M–m–miss Hawthorne, I am st–stricken dumb by your beauty, as c–customary."

"I am surprised to see you here," she replied coolly.

"Sh–sh–surely, Miss Hawthorne," he said adoringly. "You m–must realize I would follow you to the ends of the globe, if necessary, for how else shall we achieve that glorious goal we both hold so dear, our eventual union as m–man and wife?"

"Mr. Thrush," said Cecily tartly, "we have discussed this topic time and again, and time and again I have reminded you that I have never accepted any of your numerous proposals, nor do I intend to. Nor have I given you the slightest reason to hope that I will."

"Ah!" he replied, fingering his tie with such agitation that he nearly cut off his respiration, "I know you too well, you artful creature, to believe such nonsense. M–my dear m–mother has m–made it abundantly clear to me that a well-bred young lady m–must refuse a gentleman repeatedly before succumbing to his m–manifold attractions. It s–speaks highly of you that you do so, even without the guidance of a m–mother such as mine."

"I received instruction in etiquette at Mrs. Polyander's academy," Cecily said with growing annoyance, "and I have never been informed of such a dictum."

"F–f–for shame on Mrs. Polyander then," stammered Chester, struggling to untangle his tie, "for n–neglecting such a vital part of a young lady's education." He took a deep breath. "B–but, Miss Hawthorne, how peculiar you look!"

Cecily blushed, realizing how strange she must appear swathed in the folds of the amber velvet gown, her hair flowing loose down her back.

"It's—it's nothing," she said hastily, putting her hand to her hair self-consciously. "It has to do with my position here."

Chester folded his bony knuckles together, producing a loud cracking sound from his knuckles. "What, may I inquire, is the nature of your position here?" he asked, looking about the room with a sceptical eye. "How many ch–children are under your care?"

Cecily saw no reason to disguise the facts; in truth, she hoped a frank revelation might discourage Mr. Thrush forever.

"I am not a nursery governess," she said quietly. "I am employed as a model." She added, noticing the confusion which gripped him, "an artist's model."

Mr. Thrush's physiognomy went through some amazing contortions. His eyes bulged alarmingly, and his mouth twisted about so much that at times it seemed to disappear beneath his nose and at other times dive down into his neck. Meanwhile his pale bony hands wrestled each other in a silent battle to the death.

"The gentleman who owns this house is an artist," Cecily went on pleasantly, "a Mr. Devin Sheridan, who is working on a picture for the Royal Academy Show entitled, 'Pandora.' I am sitting for Pandora."

Mr. Thrush attempted to speak but only a shrill whistling sound emitted from his throat. He swallowed twice and managed to croak out, "N–n–not in the altogether?" With these words, he collapsed onto the settle and pulling out a yellow handkerchief printed with red spots mopped at his brow.

Cecily's merry laugh rang out in the room. "Good heavens, no!" she declared.

"Th–thank God!" gasped Chester. "I think the sh–shock would have k–killed off M–mother."

A long silence descended upon the occupants of the library. Chester continued to wipe his forehead while Cecily tapped her small foot impatiently on the floor. Willet, as if sensing the impasse, trotted brightly into the room with the silver tray containing the tea articles. For a few moments the familiar ritual of having tea soothed them both.

"Two lumps, I believe, Mr. Thrush?" asked Cecily, handing him the cup, a Nanking blue-and-white china cup.

"M–m–my sweetheart," he responded. "I knew that you were fond of me. M–mother always says that it is evident when one remembers the little things of l–life."

Cecily chided herself inwardly.

"W–what sort of woman is Mrs. Sheridan?" asked Chester, lifting the cup to his lips.

"There is no Mrs. Sheridan," Cecily replied frankly. "Mr. Sheridan is not, at present, married."

Chester's tea cup trembled violently, spilling tea down the front of his favourite vest, the one he wore for special occasions, the one with the purple pheasants worked over a green-satin ground.

"He is engaged?" he suggested weakly.

"Not at all."

Chester set down the tea cup and saucer and pressed one hand against his head as if in excruciating pain.

"M–m–miss Hawthorne," he said, "this is h horrible. This is far worse than I ever dreamed possible. You, a young woman of a tender age, with no parents to guide you, with no protector to w–watch over you. With little knowledge of the wicked ways of the s–sinful w–world, you are employed by a…er…ahem…a bachelor, as a m–m–model?"

Before Cecily could open her mouth he went on, "But I am, of course, with the zeal born of m–my great l–love for you, becoming overly excited. There is surely an aunt or his mother or some other f–female figure in the household to provide the proper chaperonage?"

Cecily, with a twinkle in her eye, said, "Oh, of course. There is Chlorrie, that's the cook, and Betty, the housemaid. They have been most kind to me."

"A c–cook and a m–maid," repeated Mr. Thrush in horror. "M–miss Hawthorne," he cried out, darting round the table to fling himself at her feet, "l–let me release you from this bondage. Only say you will be m–mine and I will transport you away from this— this den of iniquity, far, far away to the humble yet neat abode of my m–mother and myself, where you shall have your own s–servants, a footman, at l–least, and a girl to come in and clean once weekly. I c–cannot afford more, at the present, you understand." He took hold of one of her hands with his own large, moist one. "It will take s–some time for the s–special license of course," he continued, "but m–my m–mother would welcome you, and could acquaint you with certain details you m–must endeavour to learn—for example, that I prefer my toast to be burnt on the outside and soft on the inside and that I never take porter with my meals but always afterwards, and other such particulars."

"It's a generous offer, Mr. Thrush," said Cecily, trying to remove her hand from his grasp, "but I must decline. I am simply not interested in—"

"You c–cannot remain here, M–miss Hawthorne!" he declared, rearing back his head. "This is totally unsuitable. W–what must people think?" Cecily blushed again, for she knew well what they thought. "How can you ever hope to obtain a position as a nursery

governess again when people learn of this—this s–sordid esca-
pade?" Cecily sighed. "C–can you really reassure me that the w–
wanton and debauched ways of this profligate artist are not having
some effect upon you, and might not, at s–some later date, poison
the innocent minds and souls of the little ch–children placed in your
care? For sh–shame, M–miss Hawthorne! For sh–shame!"

"A rather strong statement to make without facts of any kind,"
came a male voice from the doorway, "but such has always been the
privilege of demagogues."

Cecily pulled back her hands from Chester's as he turned to
survey the intruder, the artist himself. He was wearing his black-
satin smoking jacket, which was embroidered with a large gold
dragon, cigarette smoke wafted from his nostrils and his dark, hair
was rumpled. Cecily had to admit that he looked like the profligate
Chester described.

"Who is this earnest young man, Cecily?" he inquired in a lazy
drawl.

"Mr. Sheridan, Mr. Thrush. Mr. Thrush, Mr. Sheridan," she said
quickly. "Mr. Thrush is a—well, a—an acquaintance of mine from—
well—from my previous situation."

"And he has tracked you here," Devin said, looking the seething
suitor up and down. "How very admirable! It shows a single-mind-
edness of purpose which is most commendable."

"S–sir!" called out Chester, wetting his pale lips nervously with
the tip of his pink tongue. "I demand that you permit M–miss
Hawthorne to depart with m–me. I intend to take her h–home to my
m–mother. We will be m–married as soon as decently possible."

"How do I know you are not some cad, planning to entice her,
exploit her and then cast her aside? How can I determine whether
or not you are profligate, wanton, immoral, an evil influence?"

"S–sir," Chester trembled all over. "I am the s–senior clerk at
Davenport and Cole."

"And I am the Queen of Sheba," replied the artist.

"This is ins–supportable!" exclaimed Chester. "Come along, M–
miss Hawthorne. This man is really a l–lunatic."

"Stop it, both of you!" declared Cecily passionately. "I have no
desire to go with you, Chester," she said, turning to him. "I do

appreciate your offer, yes I do," she glanced defiantly at Mr. Sheridan, "and I hope you will call again and we can discuss what you have said at greater length." Once more she tossed her head at the artist. "But at the present I prefer to remain here and see the job I have begun to its close, at which time," she faced Mr. Sheridan, with her hands on her hips, "I shall be only too glad to leave, not desiring to make the mistake made by so many other females. Hah!" She stamped her foot and shooed them both toward the door, and none of Chester's incoherent pleadings or Mr. Sheridan's stern reminders of his ownership of the property, stirred her in the slightest. Cecily's stubborn determination was so successful that the library door was soon slammed triumphantly shut, closing her off from Chester's denunciation of the morals of artists or Mr. Sheridan's criticism of the perversity of models.

Chapter Seven

*In Which Cecily Gains a Mother-in-law
of Sympathetic Good Sense*

MR. CHESTER THRUSH, and his mother, Mrs. Isabella Thrush, occupied the two-pair front above a second-hand clothing shop in Islington, and it was to this humble refuge that Chester retreated to lick his wounds following the failure of his mission to Number Seven Swan Walk. Broken in spirit and twitching with frustration, he stumbled up the dimly lit, narrow stairway which led to their door and, when his barrage of knocks went unanswered, fumbled in his waistcoat pocket for the key.

"Is that you, Mister Thrush? I've a messich for you from yer mother!" came a sepulchral voice from the lower hallway. It was the voice of Mrs. Meeker, the current owner of the used clothing shop, which had formerly belonged to the departed Mr. Thrush. Mrs. Meeker kept a watchful eye on the comings and goings of the upstairs tenants and served as the general intelligence as well as laundress, cook and postman.

Chester was not in a good humour for lending an ear to her well-meaning ramblings. "What is it, Mrs. Meeker?" he snapped.

"Yer mother was called away this arfternoon," she called out, "to do a spot of alterations for a lady. She went without complaining, saying how it was her duty as the two of yer could not live on yer earnings alone, and how she only wished to be of help to you in the—what was her word? Policing? No! Procession? No! Ah, pursuance of yer goals."

"When will she return, Mrs. Meeker?" he wanted to know.

"Ah, the poor woman," Mrs. Meeker's voice was heavy with woe, "I'm sure she had no notion, you know as how unheeding those great ladies can be, and yer poor mother, so frail and so long-suffering. Why if I had to work half as hard as she do to earn a living for my son what is a full-grown man, I think I'd be in my grave today, I do, all stretched out, cold and clammy in my grave."

A slam from upstairs indicated to Mrs. Meeker that Chester was unaffected by her wretched tale, but he was affected by his own wretched predicament. No hot supper, no fire in the hearth, no one to plump up the cushions of his chair or fetch his slippers; in short, no Mother. He huddled on a settee before the empty grate, contemplating the ashes and chewing on his fingernails, indulging in increasingly gloomy visions of the future. Cecily, rouged and glittering, haunting the arcade before Covent Garden. Cecily's likeness, covered only with a thin wisp of gauze, staring out at him from a thousand picture postcards in a thousand tawdry shop windows. Chester, pinched and miserable, haunting the pavement before Mr. Sheridan's house. Chester's likeness, wild and glassy-eyed, staring out from a barred attic window, where he had been incarcerated by his mother and Mrs. Meeker, who feared he would take his own life because his heart was broken. These gloomy visions were dispelled by a chatter of voices in the hallway, a huffing and puffing and rustling on the stairs, and the panting and straining of Mrs. Thrush as she tried to squeeze herself through the door, followed by the penetrating voice of Mrs. Meeker calling out, "I'll send up the potatoes and the cheese and celery directly."

Mrs. Thrush was a spry little old woman, with sharp, bright, dark eyes, plump apple-red cheeks, a ruddy nose and a small pursed mouth that had assumed a permanent expression of dignified disapproval from years of constant puckering. She was constructed in the shape of a dumpling, and she had clung to the old fashion of wearing a hoop beneath her skirts so that her circumference at the floor was twice as wide as the diameter of her waist, which accounted for her present difficulty in entering the room. Unlike other women who had appeared to glide gracefully through the decade of crinolines, Mrs. Thrush moved with a slight bounce, which action was taken up by her hoop and magnified so that she always seemed to be rocking in a particularly turbulent sea. Once she had navigated a passage through the straits of the doorway, she came sailing into the cluttered sitting room, rolling back and forth with a magnificent motion, foundering occasionally against the reefs and rocks of the furniture, and subsiding gradually to a gentle shiver when she dropped anchor and put into the haven of her rocking chair. For even when moored, Mrs. Thrush kept up a continual motion, sometimes known to cause seasickness in unseasoned bystanders. She fancied gowns that were covered with fringed decorations, always had a tasselled shawl draped over her shoulders, and dressed her white hair in tight corkscrew curls so that every part of her person jounced and jiggled constantly. On occasions, her doting son pretended that he had plans to market her as a perpetual-motion machine.

But not upon this occasion. Despite his parent's repeated sighs, Chester preferred to tear savagely at his bloodied nails and contemplate the empty grate.

"What are you up to now, boy?" inquired his venerable parent sharply, "besides mooning about like a sick calf? Don't deny that you're brooding about something. I should know when my Chester is in a fit of blue devils."

"W–where have you been, M–mother?" asked Chester gloomily.

"Why, I've been at Lady Holly's," she replied, "and a more ungrateful old busybody, I've never yet sewed for. The woman is as large as a draft horse and has her gowns made up three sizes too small to flatter her vanity. A thankless task working for her! And how she likes to talk! Gracious! I thought my ears would be burnt off altogether. I wonder how Phoebe manages."

Phoebe, well-known throughout London Society for her excellent alterations, had left the previous day to visit an invalid sister in Kent, bequeathing her clientele to her dear friend Mrs. Thrush in her absence. Lady Holly had been the first to require such services, and she was not pleased to view an unfamiliar face in her boudoir.

"Where is Phoebe?" she barked out, when Mrs. Thrush, bustling with energy and quivering with excitement had been ushered into the lavishly-decorated bedchamber.

"Ooo, my gracious goodness!" Isabella Thrush had declared gazing round-eyed at the plaster cherubs holding the swagged pink satin draperies and the gilt cornucopia above the pier glass. "What a lovely setting, Madam."

"I repeat my question. Where is Phoebe? She is the only one I permit to touch my clothing," declared Lady Holly, who was a horrible sight, seated upon a velvet footstool, her ample flesh bulging out above and below the corset which was the only garment she wore.

"Phoebe has been called to the death-bed of her favourite sister," Mrs. Thrush said brightly, "and I'm here in her place, and a welcome substitution I think you'll find it, Milady, for a faster needle is wielded by none, as I daresay you'll discover." She eyed Lady Holly speculatively. "I see you have the finest tastes, Madam, and it will be my pleasure to learn from you, an opportunity often lacking, even in the best houses of London. I don't suppose you're aware of the extent of the problem, Lady Holly, but Mrs. Captooth actually has her clothes brought in ready-made, and then, not even fitted!"

This was the sort of tidbit warranted to gain the good favour of Lady Holly.

"Indeed!" she snorted. "Well then, take in the purple gown on the bed and quickly. I don't understand why it should be that suddenly so many of my things are too big for me, but so it is."

Mrs. Thrush was privately of the opinion that the opposite was the case but said nothing to that effect. Instead she cooed over the colour. "*Lilas ancien,* I do think it is so elegant, and with the saffron braiding, so *a la mode.* And the style! A tabbed overskirt is very flattering to youthful figures such as your own, Madam."

All in all, her tongue was wielded to more advantage than her needle, and soon Lady Holly, who wanted sometimes for an audience, was divulging the trials and tribulations involved in raising six daughters.

"Fortunately," she declared with a mighty sigh, which almost knocked Mrs. Thrush off her seat as she sat perched with her short legs dangling over the edge of an oak chest, "my oldest daughter, Constance, will shortly announce her betrothal to a well-known artist—I don't suppose you've ever heard of him—Mr. Devin Sheridan. He exhibits at all the shows and knows the best people."

"What a great satisfaction that must be to you, Madam."

"And yet when one recalls that daughter's babyhood, her first dear steps, the time she nearly died of scarlatina (you know, one of my children did die of scarlatina) and her squabbles with Alva, that is the next one, well then," Lady Holly wiped a large tear from beneath her eye with her petticoat, "I wonder what I shall do without her." She burst into noisy tears, completely dampening the flannel undergarment she used as a handkerchief.

"I understand, Madam," put in Mrs. Thrush soothingly, looking up sharp-eyed from her work. "I have a son, my only child, a dear, good boy, and so thoughtful to his poor, helpless mother. Why if he should marry, I don't know what would become of me, I really don't."

"But my daughters must make good matches," stated Lady Holly, rearing back her head imperiously.

"I agree with you absolutely, Madam," replied her seamstress. "Alas, I fear there is no woman good enough for my dear Chester."

"Mr. Sheridan shall do very nicely for my Constance," announced Lady Holly. "In fact, despite a mother's prejudice, I might say she is getting a bargain. Of course, it's well known he drinks a bit too much—but then, what man doesn't?—and that he sometimes beds his models—but then, what artist doesn't? Still, Constance can overlook all that." She poked Mrs. Thrush in the ribs with one of her large fingers, a thrust which occasioned the seamstress much pain but which she bore with wonderful silence.

Lady Holly undid some of the strings of her corset, which spread apart with a creaking sound and which evidently, judging by her wriggling back and forth, provided her with greater comfort.

"Why, it was worth it all," she cackled, settling in for a good long gossip with her seamstress, "just to see Mrs. Fluster's face when I told her. I don't suppose you know the Flusters?"

Mrs. Thrush made a great show of pondering this question. She cocked her little head to one side, setting all the curls wagging, then pinched her red nose with her thumb and forefinger, a gesture indicating great thought, before shaking her head emphatically.

"No, I can't say that I do, Madam," she replied. "Is she a newcomer? Among the newly rich, perhaps?"

Lady Holly smiled a smug, supercilious smile. "A newcomer," she repeated, savouring the words. "One of the nouveau riche. A *parvenu*, perhaps."

"Yes, a *parvenu*, the exact word. You are so quick with words, Madam."

"One might say she is a *parvenu*," Lady Holly declared in the manner of giving a benediction. "Her husband," she shuddered slightly, "makes cast-iron furniture. Dreadful stuff!"

"Think of it, cast-iron furniture," said Mrs. Thrush, rocking back and forth in agreement.

"Ah, Mrs. Fluster was not pleased to hear of Constance and Mr. Sheridan," sighed Lady Holly, drifting off into her memories of the scene which had taken place nearly a fortnight earlier. "I saw the expression on her face, you know, and I can guess at the thoughts that crossed that foggy little mind of hers."

"Indeed you can. Indeed you can," chanted Mrs. Thrush.

"She thought she could find a suitable suitor for her daughter, Joconda," declared Lady Holly in triumph, "as if anyone would want that homely, prim old maid. Why even though Constance is nearly ten years older than Joconda, she's a thousand times prettier and more witty besides."

"Of course, it's well known," murmured the seamstress.

"I must keep an eye on Mrs. Fluster, however," said Lady Holly, more to herself than to her agreeable audience. "I had some scheme for doing so, but it has vanished." Lady Holly's voice drifted off and she frowned as she gazed into the middle distance. All at once she stiffened, like the wind suddenly catching a sail, and gasped out, "Of course, it was the nursery governess."

"To be sure, the nursery governess," was Mrs. Thrush's refrain.

"Yes, the nursery governess," intoned Lady Holly, rising from her seat on the footstool as if rising from the dead. "I promised Mrs.

Fluster I would find a nursery governess, and I have forgotten it until this moment. There is not a second to lose. Quick! Finish that dress. I have to be off. Good Heavens, you are a slow one!"

"I am going as fast as I can go, Lady Holly," complained Mrs. Thrush.

"You might know a nursery governess yourself," stated Lady Holly, really looking over Mrs. Thrush for the first time. "One who is looking for employment or would like to change positions? It is of the utmost importance that I find one. A very easy job, she'd have. One child, and that an infant, still in leading strings. You must know someone who would do!"

"I regret to say I don't," replied Mrs. Thrush calmly, humming a little as she pulled the thread through the cloth.

"Don't say so!" shouted Lady Holly, catching her by the shoulders and shaking her soundly. "I must have one, and find her immediately. Why aren't you done with that? Where is my maid to do my hair?" She stormed about the chamber like an enraged elephant, pulling on the bell pull so strenuously that it came off in her hand and bellowing all the while.

"Of course," Mrs. Thrush offered mildly, pulling at the thread with her teeth to make a knot. "I could ask about. You know, I recommended the man who is now the butler at Mrs. Tremblechin's."

"Never mind, never mind, woman," growled Lady Holly from behind clenched teeth. "I cannot trust someone in your position to find a suitable young person anyway. I shall have to do it myself. Hurry up there, will you? I hired someone for alterations, none of your fancy needlework."

"I am happy to announce I have finished," proclaimed Mrs. Thrush, rising to her full height, nearly half that of Lady Holly, with dignity.

It was fortunate that the maid tumbled into the room at that moment for it required the efforts of two persons to pack Lady Holly into her *lilas ancien* tabbed overskirt with the saffron braiding. Once accomplished, however, Lady Holly adopted the *grande darne* role congruent with her attire and swept down the hallway, completely forgetting her two menials.

Mrs. Thrush picked her way home to Islington without any payment and mentioned this fact to her gloomy son.

"Think of it, Chester," she said wonderingly. "A grand lady, like that, and yet she was as miserly with her money as, well, as your poor departed father."

Chester did not seem anxious to revere the memory of his poor departed father.

He sighed and began chewing on his knuckles.

"Heavens! One would think you were in love or something equally ridiculous!" snapped Mrs. Thrush, as Mrs. Meeker's eldest daughter, a pale, dark-haired girl who never uttered a word, brought in the potatoes and the celery and cheese. "Run along now, Katie, and bring me the roast fowl from the pastry cook's around the corner," said Mrs. Thrush to this silent presence.

"It's true, M–mother," intoned Chester in a hollow, gloomy voice.

"What's true?" snapped his parent. "That the roast fowl is at the pastry cook's?"

"No, I am in l–love," replied Chester, in much the same tone one uses to announce the beginning symptoms of a fatal disease.

His mother shrieked.

"Of course, you are teasing me, my darling boy," she ventured at last in a trembling voice.

Chester did not turn to view the havoc he had wrought; he was far too concerned with the wounds inflicted upon his soul.

"I am quite s–serious, M–mother," he responded. "I have declared my feelings to the object of my affections, and have asked her to m–marry me."

This time Mrs. Thrush screamed, a cry so piercing that Chester looked about in alarm, fearing that she had impaled herself on the poker she had picked up to stir the fire. The sight which met his eyes did little to relieve this impression for she was clutching the poker to her breast and making a slight moaning sound.

"M–mama, what is it?" he cried out, trying to wrestle the poker from her grasp. "M–mama, is it some kind of fit? Shall I call the doctor?"

"Heartless wretch!" screamed his mother, striking out at him with her incendiary weapon. "A fit! Fie! Why did I live to witness this catastrophe, why did I go out uncomplaining every afternoon to slave for rich ladies, only to hear my own child accuse me of suffering from seizures? Oh, woe is me!" Having thrown aside her deadly implement, she covered her august white head with her apron and rocked back and forth in silent sorrow, all of the fringes and tassels which covered her quivering as she did so.

"M–mama," Chester implored, "Take that apron from your head."

"Never," she mumbled with dignity.

"At once."

"Never."

"M–mama, I warn you—"

"You are certainly no son of mine, so little heed will I pay to your treacherous and threatening remarks," was the muffled response.

"M–mama, you are behaving like a child," declared her son, snatching her apron from her head.

"Oh, don't look at me with those matricidal eyes," she cried out, covering her face with her hands and continuing to moan and mourn.

"Egad! I'll not indulge you any f–further," Chester announced, stamping his foot, just as the eldest Meeker child glided silently into the room with a roast fowl which she set upon the table. Chester took up a knife and fork and fell upon it. For a time the only sounds were the scrape of his knife upon the plate, his gobbling noises, and the wailing of his mother.

After some time, Mrs. Thrush peeked out from between her fingers. "When," her voice quavered, "do you wish me to remove myself from the premises?"

"There is absolutely no reason for you to c–carry on so, M–mother," Chester said with a mouth full of poultry. "You will, of course, remain here. I know, Cecily, that is, M–miss Hawthorne, would want it so."

Mrs. Thrush howled and retreated behind her cambric barricade.

"I think I would prefer to go to the Workhouse rather than inflict my unwelcome presence upon my estranged son and his proud wife."

"Cecily is not proud, M–mother," put in Chester. "She is unassuming." He thought of her calm command of the tea service. "Well, if not unassuming, then m–modest." The visions of her posing

67

in the altogether flashed through his mind. "Or if not m–modest, at best, h–humble—" He recollected her haughty rejection of his declarations and lapsed into confused silence.

"What is she?" asked his mother, sticking her red nose around the corner of her apron to sniff the diminishing odour of roast fowl.

"W–what do you m–mean, M–mother?" demanded Chester, crunching on the bones of the hapless bird he was devouring. "She's a Goddess among w–women, a pearl in the oyster of L–London."

"Heavens, Chester! Can you really be so stupid?" asked his sympathetic parent. She was emerging from the trance of sorrow into which her son's words had plunged her. "What sort of family does she have? Is she a tradesman's daughter?"

"Not exactly. No."

"Then, the child of a professional man?"

"I c–couldn't say that."

"Oh, Chester, don't tell me! She's a member of the nobility. You've won the heart of some earl or duke's daughter! I knew it would be so. My darling boy. My most handsome poppet." She catapulted from her chair, and fastened herself upon his neck, rumpling his hair with one hand and dampening his neckcloth with her happy tears. "Let me think, the Hawthornes! Could that be the Duke of Drumland, no, those are the DeWinques. Perhaps the Marquis of—"

"M–mother," stammered Chester, trying to disengage her from his anatomy. "Sh–she is not a m–member of the nobility."

His mother peered at him suspiciously.

"Sh–she is a s–servant."

Isabella Thrush uttered a little scream, clutching her heart.

"Sh–she is a nursery governess."

Chester's mother rolled up her eyes and fell into a quivering heap at his feet. Her son, paralyzed with terror at this sight, remained where he was, eyes bulging from his head, throat working convulsively, until the wraith-like Katie Meeker darted in through the doorway and, in an instant, had dumped the contents of an ewer of water over Mrs. Thrush's tender grey head. She came to her senses with a shudder which coursed through her entire frame.

"A servant! Oh, Chester!" she declared in an unearthly voice. Katie Meeker vanished as quietly as she had come. "How can you do this to the dignity of the Thrushes? How can you destroy everything we have worked and striven for these past ten years?"

"M–mother, I didn't think—"

"Obviously you didn't think. A nursery governess! A nursery governess?" She paused, she frowned, her eyes brightened. "You say she is a nursery governess. Where is she employed?"

"At present, she is not, which is why—"

"Never mind that. There's not a moment to lose. Lady Holly was telling me only hours ago that a grand family called the Flusters require a nursery governess immediately. This—this—person must apply."

"W–why sh–should M–miss Hawthorne engage herself to a family when she is s–soon to be my w–wife?" asked Chester suspiciously.

"You naughty child!" exclaimed his provoked mother. "Of course, you cannot marry an unemployed servant. Do you really think a penniless young woman would wish to link herself to the Thrushes? She will need a magnificent trousseau and a kind master to give her away. No girl of any breeding whatsoever would enter the holy state of matrimony with only the clothes on her back."

"Perhaps that is w–why she was so unencouraging," mused Chester. "Perhaps she was too embarrassed by her impecunious position to m–mention it."

"Of course, no man could be expected to realize the havoc such a situation can wreak upon the female heart," declared his mother. "Now, Chester, when you go to speak to her to propose this new position at the Flusters, you must not bring up these sordid financial considerations. You must simply present this as a golden opportunity for her to learn at first hand the sort of manners and scale of living she will need to fulfill her duties as your wife. Can I count upon you to do exactly that, my darling boy?"

"Oh yes, M–mother, how wise you are!" replied the son. "M–miss Hawthorne is a fortunate young woman to be gaining in one fell swoop a husband of such merit and a m–mother-in-law with such s–sympathetic good sense."

Chapter Eight

An Unsettling Valentine's Day

THE RAIN HAD WOKEN CECILY from a light sleep close to dawn, and she had risen to watch the light creep sullenly through her bedroom window.

Yellow roses, a gift from Mr. Sheridan presented the previous day, scented the air, sweet and almost dizzying. Cecily shivered in the chill of the morning, and pulled the counterpane she wore as a robe more tightly about her shoulders. Longing for a cup of warming tea, she crept soundlessly down the winding stairs and tiptoed into the kitchen, where she found Chlorrie busily rolling out the dough for the croissants while Betty clumsily cut slices off a cold ham. They were speaking as they worked and Cecily overheard a few sentences.

"I finished it," Betty was saying as she savagely hacked at the ham, "but can you imagine? The nerve of him! I think, for all his talk, he knows nothing about women!"

"I say he'll be lucky if she doesn't—ah, Miss Cecily! What a glorious surprise! Isn't it, Betty?" The cook trod, rather obviously, on Betty's foot.

"Certainly is," said Betty with a weak smile.

"Ah, it's a cup of tea you're wanting, isn't it?" exclaimed Chlorrie, with her usual Irish warmth. "Well, the teapot's just been filled so mind your fingers, and help yourself."

"Who's lucky? Who doesn't know much about women?" Cecily asked unabashed. Betty looked at Cook and giggled.

"Ah, go on with you, girl," declared Chlorrie. "You know we're always talking about summat or other. There's little to do while we work, so we're always flapping our gums. Pay us no mind."

Cecily sighed and sipped gratefully at the warm golden brown liquid in the chipped enamelled mug she held between her cupped hands. Usually Willet brought her morning tea in a priceless blue-and-white Nanking porcelain teapot on a silver tray. Despite her protests that this practise made her uncomfortable, despite her assurances that a cup of tea in the kitchen was more to her liking, despite her unsuccessful attempts to make her point clear by leaving the tea untouched, Willet continued to present the tray, priceless teapot and all, and Cecily, becoming accustomed to late hours, found it more and more difficult to rise early enough to forestall him. Mornings like this morning were rare and treasured all the more for it.

"How is Charlie, Betty?" asked Cecily, naming the greengrocer's assistant with whom Betty was enamoured.

Betty blushed a lovely shade of red. "Oh, Miss Cecily," she declared. She rocked back and forth clutching her bony elbows. "I'm sure I wouldn't know how he is."

"Go on with you, girl," put in Chlorrie. "You went to the music hall with him just last night. I should hope you noticed how he was then."

Betty subsided into giggles again and refused to be drawn out further on the subject. Instead she wanted to know if Cecily wanted assistance with her toilette.

This was another custom which made Cecily uncomfortable. She felt, and frequently said, that she could manage very well for herself, but Betty was so eager to learn something of the duties of a lady's maid ("For I'm sure if I wait for Mr. Sheridan to marry, I'll be waiting forever," she explained) and so convinced that she could dress Cecily's hair in the most modern and becoming styles, that

Cecily occasionally relented and accepted her aid. Today was such a day, and after Cecily had finished her tea, the maid and the model hurried upstairs and, after an hour of whispering and trying on gowns and primping, Cecily was proclaimed "turned out bang up to the nines!"

"Ooo!" squealed Betty, pressing her hands to her lips as she watched Cecily try to glimpse herself in the small mirror over the bureau. "I'm ever so glad we chose this gown, Miss Cecily, for I nearly had forgot it's Saint Valentine's."

"Saint Valentine's?" frowned Cecily, fluffing up the white batiste ruching on the skirts of her coral crape dress.

"February the fourteenth," declared Betty, clasping her hands to her heart. "I do hope Charlie doesn't forget me."

"Miss Hawthorne," came the voice of Willet, who was rapping softly upon the door, "Mr. Sheridan invites you to dine with him in the breakfast room."

"Thank you, Willet," Cecily called out in reply, and suffered the jesting remarks of Betty as they made their way downstairs.

The teapot was steaming on the table. The kippers were still broiling on the sideboard. Kidneys lay sizzling upon a salver and the croissants, fresh from the oven, were snuggled into a linen-napkin nest. The table was set. The glittering colour of the goldfish matched the outlines of the coral chrysanthemums painted upon the china. Upon the window seat, where the terrier had been used to perch, the wombat jumped up at Cecily's approach and came scurrying over, to snuffle at her hem, until she bent over to cradle him in her arms. Several days after Mr. Swinburne's *faux pas*, just about the time Cecily's hot temper was cooling, the eccentric poet had returned bearing the wombat (who had not been welcome at Mr. Rossetti's house) as a peace offering. The affectionate little mammal had become Cecily's pet and was never more content than now when curled in her lap. She sat, with her forehead against the cool glass of the window, waiting for the arrival of Mr. Sheridan, studying the garden in the rain.

A mist had risen off the river and curled about the trunks of the beech trees, permitting every now and then a glimpse of bare branches and stark twigs dripping with clotted raindrops. It was more of a drizzle than a rainstorm; the drops fell steadiest from along the eave, splashing onto the windowpane and skating along it in wide silver streaks. From far off, Cecily heard the forlorn sound of the fog horns.

Suddenly she was aware of a furtive, scrabbling noise behind her, and turned to find Mr. Sheridan triumphantly tearing a piece of paper out of his drawing pad and handing it to her, a pencil sketch entitled "Cecily and the Wombat" depicting a fuzzy-headed Cecily with a long elegant neck and a friendly little creature dancing in her lap.

"It's lovely," she said with a smile.

"If you continue to look out on that gloomy scene, there'll be an even gloomier one within," he commented light-heartedly, snatching the wombat away from her and inserting him under the dome of a silver platter.

"Fricassee of wombat, my love?" he asked, displaying the platter with a flourish, "or would you prefer wombat *a la béchamel?*"

"Do be serious!" declared Cecily, without any serious intention.

"Well, then, have a seat and begin upon breakfast, my dear," commanded Devin, "for it will soon be cold, and if it is, I may consider sending old Harry the wombat to the kitchen to be served up baked and minced!"

"I do wish I could draw," said Cecily irrepressibly, "so as to capture the extraordinary likeness between you and poor Harry. Saving your greater size, there's really little difference. Oh! Harry does sport a nobler brow."

"Do you mean that?" Devin inquired in a friendly voice, helping himself to the marmalade.

"About the nobler brow?"

"No, no! Good Heavens! I'm not such a dunce as to fall for such obvious flattery. Harry is infinitely my superior, particularly in hirsuteness, and I'm told that's what susceptible females pine for." Cecily wrinkled up her nose at him. "No! I meant about knowing how to draw. You know, I could teach you!"

Cecily paused in the midst of a forkful of veal-and-ham pie. "Oh, you wouldn't want to!" she said quickly.

"Why wouldn't I?"

"Well, you shouldn't."

"Why shouldn't I?"

"Well, you know that better than I!" retorted Cecily indignantly. "That's your profession. I know nothing about it. If you stopped to teach me, well, it would be as ridiculous as if I, for instance, should instruct you in the ailments of childhood or the proper mode of carrying an infant."

"Whenever I need such an education, I'll turn to you for edification," Mr. Sheridan replied unconcernedly. "Meanwhile, it would be my pleasure to teach so lovely a pupil the rudiments of my art."

There was a timid knock upon the door and Betty suddenly appeared, holding a linen-draped tray containing a loaf and blushing furiously.

"'Ere's your Valentine Day bun, Mr. Sheridan," she mumbled, setting her offering down upon the crowded table. "Chock full of raisins," she confided to Cecily. "It's a special treat from Cook."

The artist looked confused. "Oh, Valentine's Day, it is?" he declared at last. "Most thoughtful of Chlorrie. Give her our thanks."

"Certainly, sir," replied Betty with a bob of her head before scampering away. Mr. Sheridan produced his drawing pad from beneath his chair, discovered a pencil in his inside pocket and bent over the tablet, at times, scribbling furiously, at other times nervously sucking on the tip of the pencil.

Cecily complacently finished off her pie, helped herself to a slice of the Valentine's Day bun, took the last of the kippers and drank the dregs of the tea.

Mr. Sheridan, once he had finished his magnum opus, spent several minutes, folding and refolding it into an intricate shape, a white paper star, which he handed to Cecily with a flourish.

"Happy Valentine's Day, my love," he said with a grin. Suspiciously Cecily unfolded this epistle. Within she found a sketch depicting a harried-looking Cecily dabbing an oversized brush at a canvas upon an easel while Mr. Sheridan, swathed in the velvet "Pandora" robe lounged upon a sofa, idly smoking a cigarette. The accompanying verse read:

You've much too bright an eye, my dear,
And softly heaving breast.
Your presence in my studio
Is cause of great unrest.
My trembling hands, my quaking heart,
Might best withstand the shock,
If I were on the model's throne,
You in my artist's smock.

Cecily felt her stomach (and she was quite sure it was her stomach, and not that notoriously impressionable organ, the heart) do a sudden flip-flop. For a moment she could not think of a glib retort.

"Wombat got your tongue, my love?" inquired the artist, grinning devilishly.

"Just dumb with amazement at your pulchritude," Cecily at length managed to stammer. "I believe you will have to begin again, with a new concept for the figure of Pandora."

The artist laughed with good humour, but Cecily still felt curiously uneasy. It was a friendly sort of valentine, but not the wildly romantic sort one read about in novels nor the merely polite card one expected in reality. "Shall I draw one for you?" she asked hesitantly.

"Can you?" he asked, handing over his tablet and pencils.

"I used to be quite good at floral borders at Mrs. Polyander's," was the prim reply. Cecily bent over her project, pressing the pencil heavily into the paper, furrowing up her brow with fierce concentration. It was some time before she presented Mr. Sheridan with the fruit of her labours, a poem whose lines were so crossed and blotted that it was some time before he could make out these words:

He's super-eminent and known in all the best salons,
He's touted by the *bon ton* as one whose time has come,
He's feted high and low as an artistic aristocrat,
My question is a simple one—is he a man or wombat?

Beneath the verse was a crude but graceful sketch of a wombat wearing Mr. Sheridan's brocade smoking jacket.

"Capital!" he declared with a genuine smile of amusement and pride. "You have a natural touch with the pencil. Most novices would have belaboured the subject. You've managed to capture the essence of wombat with just a few lines. However," he leaned forward, pushing aside the breakfast plates and smoothing out her sketch, "you notice here, a little bit of problem with the perspective. Observe what happens if I sit back in my chair, like so." He assumed the same position in his chair held by the wombat in the drawing. "Looking at me with your normal eyes, you see a man, in normal proportions. But look at me with painterly eyes and see what happens! My legs loom larger, my head is smaller yet, one arm seems expanded, the other shrunken. This is what gives one the illusion of distance in a picture."

Cecily was nodding bright-eyed, suddenly experiencing the altered perception he described and awed by its implications, when Willet advanced into the breakfast room.

"Good day, Miss Hawthorne," he said pleasantly. "I am afraid I must interrupt this pleasant repast, which I discover, to my great relief, was at an end anyway, for I must announce that Mr. Sheridan has a visitor in the Whistler Room." The artist scowled at his valet. "A lady, sir. Lady Corrough, who wishes to speak to you about a portrait of herself for, as she put it, a lasting memorial for Lord Corrough once she has departed."

Devin threw down his napkin in disgust. "She's so petrified at present," he declared, "there shouldn't be any problem in preserving her. Lord Corrough could mount her today on a pedestal in his park, and with that as a reminder of the follies of his youth, go out and find a more amiable companion."

Willet frowned to indicate his disapproval of his employer's rude remarks, but only slightly so as to convey his partial concurrence with the description of the caller.

"Forgive me, Cecily," said Devin, leaning forward to brush a light kiss upon her forehead. Cecily's heart, or rather her stomach, made another peculiar lurch. "We'll continue the drawing lesson later. After I'm through with this old bat—"

"You've a lunch with Lord Leighton, sir," put in Willet sternly, "and a meeting with Mr. Monceau."

"Oh, that's right," sighed the artist. "He's promised to purchase some of my old things."

"Followed by a dinner at Lady Calverley's," went on the valet inexorably.

Devin shrugged his shoulders.

"I guess I'll not be needing you to sit for me today, Cecily," he said. "You've the afternoon free. I hope it's a pleasant one."

Cecily tried to make it so, but she found that nothing soothed her fretted disposition and fevered thoughts, infirmities which she blamed upon her ill-advised consumption of every delicacy of the breakfast table. Nothing was of assistance. Not the many novels in the library, whose characters failed to touch her heart, whose events in vain sought to attract her roving mind. Not the many windows through which she gazed forlornly at the monotonously falling rain, nor the empty vistas of grey clouds and leaden skies. Not the light-hearted banter between Chlorrie and Betty, on the subject of Charlie who had sent his sweetheart a truly dreadful penny-dreadful valentine. Not the crisp suggestions of Willet, who was disturbed by Cecily's unusual restlessness, nor the antics of Harry, the wombat. Certainly not by the appearance of Mr. Chester Thrush, who was washed on to the doorstep by a fresh onslaught of showers, shortly after Mr. Sheridan departed for his luncheon.

"Take me to M—miss Hawthorne," he stammered when Willet asked how he could be of assistance. Willet ushered him into the Whistler Room with some misgivings. His misgivings were confirmed by Cecily's opening remark.

"Oh, it's you, Mr. Thrush," she said tonelessly. Willet politely withdrew—that is, he went as far as the communicating door in the next room.

"M—my angel," spoke Mr. Thrush. "Be my V—valentine." He doffed his hat, which loosed a small flood of rainwater upon the straw floor matting, and produced a large white envelope from within the lilac-and-green pheasant-covered vest. "K—kept it close to my heart," he explained.

Cecily took the missive without comment and opened the envelope to find within a very large, very garish valentine, encrusted with lace, tassels, padded satin hearts, a grinning pink Cupid and rosettes of feathers. "To One I Love" read the legend inscribed on the garland the Cupid wore placed strategically over his nether regions. Chester beamed with pride.

"How charming," said Cecily flatly. "How very thoughtful of you, Chester. I appreciate it. I really do."

"I knew you would," he said, with a smirk. "Every woman likes to be remembered on Valentine's Day."

Cecily nodded in acknowledgement, and setting the valentine on the mantel, where it offended the sensibility of the Japanese woman in the Whistler painting across the room, she resumed pacing about the chamber.

"S–something is not right!" declared Chester indignantly, watching her. "By God, if that rogue has done anything to you."

"Oh, don't be ridiculous, Chester!" snapped Cecily.

"S–something has upset you, and I'll know what it is!" insisted her gallant swain.

"I'm restless," she said simply. "It's the rain." She tossed her head nervously. "It makes me feel closed in. I need a change."

"You shall have it!" he cried. "I have found, rather, M–mother has found the perfect position for you." Cecily's eyebrows lowered. "As a nursery governess." Cecily's eyebrows lifted. "F–for a Mrs. F–fluster, a highly respected and respectable member of Society, with a home duly admired for its unique and tasteful appointments." These details had been gleaned by Mrs. Thrush from her customers over the past week. "You w–would care for one child, an infant, of very tender years, approximately one and a half of them to be pre-cise. The child's name I do not know. This family lives in S–south K–Kensington, Number F–fourteen St–Stanhope Gardens. The position is to be filled immediately."

Cecily picked at the ruching on her dress as Chester rambled on. "I would be glad to escort you there, today," Chester concluded.

"What, go out in this rain?" Cecily frowned. "Certainly not for a position I don't even want."

"But, my dear M–miss Hawthorne," protested Chester, "that was not my understanding last time we spoke."

"Perhaps your understanding was fallacious," put in Cecily coldly.

"You s–said your position here," Chester sneered at the use of the word "position," curling up his nose and upper lip in a most unpleasant manner, "w—would be only temporary, contingent upon your discovering another situation as a nursery—"

Cecily cut him off. "I have changed my mind," she said brightly. "That is a woman's prerogative, is it not?" Chester nodded humbly.

"I enjoy my work here," she said holding her head high and fixing him with a steady gaze. "I find it most rewarding, both spiritually and mentally. To live in the rarefied atmosphere of those who serve, to be a handmaiden, myself, to Art, that is my pleasure. And, who knows? It may be possible, I shall take up a little painting myself."

Chester watched her goggle-eyed. "No!" he burbled. "This is abominable. You have s—somehow been taken in by that f—fiend in artistic f—form."

Cecily's merry laugh rang out. "Mr. Thrush, you are falsifying the facts."

"I?" he cried dramatically, clasping his bony hands together so that they wrestled with each other ceaselessly. "I? You c—call yourself a m—model, you c—claim to be a handmaiden to Art. I say, rather, you are a p—prostitute!"

Cecily gasped.

"Yes, I will be blunt," declared Chester. "A prostitute to this questionable cause. Demeaning your b—body, the temple of your s—spirit, by exposing it to public and impious view. Participating in the revels of a group of debauchees. No! Don't protest. All the world knows the reputation of artists. And this is my little w—wife! The w—woman in all the w—world who I have ch—chosen to honour with my name! No! Don't interrupt! I have not f—finished."

"But I have heard quite enough, Mr. Thrush," Cecily declared. "I ask you, as a gentleman, to depart. Your presence is no longer tolerable."

"I sh—shall not l—leave until you go with me," he said boldly. One of his hands seemed to have conquered the other in their death-like combat, and now he drew the injured extremity within the protection of his coat, and extended the other to Cecily. "I sh—shall not l—leave you here to endure f—further indignities."

"Mr. Thrush, it is you that shall suffer indignities if you refuse to leave as I requested," Cecily said firmly. She was raging with indignation and attempting, with only minimal success, to suppress it. "I have only to call Mr. Willet—"

"Yes, Miss Cecily," said a quiet, self-possessed voice at the door. It belonged to the object of the previous sentence, who bowed politely to Mr. Thrush. "Allow me to show you to the door, sir," he offered.

Chester pulled at his collar nervously. "M–miss Hawthorne, f–forgive me," he said abjectly. "I've s–said things I did not mean, all in the hope of f–furthering your best interests. M–mother said—"

"Right this way, Mr. Thrush," added Willet, somehow manoeuvring between Cecily and her unwelcome guest and nipping at his heels like a sheep dog with a particularly recalcitrant sheep.

"L–let me apologize!" Chester was calling out over Willet's head as he was relentlessly pushed into the hall and borne out the door. "L–let me explain. Oh, if only you were to apply to M–Mrs. Fluster at Number F–fourteen, S–Stanhope Gardens. I kn–know everything would be for the b–best." The slam of the door cut short his plea.

Willet and Cecily faced each other in the hall.

"How fortunate you were there, Mr. Willet, just when I required your assistance," said Cecily.

"Always glad to be of service," he replied and no further mention was made of Mr. Thrush or the purpose of his visit.

Alone the remainder of the day, Cecily occasionally regretted her flying off the handle with Chester Thrush, for it was somewhat better to talk to him than to talk to nobody at all. By the end of the wearisome hours, as she sat before her dressing table mirror, giving her hair its usual hundred brush strokes, she was even talking to herself.

Suddenly there was a soft tap at her door.

"Yes, Betty," she said, wondering why the maid would be knocking on her door so late.

"It isn't Betty," said a soft voice, a male voice. "It's Devin. I have a Valentine's Day present for you. I've only just gotten back from Lady Calverley's and I want to give it to you before the day is gone by."

Cecily's heart (this time she knew it was her heart) pounded rapidly in her chest, so much so that she put her hand upon it to still it. She had not yet disrobed, only her hair was loosened, and Mr. Sheridan saw it thus every time she sat for the portrait. After a moment's hesitation she cautiously said, "Come in, then."

The artist tiptoed in, with a mischievous smile on his face, a large, string-tied package under his arm. He stopped on the threshold, while he was still engulfed in the shadows of the hall, for Cecily in her coral gown, with her hair like a fire about her shoulders, was even more wonderful a sight than Cecily posing as Pandora, and it took him a few moments, to quell the tumult of emotions that sprang into his heart.

"This is a very special gift," he said at length, finding his tongue. "Very special because I consider it to be one of the most beautiful objects of its kind that I have ever seen. Very special because, until I met you, there was no one with the beauty to match it."

Cecily was humbled by such praise and put out her hands slowly to take the package and, placing it on the bed, carefully undid the strings. A glimmer of celandine-green. The flash of satin. An embroidered chrysanthemum. She drew it out, holding it up to the light of the fire. A celandine-green satin Japanese kimono embroidered with chrysanthemums, a faintly visible and delicately repaired tear up the back.

"Why, this is the same garment you gave to Miss Flo!" cried Cecily unbelieving.

Devin frowned. "I didn't know you knew about her."

"How dare you!" Cecily cried, flinging the robe at him so that it struck him across the face. "By what right do you give me a discarded piece of clothing belonging to your mistress?"

"But it's exquisite, it's been repaired—"

"It's not exquisite," shouted Cecily, tears streaming down her face. "It's a patched-together, old, worthless piece of cloth, a relic of a sordid liaison."

"Now, look here, I meant what I said. This is most precious to me. I paid a fortune for it, and yes, I gave it to Flo, but once I saw you, I knew who I had in mind when I purchased it. And I've already had it flung at me once before. I don't need—"

"I don't need your charity," declared Cecily. "I don't need your abject explanations. I don't need your odious comparisons with that flighty piece who used to reside in this room for you to visit at your pleasure."

"Certainly more pleasurable than this," said Mr. Sheridan grimly.

"I won't be talked to like this!" declared Cecily passionately, stamping her foot. "I am not the sort of woman you take me to be. I cannot forget what I was told was right and wrong when I was young. I cannot be expected to sit idle all day, every day, without a thought in my head or a penny in my pocket. I cannot be reminded, at every turn I make, of your foul attentions, and intentions, no doubt, toward unlucky women who reside under your roof."

"This is going too far."

"Borneo would not be too far for me," said Cecily wildly. "I have been offered a position as a nursery governess in a respectable household, where the staff is actually paid wages, where young women are not accosted in their bedrooms and forced to submit—"

"You make a habit of this, don't you?" said Devin coldly

Cecily was momentarily stunned and lost her train of thought. "What? What habit?"

"You just drift about from household to household, don't you?" he questioned contemptuously. "You didn't like it at the Davenports, you came running to me. Now you don't like it here, you'll go running somewhere else, isn't that it? Never face the real problems! Never admit your errors or wait for solutions! Never see through a project to which your presence is central! No, far more preferable for Cecily to run."

"I never—" she sputtered.

"You never will succeed at finding what you want," he concluded, shaking his head. "Always fleeing, always leaving it behind. Never knowing what went wrong. I feel sorry for people born without perseverance, for individuals without backbone. At least, Flo had that—"

Cecily, in a rage surpassing all those she had ever known, picked up the nearest object, a brass candlestick and flung it at him. He caught it easily with one hand and threw it back at her feet.

"Farewell, Miss Hawthorne," he said bitterly. "Best wishes with your new situation."

Chapter Nine

In Which the Artist Is Snared by an Artful Plan

MR. SHERIDAN'S TEMPER was of a different sort altogether than Cecily's temper. While her rages were like a summer storm, dramatic, flamboyant, unpredictable, they were gone as quickly, leaving behind few reminders of the violent upheaval. On the contrary, Mr. Sheridan's anger smouldered beneath a carefully controlled facade, like a volcano bubbling and seething beneath the earth until ready to burst forth, perhaps some time after the initial incident, with a fury that threatened to engulf everything in its path.

Cecily had long been gone from the Swan Walk household by the time Mr. Sheridan gave vent to his wrath, and it was another woman, Constance Holly, who became the innocent victim.

She was sitting for him in his studio. Her mother had discreetly disappeared, after an arched remark about tracking down the source of the delightful pastries and a broad wink for her timid daughter, a wink easily perceived by Mr. Sheridan, which made Constance blush with mortification. She knew however what the wink meant. It meant that she should ask Mr. Sheridan the questions her mother had carefully prepared for her on immortality and fame, questions designed to lead to a discussion of personal perpetuation through the production of children.

But she could not bring herself to do it. Instead she sat quietly, trembling a little, wilting under Mr. Sheridan's intent though impersonal scrutiny, trembling a little in anticipation of her mother's rage at her failure to elicit a proposal.

"I fear it's cold in here," said the artist in the icy voice which had become common after Cecily's departure. "Should you like a wrap of some sort?"

The thought of the celandine-green robe danced in his mind. Betty, Chlorrie and Willet had all taken sides against him, suggesting that it was next to criminal for him to have given Cecily a gift he had already given to another woman, especially not a gift which had been rejected and damaged. He could not make them understand how fond he was of the robe and how greatly he wished to see its irreplaceable (.and indestructible) beauty clothing Cecily's remarkably lovely form, and, in consequence, he spoke to them as little as necessary. The household was in a sort of siege, and even guests, such as Constance, were aware of that fact.

"Oh, don't trouble yourself about it," she said quickly, not wanting to stir up trouble. "I am fine as it is. Not to worry on my behalf."

Mr. Sheridan went back to his labours without further comment.

Constance squirmed uneasily in her seat. She had been sitting for three hours without any refreshment or respite. Although the artist had always been relatively oblivious to the comfort of his subjects, he was now completely unconcerned. Miss Holly, not ordinarily wont to complain, recognized the grim possibility that he might never notice her discomfort.

"I would like, ahem, appreciate—" she began timidly.

"Yes, what is it?" he snapped, never lifting his eyes from the canvas.

"I'm rather fatigued, from, well, it's been a long day," she continued apologetically.

"Very well then!" retorted Mr. Sheridan. He set down his brush with a clatter.

Constance got up uncertainly, shaking out her blue-silk skirts.

The artist did not look up, choosing instead to potter about with his paints.

"Devin—Mr. Sheridan," she said softly, "shouldn't you take advantage of this recess yourself? You must be hungry or weary or—"

"Spare me your apprehensions, Miss Holly," he replied with some annoyance. "I have managed to survive the past thirty-five years without a nursemaid." He winced slightly as he thought of Cecily. "I shall manage to survive several more without, I don't doubt."

Constance, inured to peevishness and ill humours by continual association with her mother, was not at all put off by Mr. Sheridan's rudeness. In truth, she was challenged. She wished to get at the root of his discontent.

"How is the portrait progressing?" she asked.

"As well as can be expected."

"And you anticipate it will be done with two more sittings?"

"I should imagine so."

"The young woman who was modelling for you. I haven't seen her recently. Did you finish the picture? If so, I should like to see it. It must be remarkable. She was a very striking young woman."

Mr. Sheridan actually looked at her for the first time, but his eyes were curiously blank.

"You probably think that a terribly bold question," Constance added hastily, "but I was impressed by her cheerfulness and good humour—"

"Hah!" said the artist gloomily.

"And just wondered what the completed picture—"

"Hah!" repeated Mr. Sheridan more bitterly.

"Then the picture was given up?" Constance was asking, when a bold step on the stairs signalled the arrival of her mother, whereupon she promptly crumpled into her customary sitting position, shoulders rounded, head bowed, and became the meek, mouse-like daughter with whom Devin was so familiar.

"Ah! A *tête-à-tête!*" announced Lady Holly, charging into the studio, one hand lifted in the air before her on which her eyes were fixed as if she were a second-rate actor reading cribbed stage notes. "How very romantic! Pray, don't let my presence deter you in any way from your delightful lovemaking, Devin, my son, I feel I can call you my son."

"Mama!" whispered Constance, blushing crimson.

"I assure you nothing of the kind was going on, Lady Holly," said the artist.

"Nonsense! All young lovers say the same thing," was Lady Holly's airy reply to him, before turning upon Constance and saying, "You haven't forgotten Immortality, have you, you goose?"

"No, Mama," replied Constance. She fixed her soft eyes on her hands which were clenched tightly in her lap. "Mr. Sheridan, I would find it most instructive to learn of your views on Immortality."

Mr. Sheridan raised his dark eyebrows.

"Whether or not one should wish to achieve it, and in what manner," Constance added dully.

"Of course, as an artist, a guardian of Culture, a bearer of the glad tidings of the future," Lady Holly took up the topic, "you must have a fascinating opinion."

"Hardly," he stated. "As a goal, I find it impractical, yet I wouldn't deny that when I work I consider my audience to be a vast group, far greater than the number of individuals now living. If my work gives pleasure, if it has substance, then a century from now, in 1979—"

"Imagine!" breathed Lady Holly.

"A new generation will be viewing one of my paintings. It's a humbling thought." He ran his fingers through his hair thoughtfully. "I suppose that as an artist, one does one's best and hopes that those who come after share in one's perception and pleasure in creating."

Lady Holly prodded her daughter with one of her lethal fingers. Constance winced but said nothing. Lady Holly poked her again.

"I—I—suppose," Constance said at length, a bit reluctantly, almost sullenly, "that for a woman, such a feeling is associated with bearing children."

"Possibly," said Devin, who could not, evidently, have been less interested in any topic.

Lady Holly shuffled closer to her daughter and under cover of her cape-like polonaise delivered a stinging pinch to Constance's forearm.

"I—I—I don't suppose you've thought of children, have you, Devin...er...Mr. Sheridan?" asked Constance painfully.

"No, I haven't," was the curt reply.

"One should, you know," sang out Lady Holly, wagging a finger at him archly. "How else preserve the fame of the noble name, Sheridan? To whom, shall you bequeath your home, the lovely treasures you've collected, the fortune of your family?"

"I was not aware of the Sheridan fortune," the artist said with interest.

"Well, you know," Lady Holly wrinkled up her nose, a manoeuvre which was apparently so difficult that she left it in that position for the remainder of the visit, "the commissions you earn on portraits, the prizes for competitions, the prices your works fetch in the galleries. It all must add up to quite a tidy sum. And who better to lavish it upon than little emblems of domestic bliss, small messengers sent from the Beyond to flock about the feet of you and Constance as you sit around your humble hearth—"

"Oh, Mama!" exclaimed Constance in a tiny voice.

"Do I understand you to imply that your daughter is to be the mother of my yet unborn descendants?" inquired Devin. "I have not yet heard of a wedding, nor, for that matter, an offer."

"I thought the wedding would be at Saint George's," Lady Holly declared heartily, "though I know it's become unfashionable of late. Still, it is quite a nice-sized church, and we have so many friends and relatives we must invite—"

"Enough!" roared Devin, enraged. "By God, woman, I've stood about as much of your interfering, meddlesome, irresponsible, small-minded schemes. You have the audacity to throw your daughter at me in the most blatant manner," Constance began to cry silently, "despite her complete absence of any regard for me at all—"

"That's not true," broke in Constance, sniffling and glancing timidly at her mother as she spoke, "I am very fond of you, Mr. Sheridan, indeed—"

"Miss Holly, I think this matter is between Lady Holly and me."

"There I think you are wrong," said Constance, rising to her feet and glaring at both of them. "I may have been a pawn of my mother's—"

"My own child, a viper in my bosom!" shrieked Lady Holly.

"I may have been a troublesome annoyance to you, Mr. Sheridan, a pitiful object to be placated with crumbs of your attention—"

"Look here, I said nothing of the—"

"But I am also a human being, with dignity, with feelings, with purposes and goals in life. It's not merely my mother's doings, I do wish to be married." She began to cry again, but with complete abandon this time, noisy sobs, racked with hiccoughs.

"Hush, Constance!" hissed her mother.

"Maybe that seems shameless to you, Mr. Sheridan," cried Constance, "but maybe you don't know what it is to be a thirty-two-year-old spinster—"

"I've always told you to state your age as twenty-seven, Constance!" interjected Lady Holly sharply.

"But I am thirty-two, Mother!" she said, whirling about, "and getting no younger. Thirty-two years of living at home with five sisters, all frustrated and bitter, thirty-two years with a mother who talks of nothing but disposing of me to the highest bidder, thirty-two years in a world where the only men I see daily are the butler and the hack-driver who waits at the cabstand across the street."

"Now, calm yourself, my dear Miss Holly," said Devin, putting his arm about her and leading her back to her seat. "Surely you go out to parties, the Opera, plays—"

"Surely!" agreed Constance with venom. "And what happens there? I'm talking to a gentleman, I have finally conquered my timidity sufficiently to strike up a conversation or to answer his very conventional inquiries, when another woman, a winning, fascinating little woman, a woman who giggles and protests her helplessness, wanders by and lures the gentleman away. Why even your model, that young girl with the red hair. When she was in the room you never even noticed me!"

"Constance!" exclaimed Lady Holly. "Never compare yourself to such women!"

"I think I should go into a convent!" declared her daughter hysterically, "or become a nurse." Her sobs became more uncontrollable and her head fell back alarmingly against the sofa. She clutched at her side.

"Oh, it's one of her fits!" remarked Lady Holly. "Now see what you've done, Mr. Sheridan, by spurning my daughter after placing her in such a compromising situation."

"Hardly a compromising situation," he retorted, "when the implications were all introduced by you. But never mind that! Good Heavens!" He stared aghast at the helpless form of the twitching girl. "What does one do for her now?"

"Move aside," she commanded not giving him a chance to comply but elbowing him aside with her bulk. "I must loosen her stays and have your man send up some *sal volatile*, some smelling salts and some cold water."

Shaken out of his recent apathy by the alarming turn of events, Devin went galloping down the stairs, rather than wait for Willet to respond to the bell (little knowing that Willet was, of course, listening to the entire scene from his favoured vantage point in the corridor), and in consequence of Willet not being able to be located, went racing back up again, clutching the required items only to discover Willet, kneeling alongside the overwrought girl, splashing water upon her face. Lady Holly snatched the smelling salts from the artist's arms and applied it promptly to Constance's nose. One of these two remedies appeared to be efficacious. Constance calmed down, her eyes cleared, she raised herself up a little on her elbows, met the concerned eyes of the observers and promptly fainted.

The cold water was splashed upon her again. The smelling salts were once more applied. Devin, finding that he had forgotten a spoon for applying the *sal volatile* dashed back down to the kitchen, returning to find that Constance, having been brought to her senses for the second time, was overcome with mortification and shame and refused to allow him in the room. As the room in question was his studio and workplace, this maidenly modesty was rather inconvenient. Still, Mr. Sheridan felt that he had played a part in her collapse, nay, that he even owed her an apology for his trifling treatment of her real concerns. Lady Holly saw the softening impulse in his eyes and, always quick to take advantage where her daughter's matrimonial status was involved, took him aside while Constance was assisted to the waiting carriage by Willet.

She dabbed at her eyes with an oversized handkerchief.

"Mr. Sheridan, you must forgive my Constance," she said in maudlin tones. "She was distraught, overcome, choked, if you will, with her unexpressed sentiments, those feminine feelings that in her, alas, seem doomed to die an unnatural death, forever unventilated!" She snorted noisily by way of a sob.

"Lady Holly," said Devin sternly, "your daughter is a fine woman, with all the tendernesses and strengths of a true member of her sex. If you would let her flower in the true form of her beauty, rather than torturing it into unnatural patterns of growth, she should have little trouble in making a satisfying marriage and becoming an excellent wife for some lucky fellow."

"Don't think I haven't tried!" snuffled Lady Holly. "Don't think I haven't exposed her to the cream of the limited circles within which we move!" she cried in anguish. "Never say that I have been remiss as a mother and guardian of my children's well-being. Never say so!"

"I do say so."

"Oh, monster! Oh, brute! You reduce my simple pet to hysterics and swoons and fits and tears, then castigate her mother for lack of feeling! What an unsensitive beast is man!"

Mr. Sheridan ran his hand through his hair.

"My poor darling!" continued Lady Holly, one eye looming large over the horizon of her handkerchief. She waited for her pathetic words to take effect. She had not long to wait.

"Perhaps there is something I can do," sighed the exasperated artist. "It pains me to see such a fine girl in so much distress."

"Then you will marry her! I knew you were a gentleman!" declared Lady Holly, emerging from her camouflage dry-eyed and radiant.

"No! Good Heavens, no!" ejaculated Devin. "I only meant that I could take her under my wing, as it were. My acquaintances are, perhaps, more varied than yours. I feel certain there is someone among them who could appreciate Miss Holly for her own admirable qualities."

"Yes?" asked Lady Holly meaningfully.

"I could escort her to various functions, introduce her to hostesses I know. In turn, she would be doing me a favour for there is nothing I detest more than being seated beside some simpering young miss whose mother is waiting with bated breath for a declaration of interest. With your daughter as my social partner, I would be spared the tedium of many otherwise stultifying affairs. Yes, I believe we could reach some agreement on such terms."

"It is done!" declared Lady Holly, putting forth her big hand and crushing Devin's slender one in her own meaty clasp. "I shall inform Constance. She will be overcome! You are too generous!" She pranced out of the house to join her daughter in an obscene parody of a skip.

Devin Sheridan sighed and wondered if he had done the right thing.

Within the confines of the carriage, Lady Holly embraced her daughter.

"You have done it, Constance!" she exclaimed. "You have won Mr. Sheridan's heart! I knew you were capable of it, with, naturally, my sage advice. What a masterful stroke that fit was!"

"Mother! What are you saying?" asked the affronted daughter.

"Mr. Sheridan will soon be your affianced husband," proclaimed her proud parent. "He wishes to take you about, introduce you to his friends, show you off in various gatherings. Within a matter of months, the engagement can be made public. Oh, Constance, what an artful little minx you are! Just wait until your sisters hear of this."

Chapter Ten

Relates the Perils of an Aesthetic Household

CECILY HAD BEEN TERRIFIED upon her first acquaintance with Number Fourteen Stanhope Gardens, and the Flusters who resided therein. Live peacocks that ran about the corridors screeching, bearing odd names such as Cadwallader and Brunhilda. A complete suit of armour in the hallway. A six-foot, seven-inch footman in velvet doublet and pink plush knee breeches. Acres of porcelain and oceans of peacock feathers.

She had been interviewed by a stern bespectacled woman with a pinched face and scraped-back hair, who she at first took to be the housekeeper and later learned was Miss Joconda, the daughter of the house. She had been approved by the ethereal Mrs. Fluster, with Mr. Fogwell in attendance, nodding his acquiescence. She had been shown to her room, a medieval–looking chamber on the upper floor, by a pert young maid who said her name was Nessie Caper, and who claimed to be the only female servant in the house. She had been brought in to see her infant charge in the oppressively cluttered nursery, and suddenly, all her fears and trepidations vanished. For here was a child who required all of the cares and attentions she had been taught to give at Mrs. Polyander's Academy. Here was a young being who had been so isolated that the child cringed in terror from friendship and cowered at a kind word. Here was a fretful baby, whose health could be strengthened in every manner, who could be cosseted with all the delicacies Cecily knew how to concoct. Here, at last, was a project deserving the entire mind and soul of Cecily Hawthorne.

And Cecily was glad that her labours were so enormous and so demanding. For possibly, they would enable her to forget her luxurious interlude in Chelsea, forget the unkind words of Mr. Sheridan and forget the failures of her previous endeavours. She applied herself diligently to Amaryllis, usually known as "Baby," referred to by Nessie Caper, as the "infant burden."

"'Pon my word, her Mama's ashamed of her very existence," explained Nessie, pointing at the timid infant, who sat primly on a chair clutching her favourite toy, a threadbare rag doll, unimaginatively named "Dolly."

"Can you imagine her horror at finding herself in a delicate condition and she forty-five?" Nessie didn't wait for Cecily's response. "Well you can guess, I'm sure, her predicament. Two grown children and suddenly, a blessed event. I tell you, the Missus isn't the sort to be a devoted mother. She was exasperated. Denied it up to the moment of her confinement. Mind you, I don't know this at first-hand, but I get it from reliable sources. I've only been here a quarter and considering leaving myself. It was 'Find me a wet-nurse!' 'Occupy the child, somehow!' 'I don't want to see her belowstairs!' and I'm a housemaid, not a nursemaid. I told her so. Repeatedly, I told her, 'I'm not a nursemaid, Madam.' But what with money being so tight in this here establishment, they paid me no mind. If it hadn't been for that interfering old harpy, Lady Holly, they'd never have hired you. But Mrs. Fluster couldn't afford to have society learn of their financial prevarication. There was nothing for it but to get a nursemaid. And I sez a loud and fervent 'Halleluiah!' This child is a monster! A veritable monster!"

Baby nodded solemnly in agreement. Cecily put a protective arm about her but the infant shrugged it away and popped her finger into her mouth.

"Take that!" declared Nessie. "I put bitter aloes on her thumb. A friend of mine, she works for the Earl of Corrough, said it never failed to break his brats of the nasty habit. But on Baby? Nothing! She sucks her thumb even more, if that is possible. I think she likes the horrid stuff! She's never slept through a single night, and I must lose my sleep because of it.

Think on it! I'm the one who must be up before dawn to light the fires and fetch the water, and yet, because this wretched child has nightmares, I am expected to minister to her the whole night through! What if Alf—he's the footman. Athelbert they call him, we all must have some poetical name to suit the Missus—should fancy a little of my time? Well, I'll tell you, I have no chance for romance. How's a girl supposed to meet the man of her dreams? And as to nursery meals! This wretched child can only eat the mildest substances. That's what she's lived on since her birth. Course, I administer some cordials now and then, as much as I can get away with. That's my only opportunity to sleep. But even laudanum has little effect upon this one. I tell you, quite plainly, open and above-board, I don't like children. I told Missus that when she hired me. Drooling little beasts, always whining and wanting attention. If I wanted to be a nursemaid, I said, I would have hired in as a nursemaid. I'm ever so grateful you're here, Cecily, I may call you Cecily? Good! None of this hoity-toity stuff between us, right? But I expect you to keep your hands off Alf—Athelbert! I warn you, fair and square, he's mine. Understood?"

Cecily nodded her agreement.

"Right! Then you handle the little monster and I'll see to the housecleaning, though I don't know why I bother when I haven't seen a farthing since I began."

"I was told this was a wealthy household," said Cecily indignantly. "I wouldn't have taken on the position otherwise, for I haven't been paid for the last two months."

"Well, looks like you were given bad information," retorted Nessie, with a shake of her blond curls which set the blue ribbons in her cap fluttering. "Promises! Promises!

That's all we get, by we, referring, of course, to me and Athelbert and Cook and Susan, the scullery-maid, for that's all of us. Oh, Mrs. Fluster's maid, that nasty, meddling Spinks. When Mr. Fluster's ship comes in, they say—he's the director of a manufacturing concern though no longer active in the company—yet his ship must still be out on the Indian Ocean for all I know!"

"This is terrible!" cried Cecily.

"There's good grub," Nessie explained. "Miss Joconda, she's Mrs. Fluster's eldest daughter, sees to that. She and her mother are violently opposed. Missus says it's unnatural for an unmarried woman to be so involved with all the management of a household, the cleaning and the cooking, the way Miss Joconda is. They hate each other. You should hear them quarrelling. Sounds like the Battle of Waterloo. Yet it's fine for us. The menus are superb; the dishes divine. There's not another house to match it in all of London. On the other hand, and there always is another hand, I've found, it means Miss Joconda is always poking her nose in where it isn't wanted—for instance, criticizing the polish I use on the fireplace grates or telling me, me who's been a housemaid for the past seven years, that I don't light the fire properly! At least, you'll have little dealings with her, for she knows nothing about nursery-maiding, no more than I. Yet like I said, we have good food and very generous they are with perquisites, which you must admit are the back and bone of a servant's existence. This gown I wear was once the Missus'!" She waved her lilac silk skirt in the air. "Alf says when I wear it he cannot concentrate on his duties properly."

"It's very lovely," agreed Cecily, who had to admit that everything about Nessie, from her mop of golden curls to her daintily-clad toes, was exquisite. Never had she seen such a beautiful girl employed in domestic service, and she knew the usual reason why this was so.

"Is there a son in the house?" she asked.

"Oh, Cedric!" declared Nessie, with a scornful look. "He's nineteen and the apple of his mama's eye. She thinks he can do no wrong. A more arrogant, ignorant, silly, ridiculous young fool, I've yet to see. Don't set your cap for him," advised Nessie. "He hasn't a thought in his head for anyone but himself. His parents think to set him up with an heiress, a rich American girl named Flutterby. Poor girl! She actually thinks he's some sort of romantic hero! I suspect, though, marriage to her would be the best he can do. He's not fit for anything, not military service, nor a place in the government.

He goes about mouthing poetry! Faugh! When has poets ever earned their own living? Though I must admit, Cedric's the only one in this household who still labours under the impression that his papa made all their fortunes. No, marriage to Miss Flutterby would be the only thing to put him out of his misery. I doubt, mind you, that they can carry it off successful–like. Sooner or later she's sure to notice something amiss and then—pffft! Good-bye American dollars! And with that, down we all tumbles! It's sort of assumed that we all put on a good front, for elsewise, what was this all for?"

Though she did not sanction Nessie's philosophies, Cecily found it easy to fall into the same patterns of compliance. Ever in the back of her mind were Mr. Sheridan's charges of her instability, and she was determined to prove them untrue, at least to herself. And then, the infant burden was beguiling in her own right.

It was many days before she would let Cecily approach near enough to comb her matted blond curls or wash her begrimed little face and many days again before she would respond to her name (Cecily called her "Amy" finding "Amaryllis" too big a mouthful).

Every minute of her waking hours, and many of them, as Nessie foretold, occurred during the middle of the night, Cecily was absorbed with her charge, and only slowly did the baby come to count upon Cecily's presence, toddling to her with toys, running to bury her head in Cecily's skirts whenever she heard footsteps in the corridor. During the first week of Cecily's stay, Mrs. Fluster never appeared in the nursery, and the only visitors were Nessie and Cedric, come to see the new nursery governess for himself.

He was a lanky young man, with longish fair hair curling about his ears, and light-coloured blue eyes with a tendency to cross slightly. His costumes were the most outlandish Cecily had ever seen, and this was amazing, she thought, considering she had been in the company of artists and poets, notorious for their eccentricity. Cedric favoured striped stockings, scarfs dangling about his neck and, when with the fair sex affected a fashionable lisp.

"Mith Thethily," he had drawled at their first meeting. "A lily in a garden of prickly rothes."

Cecily, well-schooled by Mrs. Polyander in methods of avoiding the son of the household, merely nodded and handed Baby another piece of the puzzle they were completing.

"I thall write a thonnet to your pulchritude," Cedric announced. "I thall compare you to a well of thpring water in a thorched desert, to an Arabian theed in an enclosure of camels."

Receiving no response he flung himself down upon the hearth rug and adopted a pensive pose. Cecily bent closer to the baby, saying, "Now, Amy, say hello to your brother!"

Amy regarded Cedric with wide, mournful eyes before burying her head in Cecily's lap.

"Ah, how I thould long to follow her excellent example," proposed Cedric. Cecily, remembering Mrs. Polyander's injunctions, ignored him.

"Amy, be a good child, there you are," she crooned softly, for the baby had lifted her tousled head. "Do Miss Hawthorne a favour and say hello to your brother. He must be going, and he came expressly to greet you."

Amy wrinkled her nose descriptively. "No!" she said distinctly and shook her head emphatically.

"The only word she knows," explained Cecily apologetically.

"No!" repeated the child with pride.

"I'm afraid your presence is overwhelming to her," Cecily said calmly. "She's so little used to company. She does better when with one person."

Cedric remained where he was, regarding Cecily through a monocle he wore draped across his lapel upon a black satin ribbon.

"I must ask you to leave," she said firmly, "for it's time for Amy's nap."

Amy began to cry. Cedric did not move.

"She's a very sensitive child," said Cecily, in as authoritarian a voice as she could muster, "and when it's time for her nap she's even more excitable."

Baby wailed. Cedric leered at Cecily complacently. Fortunately, Mrs. Polyander had devised a stratagem for just such a predicament.

"I fear Amy has been troubled with a cough recently," said Cecily casually. "I must dose her with an emetic. If you would hold the basin, while I administer the ipecacuanhanic wine—" Before she had finished her sentence, Cedric had vanished, and Cecily thought again, with a sigh of gratitude, of the invaluable down-to-earth precepts of Mrs. Polyander. She wished, somewhat ruefully, that she had thought of consulting that redoubtable matron before leaving Mr. Sheridan's employ so precipitately, but after a moment's daydreaming, shook herself soundly out of the clouds, telling herself sternly that Mrs. Polyander could hardly have sanctioned art modelling as a profession, and applied herself to the realities of a nursemaid's job.

Cedric, meanwhile, strolled down the curio-littered corridors of "Fluster Fancy" (as his mother quaintly referred to their home), hands in his pockets, whistling a music hall tune. "Demmed fine figure of a gel," he said aloud, reviewing Cecily's charms in his mind. "But a dem sight too wrapped up in her work." Cedric found it difficult to comprehend the attachment such persons formed to their duties. Surely all the world could see that the important things in Life were not the things one did, but the luxuries one appreciated: fine wine, beautiful women, an elegantly cut jacket, a noble cigar, a run of luck at the gaming table. In this, he was his mother's son, moulded and influenced by her principles until he emerged a perfect embodiment of her ideals. For his father, he had only contempt. If one had managed to raise oneself from a humble position and a disgraceful family, then surely one should be grateful for one's good fortune and view the past from the proper perspective—as beneath one's notice. But Mr. Fluster was too fond, by far, of recounting the obstacles he had encountered on the ladder to success, too soft-hearted to refuse the demands of the disreputable-looking individuals who occasionally applied for his assistance claiming some degree of relation. Whenever possible, Cedric ignored his father and when he saw him coming his way, as now, headed with as much initiative as he was capable of (which was very little), in the opposite direction.

On this occasion he was too unhurried in his movement, and Mr. Fluster, a small, rotund and balding little man, bounded like a rubber ball into his path and said cheerfully, "Oh, there you are, son. I must have a word with you! Come into my study."

"Governor," drawled Cedric, barely concealing his indifference, "I must defer our little chat to another time. I have a most pressing engagement elsewhere."

"Not more pressing than the business we have to discuss," said his father firmly, for he had not achieved his singular good fortune without diligent application and persistence, traits which he seldom used in his relationships with his children, but which were available when necessary. "It will take only a moment. Besides, you surely aren't dressed to go out!"

"I beg to differ, Governor," replied Cedric in the same lazy manner. "This is the height of fashion at the moment." He contemplated his father's spotted waistcoat and ill-fitting shabby coat with heavy-lidded disbelief.

Mr. Fluster had not been a handsome man when Mrs. Fluster, then Sophronia Bendle, the third daughter of the Fourth Earl of Gammage, decided to marry him. As she was also a small person, his lack of stature had not bothered her, and she anticipated that within the confines of marriage she could reform his execrable taste in clothing. His prominent blue eyes, which she had at first thought direct, and now considered protuberant, and his thick shock of fair hair had been points in his favour. Unfortunately, the hair had been a sacrifice to the demands of the Firm, and within a few short years he was completely bald on the top, though his thick blond moustache and his heavy sideburns remained to bear witness to his former crowning glory. His physique had once been most admired in the drawing rooms of London, and all in all, despite his humble origins, and perhaps because of his astounding wealth, he had been one of the most eligible *partis* in Sophronia Bendle's circle of acquaintances. Alas, the years had also taken a toll upon his waistline, and now his lovely wife and fashionable son could not bear his presence in their drawing room, excusing him from many of the Flusters' social invitations on the grounds that he disliked entertaining. Having retired from the Firm, which had been his life's blood and given little other direction to turn his remarkable talents, he had become a crotchety, sentimental old man, given to maudlin attachments to his pet dogs and a ridiculous infatuation with his infant daughter.

"Have a seat, Cedric," he said apologetically, indicating an easy chair in his study, a chamber crowded with mementoes of his business years, blue-bound ledger books, sheaves of bills and receipts, framed photographs of the warehouse and a certificate of merit from the late Prince Albert on the Firm's display of manufacturing equipment at the Great Exhibition of 1851, the year before his marriage and perhaps the pinnacle of his success. "I have some excellent Havana cigars. Care to try one?"

Cedric nodded his acceptance and was soon enveloped in a cloud of bluish smoke.

Mr. Fluster sat down in the chair behind his desk, a mammoth cast-iron desk which had completely filled his office at the Firm and which had been transported to Fluster Fancy upon his retirement. He straightened a pile of reports, moved his paperweight from this location to that, ran his finger along the blade of his letter opener.

"I find it most difficult to say what I find it necessary to relate," he began hesitantly.

"Then, Heavens, Governor, don't say it!" was Cedric's casual reply.

"But I find it absolutely critical," responded his father, "to the well-being of the family, which is, of necessity, my most pressing concern."

Cedric coughed.

"You know, of course," continued Mr. Fluster, "that when I left the Firm, after fifty years of devoted service, half a century of dedication and application—"

"Yes, I know all that," put in the son.

"Well, I left it in the capable hands of my partner, the very able Mr. Muddle, a most excellent director in his own rights—"

"The man had no sense at all of Culture," interrupted Cedric.

"Regardless," went on Mr. Fluster sternly, "he had a good head for business and had developed several new markets for Fluster and Muddle, as well as maintaining our high quality and insistence upon honesty with our distributors and the public. I wish the same could be said for his son, Esmond Muddle, Jr."

"An unmitigated ass," was Cedric's opinion. "He was black-balled by the Aesthetes Club. I won't say that I was responsible, because I wasn't, but still I should have voted so myself if Fitz-Boodle hadn't done so!"

"It is, of course, beyond the scope of my present duties to step in and resume active management of Fluster and Muddle, despite the unforeseeable and sudden death of my dear friend and partner, James Muddle—one might almost say tragic death."

"I should say so!" snorted Cedric, for Mr. James Muddle had been crushed beneath a beer barrel which escaped, on a steep hill, from the deliverymen who were unloading it from a dray. The contemplation of such an unaesthetic death gave Cedric nightmares.

"Nevertheless, it would not at all be taken amiss if my son, as the indisputable heir to my...ahem...well, one might call it a Business Empire and be not far off the mark, as I said, that my son should step in himself—"

"Never!" declared Cedric shuddering. "I? Be involved with a manufacturing concern?"

Mr. Fluster attempted to look severe, a feat, perhaps not so difficult to achieve if one has a large Roman nose or bushy eyebrows or a particularly crag-like forehead, but very challenging for an individual with a face like a pink cherub. He failed in the attempt.

"Now, see here, Cedric," he said, "such an attitude is fine when one can afford to think that way. I would be the first to admit it's usual (though the last to understand why) some people think it satisfying to have nothing to do but gad about to parties and sit and smoke at clubs and prate endlessly about Art and Poetry. But if you continue to ignore the very treacherous circumstances which are unfolding under our feet, threatening the foundations, if I may be permitted to employ a simple metaphor, of our security, you will soon find yourself unable to live in such high style."

"I should be black-balled by the Aesthetes if it were to become known that I had anything to do with the production of cast-iron furniture!" exclaimed Cedric indignantly.

"You already have something to do with the production of cast-iron furniture," said Mr. Fluster, somewhat more harshly than was his wont. "Without the Firm you would not have the luxury to pursue such idle undertakings."

"Idle! My dear governor!" drawled Cedric. "You simply have no conception of the arduous demands of club memberships. First, one must dress oneself, keeping in mind the latest dictums of that capricious Mistress Fashion—that is the undertaking of half a day. Next, one must get oneself to the club somehow. That too is more difficult than the average John Bull believes. A cab won't do. No—"

"Enough!" snapped his father. "You have not a serious bone in your body. I might as well be speaking to Ralph." Ralph was Mr. Fluster's pet retriever, who was slumbering before the empty hearth. At the mention of his name, he came bounding up, slobbering at his master's hand. "Good boy, Ralph," said Mr. Fluster fondly. "I tell you, Cedric, if you don't interest yourself in the Firm, we will be penniless before long."

"Penniless, Governor! How you exaggerate!"

"It's fine to be so scornful. It's fine to talk so foolishly!" Mr. Fluster was becoming excited and bobbing up and down in his seat. "The good name of Fluster, the lives of everyone under this roof, the preservation of the innumerable furnishings and accoutrements we have purchased over the years, all rest on your shoulders, and you worry more about the width of your lapels."

"You noticed," said Cedric with a frown. "I told my tailor they were a trifle too broad but he insisted they were fine."

"I warn you, Cedric," admonished his sorely-tried father, "that if you persist in this schooled ignorance—Here! I have it! Let me show you the state of affairs!" He tugged at an over-sized leather volume underneath a stack of bills and pushed it towards his son, hunting among the paraphernalia on his desktop for his spectacles.

"Figures give me a headaches, governor," whined Cedric, "unless, you understand, the figure is on a woman. Dashed attractive gel that is up in the nursery at the moment."

Mr. Fluster fell back in his chair with a moan. Again he exhorted himself to treat the matter at hand in the same dogged, determined way he had mastered all of his business problems, and he reviewed some of his well-tested principles of success. If one solution is impossible, propose another. Yes, that was it! Cedric might prefer the second alternative, at any rate.

"Cedric," he began slowly, clapping his pudgy hands together softly, "what are your intentions toward that American girl, the one who is pursuing you so avidly, what's her name, Flutterby?"

"Veracity, Flutterby?" repeated Cedric in tones of incredulity. "I have no intentions toward her, whatsoever. And mind you, that is not a comment I make lightly about a female. In the normal course of events, my intentions are strictly dishonourable."

"You know, it is your mother's fondest hope that you should marry the girl."

"Marriage?" Cedric snorted. "Mind if I have another cigar, governor?" He helped himself. "Thank you."

"Mrs. Fluster feels that Miss Flutterby would be only too happy to reside here, in London, perhaps make this her home, and naturally, if she were your wife, given the fortune her father is said to have amassed, and all at her disposal, why it stands to reason she'd be able to maintain this household, pay the servants and such—it's been months since they've gotten any wages—maybe even contribute some amount to the Firm until it gets back on to its feet again."

"Marriage?" Cedric seemed unable to get past this dreaded word.

"Mind you, I think such a plan is, well, frankly, unethical," went on Mr. Fluster, "and I've told Mrs. Fluster so myself. The poor girl should certainly be placed under no obligation to assume our debts, nor should she marry into a family in as desperate straits as we are without a sound understanding of our financial picture. Regrettably, Mrs. Fluster does not agree with me on this issue, and I have always permitted her to have free rein when it comes to matters of social intercourse. However, if that seems a better alternative to you, my son, perhaps you might make yourself more agreeable to this young woman, what's her name, Flutterby, and see if any more intimate feelings develop as you go along."

"Marriage!" reiterated Cedric, his horror-stricken eyes emerging briefly from the fog of cigar smoke to stare at his father.

"Damn it all, Cedric!" declared Mr. Fluster, slamming down his fist on the desk, which elicited a shrill bark from Ralph. "What can I say to make you comprehend the utter seriousness of our circumstances?"

"One should never be serious, governor," drawled Cedric, unfolding himself languidly from his seat and drifting in a cloud of smoke towards the door. "Seriousness makes one old, and one should sooner die than be old."

His highly effective exit was marred somewhat by his stumbling over a homely and, what was worse in Cedric's eyes, common-looking stranger in the hall.

"I'm l–looking for the h–housekeeper's room," stammered the stranger, who was our old friend Mr. Chester Thrush, choking from the fumes of the cigar smoke.

"Third door on your right," directed Cedric, "and if you'll take a word of advice, never, I repeat, never wear that waistcoat in combination with those trousers again. In fact, if you'll be very obliging to the souls of the multitudes, you should burn them both." He sauntered off down the hall, streamers of smoke trailing behind him.

Chester remained rooted to the spot for some time, quivering with indignation for he was wearing his favourite crimson waistcoat with the little white compasses with his natty grey-and-orange hound's-tooth–check trousers, but the sound of incoherent mutterings coming from the room which Cedric had vacated filled him with a horror that the young man had actually carried out his threats and burned someone else's apparel and, having no desire to meet a naked stranger, in this strangest of strange households, he bolted for the third door on the right and stepped inside, pulling the door shut behind him.

For the first time since he had arrived at Number Fourteen Stanhope Gardens he felt safe. The appearance of the outside of the house—clumps of unearthly lilies, terracotta gargoyles and a brass gong for a bell—had been disconcerting. The behaviour of the oddly garbed footman, for Athelbert was following some of Miss Flutterby's suggestions as to the democratization of the class structure and refusing to announce visitors, was demoralizing. And being left in the entry hall with a peacock had been humiliating. But having survived these hazards and the obstacles of spindly-legged tables, waving tapestries and the aesthetic madman, he found himself in a chamber containing only good solid, stolid furniture and a pleasant, practical-looking woman. It was a bit odd that all of the furniture was made of cast iron, but he decided not to let this fact bother him.

"The housekeeper, I presume," he said, with a little sigh of relief as he removed his bowler hat and sank down upon an unyielding iron sofa.

The young woman who was poring over a crimson-bound volume and several scraps of paper looked up and removed her bifocals, an act impossible to explain since it rendered her nearly blind. Chester Thrush was now to her a pale blob, with a pair of blue eyes wavering indistinctly below a crop of sandy-coloured hair and above a small, pursed, pink mouth. "How do you do?" she said softly.

"Mr. Thrush," snapped Chester.

"Very well, Mr. Thrush, how can I help you?" replied Joconda, who Chester could see quite clearly and whose appearance he found extremely correct. She wore a neat, black silk gown, ornamented only by a flawlessly white starched collar and cuffs. Her dark brown hair was bound back tightly and her plain even features were unexceptionable, saving their absolute lack of notability. Chester found, to his pleasure, that this sort of woman inspired in him a self-assurance usually missing in his dealings with the fair sex.

"I have come to see you regarding Miss Hawthorne," he said sternly, inserting his thumbs into his waistcoat pockets and assuming what he hoped to be a debonair and jaunty pose.

"Oh!" The bifocals were returned to their perch on the bridge of her nose.

"I came to inquire as to her suitability for this position," Chester said.

"I don't see what business that is of yours, Mr. Thrush."

"I assume her recommendations were in order."

"None were necessary."

"What did she tell you about her last employment?"

"I did not inquire."

"Well, young woman, I would suggest to Mrs. Fluster very strongly, and I believe she might listen to me as I am the chief clerk of the well-known firm of Davenport and Cole, that she not only might like to review the hiring of Miss Hawthorne, but also of her housekeeper."

"You might very well suggest that to Mrs. Fluster and she might very well listen, but I highly doubt that she would dismiss me."

"You have her in some sort of deceitful bondage to you, I perceive."

"Not precisely, Mr. Thrush, unless a filial relationship is considered a deceitful bondage. I am Mrs. Fluster's daughter."

"Great Scott!" exclaimed Chester, his mouth dropping open. Joconda removed her bifocals once again. "Why didn't you tell me? M–my God, you let me labour under this dreadful misapprehension. Can you forgive me, Miss Fluster?"

"Miss Joconda Fluster," she replied calmly, "though I prefer to be called Jane, which is my name—or was until my mother changed it during her Aesthetic period."

"F–f–fine. C–capital," he stammered. "I fear I must be g–going. I see I've interrupted what must be some very pressing matter."

"Oh, that," Joconda glanced down at the scraps of paper which littered her desk. "Perhaps you can help me. I am having difficulty choosing a menu."

"Ah, one of my talents," Chester said complacently, settling back again, though an iron grape leaf on the back of the sofa made unpleasant contact with his spine.

"We are having a large dinner party," Joconda explained, frowning a little, "and the planning, as usual, devolves upon me. My mother refuses to assume responsibility for the smooth operation of the household. She prefers to pretend that the servants will conduct themselves properly, the produce will be selected carefully, the best cut of meat will be used and the correct vintage of wine will be chosen without any supervision whatsoever. I know better."

"I quite concur with your opinion, Miss Fluster," said Chester.

"Well the problem is this. We must serve only the best dishes at this particular dinner in order to impress a young American woman who, if you want my frank opinion, wouldn't know a banquet from a picnic. Nevertheless, one wishes to always show one's table at its best. Now, what I must decide—these questions seem so insignificant to others, but I'm sure you'll agree with me as to their importance—is whether or not to serve *tendrons de veau* with purée of tomatoes or sweetbread cutlets, with *poirade* sauce, for the entree—with larded fillets of rabbit?"

"Oh, the sweetbread cutlets, without a doubt," replied Chester.

"Ah," Joconda chewed her lower lip. "I believe you're right, Mr. Thrush. Yes, that will suit nicely." She scribbled it in. "Then, since that choice was so happy, perhaps you have an opinion on the second course. We're having roast fowls, a boiled ham and—"

"You need a stewed rump of beef," declared Chester stoutly.

"Quite! The very thing!" declared Joconda. "I'll have it served *a la jardinière*." She sighed and removed her bifocals once more. "I only wish you could be there. Mrs. Grunion has such a way with stewed rump of beef *a la jardinière*, and her larded fillets of rabbit are divine. What did you say is your profession?"

"Chief clerk, Davenport and Cole Limited," announced Chester, puffing out his chest.

"It would never do," mourned Joconda. "This is strictly an aesthetic dinner. We're even having roast peacock for the third course removed by rhubarb tart *a la* Turner, my own invention."

"*A la* Turner?" inquired Chester, rubbing his nose.

Joconda's eyes brightened. She straightened her habitually hunched shoulders. For a moment she was as radiant as a bride.

"You mean you really don't know who Turner is?" she asked breathlessly.

"You mean to say Turner is a man?"

"Oh!" she gasped, a sigh of pure rapture.

"Turner, Turner, Turner, no I can't say that I have ever heard of him," Chester admitted.

"You've never seen any of his paintings?"

"Paintings! Ah, well that makes it dear to me. Artists! A trifling pack of mountebanks and mealy mouthed miscreants," stated Chester with vehemence. "I avoid any acquaintance with artists. A dangerous, immoral, depraved lot!"

"Mr. Turner isn't alive," explained Joconda. "He's been dead some time, but the National Gallery is full of his works."

"Bah! Art! I haven't time for it!" snapped Chester. "I have enough to occupy myself, thank you, with the financial obligations of an entire great firm resting upon my shoulders, not to mention the care of my sainted m—mother and the antics of my fiancée...er...Miss Hawthorne to keep me busy."

"You said that you had some concern about Miss Hawthorne's suitability?"

"Well, ahem, Miss Fluster, I rather fear it would take up too much of your very precious time. Would it be possible for me to meet you upon some other occasion and then to go into it more thoroughly?"

"At your convenience, Mr. Thrush," replied Joconda. "I will be free at this time next week—"

He looked at her reproachfully.

"Or perhaps Friday afternoon."

"Much more preferable, Miss Fluster," he said fervently.

"Then Friday it shall be," she said with a smile, shutting up her ledger in which she had annotated the appointment with a great bang. "I shall be looking forward to speaking with you again, Mr. Thrush. Perhaps you can help me with my menus."

"It would be my great pleasure, Miss Fluster," he replied with a gallant bow, and backed out of the door, beaming like a lantern.

Chapter Eleven

Cecily Is Schooled in the Conventions
of Romantic Novels

"SIR, YOU HAVE BEEN SEEING a good deal of Miss Holly recently," Willet observed one morning as he brought in the mail to Mr. Sheridan, who was idly daubing at a painting alone in his studio. It was a grey, sullen, overcast day with the promise of rain in the air, and Mr. Sheridan's mood evidently matched the climate.

"Hunh," he mumbled.

"A pleasant young woman," commented Willet. "I must point out, sir, that this is the third letter from Lord Throttle regarding the portrait of his wife which was to have been delivered last month."

"Let the old trout stew a bit longer," was Devin's unsympathetic response. "I still must doctor up the background in some colour that won't render Lady Throttle's complexion sallow, which it is anyway."

"Miss Holly's portrait is progressing nicely, though," offered Willet.

"As well as can be expected."

Willet busied himself straightening out a heap of entangled frames. He wanted information as to his employer's intentions regarding Miss Constance Holly, but as the observant reader might have noted, was having trouble eliciting such information. He tried another approach.

"I expect that once you are married, sir, you won't be requiring my services."

"What?" Devin looked at him as if he had gone mad.

"I mean to say, sir, it's understandable you might prefer a younger person, someone personally chosen, perhaps, by Miss Holly."

"Willet, if you are trying to tell me something, I suggest you say it as directly as possible for I am not in the mood today to beat around the bush."

Willet looked aggrieved. "Merely making conversation, sir," he said.

"Good!" Devin responded. "I thought possibly you were curious as to the exact nature of my liaison with Miss Holly."

"I wouldn't call it a liaison," Willet said with polite shock, "More a courtship, isn't it, sir?"

"Ah, so you are interested in a definition!"

"Mr. Sheridan, I am sure you are aware that my duties necessitate my comprehension of certain facts without which this household could not function."

"My intentions, whether honourable or not toward any young woman do not seem to be within the realm of those facts."

"I beg to differ, sir."

"Well then, differ, Willet."

"Knowledge as to your future plans would alleviate certain anxieties budding in the bosoms of various members of the staff."

"What anxieties, Willet? The anxiety of not having sufficient material for gossip?"

"Sir," said Willet reprovingly, "certain members of the staff fear they might be turned out by a new mistress."

"You may alleviate their anxieties, Willet. None of you will be dismissed."

"Then you do plan to announce your impending nuptials with Miss Holly?"

"Willet!" exclaimed Mr. Sheridan, exasperated. "I have dealt with you patiently, I believe, up to this point. Now go away and let me be alone. I have work to do."

"Very good, sir," said Willet mournfully. As he stepped forward to retrieve the letters he had brought, he glanced at the canvas upon which the artist was working. It was the "Pandora," half completed. Cecily's face, neck and shoulders were rendered in exquisite detail. Her eyes were opened wide, in a soft alarm, her hair streamed like a fiery river, curling around and lapping up against her vulnerable shoulders. Except for a few chalk marks here and there, the remainder of the canvas was blank. Mr. Sheridan, though seemingly adding to it, was actually picking out the highlights in Cecily's hair, with a fine brush.

"A very remarkable young lady," Willet said, shaking his head. "A pity the portrait will never be completed, but I suppose it's preferable for her to be once more engaged in her chosen pursuit."

"Then you have news of her?" asked Devin, suddenly alert.

Willet nodded his head mutely and proceeded toward the door.

"Just a minute, Willet. Where is she? What is she doing?"

"I am not able to divulge that information, sir, without first receiving permission from Miss Hawthorne."

"Don't be absurd, Willet. You know I mean her no harm. In fact, I intend to give her the wages I owe her."

Willet merely regarded him without speaking.

"Did she return to the Davenports?" speculated Devin. "No, I'm sure that harridan would not have taken her back. Where then? To that Academy where she was trained?"

Willet maintained his silence.

"Damn it, Willet!" the artist threw down his brush. "You tell me that it is your role in this household to collect all the pertinent data. Don't you consider it advisable for me to share in some of this knowledge?"

"Possibly, sir."

"Well, then, just the whereabouts of Miss Hawthorne. I'll send the wages by messenger. I swear I'll not bother her in person."

"Perhaps we can make some sort of compromise, sir."

"Compromise, Willet? I don't understand you."

"An exchange, as it were, of information."

Devin threw back his head in a loud whoop of laughter.

"Now I know why the Sheridans have always accomplished so much," he declared, strolling over to throw his arm about his faithful servant. "We've always had a Willet on our side. Very well, you've won! I'll reveal to you the details of my conference with Lady Holly regarding Constance, and you'll tell me how Cecily is doing, wherever she is."

"There was a time, sir," Willet confessed, "when we thought you would never mention her name again. You turned the portrait to the wall, had the bedchamber stripped of all its possessions, you were not yourself, sir. No female has ever, since the day I first entered your employ, caused you to act in such a rash and ungovernable manner."

"Few females, except Cecily, are so rash and ungovernable to begin with. But I can see it now for what it was. Do you realize, Willet, I was falling in love with the girl?"

"I realized that, sir."

"Did you now? That's extraordinary. I only realized it myself the last several days. Still, I assure you, there's no danger any longer. We are quite obviously temperamentally unsuited, not to mention the larger barriers of upbringing and education. Of course, there is only one position which a woman of her social class could occupy in my life, and she made quite clear to me her disinterest in that position. No, her departure is really a saving grace for us all."

"For you, perhaps, sir. I believe I speak for Cook and Betty when I say that the staff has truly missed her."

Mr. Sheridan was silent for a moment, thinking of the lonely breakfast room, the empty studio, the absence of a cheerful voice, the lack of a light footstep in the hall.

"You promised to tell me her direction, Willet," he said at last shaking free from his reverie.

"Not until after you have elucidated your feelings for Miss Holly."

"Quite simple, actually. I told her Dragon of a mother that I would escort her about, introduce her to some of my friends. I expect someone will see her, fall desperately in love and propose marriage on the spot." Willet looked sceptical. "I think she's a fine young lady and deserves a chance to shine on her own without the constant dampening of her spirits by that human wet blanket, Lady

Holly. She's really quite delightful when away from her mother's side. Not—" he noticed Willet's narrowing eyes "—that I have any romantic interest in her myself whatsoever."

Willet nodded.

"You approve, don't you, Willet?" asked the artist suspiciously.

"Sir, I merely concur with your judgement. Miss Holly and you would not, if I may be permitted to say so, make a happy pairing."

"And why not?"

"I believe, sir, that Miss Holly would always fear that she was being foolish or thick-headed or disappointing you in some other way, an impression that would have been exacerbated rather than alleviated by time. On the other hand, I think you would have been bored."

"Bored? By someone so soothing, so pleasant, so agreeable in every way?"

"My point exactly, sir." Devin reflected on this for a while, before saying in an annoyed voice, "And what of Cecily?"

"Miss Hawthorne is at present engaged as a nursery governess."

"Well."

"For a family known as the Flusters. They own a large house in South Kensington."

"And the address?"

"Numberfourteenstanhopegardens," said Willet all in a mumble.

"Heh?"

"Numberfourteenstanhopegardens," repeated Willet, slurring his words even more desperately, and like a frightened rabbit startled by a farmer, he made a dash for the cover of the stairs. Devin Sheridan watched him go without dismay, for despite Willet's earnest efforts at obfuscation, the artist's sharp ears picked up the information he required, and less than two hours later he was sauntering up the steps which led to the front door of Number Fourteen Stanhope Gardens.

Unlike Chester Thrush, he was not intimidated by the bizarre trappings of Fluster Fancy; instead he scorned them. Imitation crockery, hideously sentimental pictures, ungainly furniture and a tendency to overindulge in aspidistras were his judgements as he loitered in the Early Italian Drawing Room awaiting the arrival of the mistress of the house. The Fluster family banner particularly offended his eye and he was staring at it when Mrs. Fluster swept into the room, robed in a filmy gown of peacock-blue with gauze veils wafting behind her. An enormous cross of gold inlaid with sapphires and pearls lay upon her faultlessly ivory bosom, and her fingers glittered with other gems. Behind her, like a shadow, came Mr. Fogwell.

"Ah, you are admiring our coat of arms," sighed Mrs. Fluster. "It is too, too ennobling, is it not?"

"I've never yet known a family to sport a pig as its heraldic animal," said Mr. Sheridan politely.

"A pig? You take it to be a pig?" cried Mrs. Fluster with a worried frown. "Pemberton, do you think it resembles a pig?"

"No, Milady," replied Mr. Fogwell.

"The body did get to be a little too thick," fretted Mrs. Fluster, "and the eyes came out much smaller than I intended, and I hoped for a lovely crimson colour in the satin instead of that pinkish tone, but still no one has thought it was a pig until now."

"I beg your pardon," said Devin. "Now that I examine the work in question more closely I see it is a…er…ah—"

"A griffin," prompted Mr. Fogwell.

"Ah, yes, definitely, a griffin, sitting upon a mushroom."

"No, no, no!" shrieked Mrs. Fluster, putting one pale hand to her forehead, "not a mushroom. Good Heavens! It seems it is my fate, as it is of all artists, to be unappreciated in my own time, misunderstood, my spiritual concepts reduced to earthly considerations."

"That, my dear sir," put in Mr. Fogwell pleasantly, "is a boulder."

"Quite. Quite. The resemblance is remarkable," agreed Devin. "It really should be hung much closer to the light so that all of your visitors can admire the creativity and craftsmanship involved."

Mrs. Fluster inclined her head on its long graceful neck in acknowledgement of this tribute. "Do be seated, Mr. Sandman," she said graciously. "I do so like to visit with individuals who share my absorption in the finer aspects of life, the aesthetic considerations, as it were. I live only for Culture, my dear sir, only for Culture."

"I will accept your kind invitation," replied Devin gallantly, "but must correct your pronunciation of my name. I fear the footman has gotten it wrong—"

"Athelbert has been so impossible since Miss Flutterby got to him," mourned Mrs. Fluster. "Half the time he refuses to answer the bell, and then when he does he either leaves the caller standing in the entryway or leads him into the kitchen for some small beer."

Devin smiled. "My name is Sheridan," he said, "Devin Sheridan."

"The artist!" cried Mrs. Fluster, sinking onto a nearby armchair and pressing her hand to her bosom. "The well-known portrait painter. What a privilege! What an honour! What a distinction! Oh, Pemberton, think of it! The famous Mr. Sheridan coming to me, requesting me to sit for him, having doubtlessly heard stories about my beauty—people will talk, Mr. Sheridan, no matter how much I ask them not to do so—and wanting to see for himself if they could be true! Oh, the absolute wonder of it! My heart is fluttering about madly, Mr. Sheridan, like a caged thing!"

"Your sensibilities do you credit, Sophronia," said Mr. Fogwell, bringing her a footstool for her tiny feet, which she displayed rather ostentatiously, murmuring as she did so that Mr. Sheridan would think her bold though many people had commented upon the fineness of her ankles and even said her feet were her best feature. Devin merely nodded by way of an admission of this truth.

"Allow me a few moments to gather my scattered thoughts, which drift about in my mind like the passionate leaves of autumn," requested Mrs. Fluster.

"Certainly," responded Devin, perceiving that he was not going to have to take any active part in this conversation.

"I have heard so very many things about you, Mr. Sheridan," began Mrs. Fluster, once the leaves had settled into heaps, "so very many paeans to your talent and your discrimination and to the high calibre of your patrons. One hears that you are dedicated to your work alone, that none of the siren calls that tempt so many lesser mortals to marriage and family and other traps which Life lays for us can tempt you from your appointed sphere of expression. I, alas! Though I once longed to be an Artist, though I have always felt the production of beautiful moments to be my calling, I, alas, have succumbed to these temptations, in the person of Mr. Fluster and my children."

"Yet—" began Mr. Fogwell.

"Yet," Mrs. Fluster took up the refrain, "I have filled those moments which I can snatch from the tedium of Daily Life, the endless round of parties and social occasions and concerts and lectures, I have cluttered them—would clutter be the right word, Pemberton?"

"Suffused," he suggested.

"Ah, very nice, suffused them with my own humble offerings to our common Muse. The banner," she waved a hand at it, "the collection of priceless porcelain, the miniatures of my children I painted on ivory, the harp sonata I composed—no! Don't ask me! I really cannot perform it upon such short notice! I have, in short; done my best, Mr. Sheridan, and what more can be required of a being so frail, so transient?"

"Nothing," he murmured. "As a work of art yourself, you stand in need of no endeavour, no addition."

"Listen to him, Pemberton!" cried Mrs. Fluster. "Whoever said that artists were uncouth beasts, untutored in the social graces, unable to form a pretty compliment when the occasion demanded one?"

"Not I," said Pemberton.

"It was that nasty, meddling old harridan, Lady Holly," declared Mrs. Fluster vehemently. "Do you know her, Mr. Sheridan? A more obstinate, puffed-up old Philistine I have never met, and yet this creature, I dare not call her a woman as it would be an insult to the sex, this creature dares to hold herself up as an Arbiter of Culture, as an example for the Masses! Well, you must know her, Mr. Sheridan, for she claimed—I am almost embarrassed to repeat this for I know how it must pain you that your name is bandied about and linked with such personages—she actually insisted that you were planning to marry her daughter—what's the girl's name? The one that looks like a sheep and acts like a turtle?"

"Constance," said Pemberton quietly.

"Yes, that's it, Constance," continued Mrs. Fluster. "How odd that you would remember it, Pemberton, you've only met her that one time. Constance, an unremarkable name, not like Joconda, that is my daughter, Mr. Sheridan."

"Joconda is a quite striking name," said Mr. Sheridan.

"Yes, unfortunately, she does not live up to it," complained Mrs. Fluster. "She actually prefers the kitchen to the concert hall and cherishes her Mrs. Beeton rather than Tennyson. Can you imagine such a thing, Mr. Sheridan?"

"*Chacun à son goût,* as the French say," he replied.

Mrs. Fluster furrowed up her pretty brow.

"Each to his own taste," translated Mr. Fogwell.

Mrs. Fluster smiled. "Now tell me, Mr. Sheridan, are these awful rumours true? Are you actually going to give up your solitary and marvellous life to cater to the whims of a girl called Constance?"

"Lady Holly did, I believe, at one time," said Devin seriously, "entertain hopes that I would offer for her daughter, who, incidentally, is sitting for a portrait for me, but, to my great loss, I fear, for Miss Holly is a charming companion, it has been settled that we shall be merely friends."

Mrs. Fluster took this in for a few moments, holding aloft one white hand to indicate the need for silence.

"And how can I be of service to you, Mr. Sheridan?" she asked at last. "For it is my purpose in Life, as I see it, to foster the progress of Art everywhere, and therefore to cater to Art's domestic attendants, the artists, no matter how personally exhausting it may be. Shall I sit for you here in this highly inspiring atmosphere? Shall I wear this gown, or perhaps, one of the medieval ones? I have gowns of languorous velvet and colours warranted to melt the soul. I have gowns as soft as a baby bird's feathers and gowns as strange and intense as a choir at midnight in an abandoned chapel."

"I really hadn't thought—" began Devin.

"You came to mull over the potentialities," said Mrs. Fluster. "Ah, I know the artistic mind so well, you wanted to study me first in my own environment, in my habitat, as it were, to let the creative mind dwell upon the many, many ineffable considerations, which cannot be decided upon ahead of time, like so many bankers establishing a policy, but must be revealed to us by our Divine Mistress."

Devin nodded. A quick consideration of the possibilities deriving from Mrs. Fluster's misunderstanding helped him to recognize the distinct advantages of having a constant access to the Fluster household. But he could spend hours, endless, wearying hours listening to Mrs. Fluster ramble about her views on Culture without ever catching a glimpse of Cecily. He must think of some way to involve Cecily.

"I am most interested in doing a portrait of you, Mrs. Fluster," he said.

"See! I told you, Pemberton!" she declared with a little giggle.

"I am sure," continued Devin, "it will be the talk of London. Perhaps the Queen will purchase it and hang it in the Palace!"

"Oh!" sighed Mrs. Fluster, rendered speechless by this thought.

"I must explain," Devin went on, "seeing as you are one who understands the ways and motives of artists, the conception of the painting. I trust it will not bore you if I go into the more abstruse theory behind my desires to do this portrait"

"Oh, no!" she proclaimed. "I am, of course, most sympathetic to such a notion. In fact, I would insist upon it."

"I have for a long time been desiring to do a portrait of a mother and child."

Mrs. Fluster frowned and looked at Mr. Fogwell uncertainly.

"But, unfortunately, I could not find the proper subjects," Devin continued. "It was necessary for me to find a woman as beautiful as any woman in London, a woman seemingly unaffected by the passage of Time or the many cares and worries of the maternal state. And therein lies the heart of the difficulty, for how to find a woman with a child who was yet as lovely and virginal as she had been at sixteen? Then someone told me of you, Mrs. Fluster, and I see for myself that they were right."

Mrs. Fluster smoothed out her frown but was still unable to respond.

"You have an eternal beauty, a beauty untroubled by the grosser concerns of Mankind, a beauty so affecting and rich, yet simple in its very wealth," Devin didn't know what he was saying, but he saw by her expression that his words were achieving their desired effect. "And yet I am told you have a child, a young child? I ask myself, 'How can this be?' It must be an error, and yet, if it is, how melancholy I shall be. It will mean I must continue my tiring search."

"No, oh, no! Search no longer!" Mrs. Fluster was unable to contain herself. "You have found her. I mean, me! I am that woman. Oh, I have no doubts about it! But tell me, Mr. Sheridan, as one artist to another, surely you don't plan to paint the child, perhaps just the mother looking over the baby's things, the little gowns, the teething ring, ah yes! I see your bold conception now. A mother, a lovely, elegant mother, pausing in the gloom of twilight and fingering the little things which speak to her of her femininity, her bliss."

"No, it is to be a portrait of mother and child," insisted Devin.

"Oh, but Baby will never do!" wailed the proud mother. "Why she would spoil the whole picture. She's quite a common-looking child, nothing exceptional there. The presence of a child will mar the whole picture, as I conceive it!"

"Ah, but not as I conceive it, my dear Mrs. Fluster," put in Devin hurriedly. "But possibly you are right. I see you have superior instincts in such matters. If the child is truly plain, and I find it difficult to believe that with such a mother she could be plain, then I must abandon this cherished dream forever. For if you are not to be my subject, having met you, how could I look elsewhere? Well," he arose from his seat, "I fear I have taken up a great deal of your time already. Permit me to take my leave and thank you for your kind—"

"No, no, no! Not so hasty, Mr. Sheridan," cried Mrs. Fluster. "I shall have Baby brought down immediately and you can see for yourself. She is not an ugly child, I think anyone would concede that it would be hard for me to produce an ugly child, and yet, she is so—so—earthly, so—well, you shall see for yourself! Pemberton, ring for the maid and have her send down the nursery governess with Baby."

Mrs. Fluster placed a special emphasis on the words "nursery governess" feeling grateful that they had so recently hired such a person, and Devin could not repress a smile and a certain general restlessness.

Mr. Fogwell arose to go do his hostess' bidding, and Mrs. Fluster engaged Mr. Sheridan in a discussion of the merits of various sorts of paints, a discussion on which he found it painfully difficult to concentrate. At last, there was a light step in the corridor and Cecily came drifting into the chamber, carrying a little blond child in her arms.

Mr. Sheridan had no eyes for the child. He saw only Cecily, her gold-red hair piled loosely upon her head, escaping here and there in wisps which caught the light of the candles lit in the room, Cecily, magnificent and glowing in her yellow-cashmere gown, Cecily, whose exuberant spirits and vivid colouring made Mrs. Fluster and Baby pallid and effete by comparison.

To say that she was shocked to see him is to state the obvious. She froze upon the threshold, her wide, expressive hazel eyes growing wider and more expressive. She nearly dropped Baby.

"I see you are very taken with Baby," said Mrs. Fluster, noting the intensity of Devin's gaze but not its direction.

"A lovely child," murmured Devin, unable to wrest his attention from the tempting curves revealed by Cecily's snug basque and low corsage.

"If you think so," put in Mrs. Fluster tentatively. "I do suppose she has my hair and my eyes, thank God, and also my complexion— I have been told my skin is as fair and smooth as a baby's repeatedly. But to sit for a portrait with her, she's so wriggly and squirming, like a little eel, and sure to drool upon my gown. I don't think it's possible, Mr. Sheridan."

Cecily looked at him with incredulity, and a little of rebuke in her eyes.

Devin heard the doubt in Mrs. Fluster's voice and, having seen Cecily for himself, vowed to make this crazy project work. He applied himself to that task.

"This child is exquisite!" he declared. "A perfect replica, in miniature, of her mother. It is breath taking! Absolutely astounding! I've never seen such an attractive child, and to have the good fortune to find a child that so closely resembles her parent! It must mean this portrait is meant to be! This must be the *magnum opus* I have been building towards throughout my career!"

Cecily shook her head in disbelief. Baby took a careful look at the artist and began to cry. She buried her head against Cecily's neck, clinging pathetically. Her screams made it difficult for Mr. Sheridan to continue, but continue he did.

"I shall not be able to sleep, eat or drink until I commence on this painting!" he announced dramatically, running his hands through his hair, the perfect picture of the exasperated artist. "I must run out immediately and return with my paints. Not a moment must be wasted!"

"Mr. Sheridan!" declared Mrs. Fluster, her head rearing back a little on her proud neck, "I am flattered by your enthusiasm, and I must confess, I share in it, as one who is not unfamiliar with the artistic impulse. When it carries one away. Ah, to what celestial realms we are transported! Still I must insist upon some attention to the unfortunate practical aspects of Daily Life. My social calendar is thronged with commitments, and I must review it carefully to determine when I can grant you a few moments of my time. Pemberton, do bring me my appointment book! Now, let me see, Mr. Sheridan, the meeting of the Ladies Auxiliary for the Decoration of City Streets, then a meeting for the Medieval Chorus, an engagement with the Corroughs and another with the Tremblechins, here is a dinner for Miss Flutterby, we need another—Ah! Mr. Sheridan, may I request a simple favour, a mere trifle, as you have just requested one of me?"

"Anything you wish, Mrs. Fluster."

"We are having a small, intimate, aesthetic dinner party here, four days from today, March first. Could you, would you attend?"

"It would be my pleasure, Mrs. Fluster," he replied.

"You may bring anyone you choose," she said gaily, "we are always glad to entertain the cream of the artistic world, the literary elite, the—"

"I should be glad to bring Miss Holly, the young woman we spoke of earlier," said Devin, little thinking of Cecily's reaction. She blushed a deep shade of crimson.

"Miss Holly?" queried Mrs. Fluster with a wrinkling of her nose. "I suppose that would be permissible—"

"It is her birthday," explained Devin, glancing apologetically at Cecily, "and I had promised to spend the evening with her. I imagine one of your dinner parties, Mrs. Fluster, would be just the thing."

"We shall see," said Mrs. Fluster in a discouraging voice. "Now let me find some time for the sittings. Miss. Hawthorne must you stand there like some sort of statue! Remove the child immediately. I really believe she has colic again. You must give her a dose once you have her upstairs!"

"Yes, Mrs. Fluster," said Cecily. With one last contemptuous glance for Mr. Sheridan, she whirled about and left the room, running soundly into Nessie who was peering in through a crack in the curtain.

"Hey, look where you're going!" exclaimed that young lady in a piercing voice. "You've no mind to go running over innocent young women just because a handsome gentleman gives you a bit of an ogle!"

"Nessie, for God's sake, be quiet!" hissed Cecily. "They can hear every word you say."

"Rubbish!" declared the maid trotting after Cecily as they proceeded toward the nursery. "Coo! Wasn't he a swell–looking chap! I wonder who he was and what he wanted with the Missus!"

"He's Mr. Sheridan, the well-known artist," said Cecily primly, "and he claims he wants to paint her portrait."

"How the devil do you know all that?" inquired Nessie. "You're a deep one you are! I daresay, you're thinking of setting your cap for him."

"Don't be ridiculous!" snapped Cecily. "What would I want with an artist? Everyone knows they're arrogant, selfish, thoughtless beasts!"

"Fancy this! You've been smitten!" declared Nessie, delighted. "We read about love at first sight in those romantic novels, and it always begins like that. The heroine thinks the hero is detestable. They fight like cats and dogs, they misunderstand each other, all sorts of obstretchers—"

"Obstacles," said Cecily.

"Obstretchers are set up in their way, and then, one moment they look at each other, with eyes full of passion and longing and desire, and throw themselves into each other's arms."

"I can assure you," said Cecily, "that such will not be the case with Mr. Sheridan and me." She set down Baby who had ceased crying as soon as they entered the nursery, and busied herself setting out the child's bowl, bib and spoon.

"How did you know his name?" inquired Nessie, eager to ferret out the details of this glorious passion.

"I've met him before," replied Cecily imperiously. "Now enough of your impertinent questions. I don't have to answer any"

"Then I s'pose you knows this Miss Holly he's going to bring to dinner," went on Nessie, undaunted. "Who's she, I wonder?"

"A little nobody," said Cecily, catching hold of Baby and fastening the bib about her neck. "A pleasant little nobody, I must admit, quite good-tempered."

"Ah, the other woman!" sighed Nessie.

"Nessie, do go leave me alone!" declared Cecily. "I have to give Baby her dinner, and I'm sure you've work to do."

"There you're wrong, you know, Miss Cecily," replied the housemaid, shaking her curls at the governess. She lounged fetchingly against the mantel. "You're the artful one, trying to set me off, but I'm like a bloodhound when my nose is to the scent of true love. What was the circumstances of your meeting? Did he spy you stepping down from a cab before the Opery? Did he grab you in some dark hallway when you were bringing the children in to dinner at some other household? That's the way it was with me and Mr. Lancet at my last position. A lovely man, he was, a chemist's assistant and like to get his own shop, sooner than not. But he had no respect for a poor working girl. He cost me my position, and I sent him off on his ear. I have it! This artist saw you walking in the Park and halted you in your path, saying that you must sit for him for a portrait!"

Cecily looked startled. "How did you know?" she asked.

"That's the way it always happens in novels," explained Nessie. "Then you fell in love as he painted you, alone with each other, only mutual reserve preventing you from indulging in your wildest desires! Did he kiss you?"

"No, not really," said Cecily musing. "Not a real kiss."

"Ah, he respects her virtue despite the tumultuous clamouring of his heart!" breathed Nessie. "A wonderful story! Then he follows her from household to household cross the wide panama—"

"Panorama," corrected Cecily.

"Panama of London domestic employments," Nessie elaborated, "till one day, friendless and desolate in a strange situation, she admits her overweening passion and tumbles into his straining embrace, feeling her heart beating against his as he—"

"Impossible, Nessie!" Cecily was becoming annoyed. She removed Baby quite firmly from beneath the cot where she was playing. "He's a prominent artist and I'm a nursery governess, the daughter of a housekeeper. No, if he marries it's likely to be to Miss Holly." Her voice choked a little in uttering those words.

"Coo! Who said anything about marriage?" Nessie wanted to know. "Artists aren't the marrying sort. But he could set you up in a little cottage, with your own pianer and some canaries in the window—"

"Nessie, how many times must I tell you! The man is a mere acquaintance. I have no tender feelings for him whatsoever. As a matter of fact, I despise and detest everything he stands for. I can barely tolerate being in the same room with him and I certainly have no desire to tumble into his arms or look at him with eyes full of passion. Don't stare at me so! I assure you, the man leaves me absolutely cold! Now do run along, there's a good girl, and ask Mrs. Grunion if the nursery luncheon is ready."

Nessie was not convinced. She turned to go but paused on the threshold to wag her finger at Cecily.

"It's obvious," she said, "that you haven't read any romantic novels."

Chapter Twelve

A Dinner Roundelay for Ten

"JOCONDA, MY DEAR CHILD, who was that unusual–looking person I saw leaving your office a moment ago?" asked her mother, drifting through the doors to the housekeeper's room on the afternoon of March 1, and finding her normally composed daughter alternately turning pale and bright red.

"That must have been Chester…er… Mr. Thrush," said Joconda, striving to maintain her usual composure. She placed her bifocals quickly upon the bridge of her nose. "He is an acquaintance of the nursery governess. He's been so good as to help me with various small details pertaining to the dinner. He has most extraordinary good sense when it comes to the arrangement of domestic matters."

"Humph!" was Mrs. Fluster's considered opinion. "Well, my dear, it was the dinner which I wished to speak with you about." Mrs. Fluster played with the tassels on her bronze satin stole. "I wished to impress upon you the utter importance of this event in terms of our future. Why, if it is not a success we will soon all be sitting on cast-iron sofas, and eating off cast-iron tables, and sleeping in cast-iron beds! 'Why?' you might inquire, and I would reply, because if Miss Flutterby does not become affianced to my dear Cedric—the boy is being a positively sacrificial lamb, he is—we will be reduced to living on your poor dear Papa's manufacturing products. We will have to eat cast-iron roasts with cast-iron utensils and imbibe cast-iron wines."

"I realize, Mother, the importance of the occasion," interrupted Joconda, unimpressed with her mother's depiction of a cast-iron future. "If I did not, I would not have been labouring so hard this past fortnight to ensure that everything is perfect. I have instructed Mrs. Grunion to half-roast the rump and afterwards stew it in a little Madeira, rather than merely boil it. The fowls have been killed several days and are now ready to be picked and dressed. I have made sure to purchase only the best salmon. I felt the belly of each myself to be certain it was firm and thick. Red gills alone are not proof of goodness, you know."

"Enough, Joconda. Spare me!" cried her aggrieved mother. "Do you really think I wish to concern myself with these tawdry details, these sordid reminders of our more corporeal nature? If we must eat, let it be with dignity, maintaining a delicate mystery regarding the sources of our nourishment."

"Very well, Mother."

"Now, as to wine, I shall leave it to your excellent judgement, which wine we shall serve with—"

"Mother, that is something I expressly wished to discuss with you."

Mrs. Fluster lifted her perfect eyebrows.

"It seems the vintner refuses to extend our credit further. He maintains that he has been more than generous in permitting us to add to our account with him despite the fact that he has not been paid this twelvemonth."

"Oh, the wickedness of these tradespeople!" declared Mrs. Fluster. "Do they think we are made of money? Do they think we really interest ourselves in these petty matters—bills and charges and accounts and such like? For shame! For shame!"

"Mother, if we are to have wine with dinner, we must get it from somewhere."

"Alas, economic considerations will intrude where they are not wanted. You must find out, Joconda, where Lady Holly orders wine and tell her vintner that she has recommended him to us, and we would like to sample his wares."

"Mother, we have already used Lady Holly's vintner, last year. He also refuses to extend our credit."

"The insolence!" cried Mrs. Fluster. "I think the lower classes were put upon this earth merely to worry us and prevent our spirits from journeying to their proper abode, the sphere of Contemplation and Culture. Find out where Mr. Sheridan gets his wine and use that merchant!"

"How am I to find that out, Mother?"

"You'll think of a way, I trust, Joconda. Your mind seems more attuned to these fleshly matters. Now, as to the waiters, what did you have in mind, my dear?"

Joconda frowned and studied a sheet of paper which lay upon her desk. "Well," she replied slowly, "with Athelbert at the head of the table behind Mr. Fluster, I had thought we would use Nessie to assist him."

"Nessie! That goose of a girl! Why, surely, Joconda, you remember my mortification the night she dropped the turbot right in Lady Corrough's lap. No! She will never do!"

"Mother, you know as well as I, we have only the footman and Nessie for servants. Mrs. Grunion must keep Susan in the kitchen with her to aid in preparation, and I really don't see what other choice we have."

"The nursery governess! That rather fresh-looking young woman who looks after Baby. She couldn't be more fumble-fingered than Nessie, and she's a great deal less likely to flirt with the guests. Why don't we have her to assist Athelbert?"

"Mother, you cannot expect me to ask a nursery governess to wait on tables?"

"Why not? She's a domestic servant, Nessie's a domestic servant. What could be the objection? You don't imply that she would consider herself above the duties. If she does give herself such airs, well, I would have no use for her in a household like this, where we must all, Heavens knows, make sacrifices in order to insure our very survival!"

"Well, if Miss Hawthorne waits on table, and she has a perfect right to refuse, there's not a word in Mrs. Beeton about nursemaids ever waiting on tables, if she does accept, then what will become of Baby?"

"You worry yourself about the most inconsequential things, Joconda. You must take a rest from all of this managing and super-intending. Before we hired Miss Whatever her name is, Nessie watched over Baby and nothing dire ever happened—"

"Except Baby's falling down the stairs and tumbling into the fire," put in Joconda primly.

"You make such a mountain out of a molehill, my dear. Baby's curls were slightly singed, she sustained no serious injuries, and surely for one night Nessie could be trusted to see that no such incidents recurred. You must not be such a pessimist, my dear. You must anticipate the best, not the worst, outcome. You must strive to fasten your thoughts about truly superior principles, not mundane details. Which reminds me, my child, there is someone I wish you to be particularly attentive to at tonight's dinner."

"I am aware, Mother, that Miss Flutterby is the object of this occasion and—"

"No, no, no! Joconda, why must you always be at odds with me? I sometimes believe you were sent to me as my very own cross to bear. No, it is a gentleman I have in mind. His name is Mr. Sheridan, and you must strive to be agreeable to him."

"Mother, you expressly informed me that Mr. Sheridan is bringing Miss Holly as his companion. Now, why on earth should I try to be agreeable to him?"

Mrs. Fluster sighed. She inserted the end of her stole in her mouth as if to stifle an angry outburst. When she withdrew it, mark-ed with the imprint of her perfect teeth, she sighed and said, "Mr. Sheridan has already made it quite clear that he has no romantic interest in Constance Holly—a common name, don't you think?— in Miss Holly whatsoever. That means that his attentions are free to be placed elsewhere. And I see no reason why, if Constance Holly can catch his eye, you shouldn't be able to do the same. She's at least ten years older than you and not half so prepossessing."

Joconda slammed shut the volume which lay open on her desk. "Mother," she said crisply, "you contradict yourself. First you inf-orm me that Mr. Sheridan has no interest in Miss Holly, then you tell me that she has caught his eye favourably. Let me assure you, whatever your explanation, and I'm sure you have one, you always do, that I categorically refuse to flaunt myself before him the way you do. I am not beautiful like you! I am not aesthetic like you! I am not spiritual like you! I am not able to charm like you! I shall never be like you, and I will not," she slammed her hand down on the desktop emphatically, "compete with you for the attention of all of the gentlemen who come to this house."

"Joconda, what do you imply?" asked her mother in shocked tones. "Surely, you don't accuse me of flirting? Why, I am old enough to be Mr. Sheridan's mother, and happily married to your dear papa these past twenty-five years."

"Then, why is it I see Mr. Fogwell's name pencilled in on the guest list?" asked Joconda.

"Joconda, my sweet Puritan," declared her mother, rolling her perfect blue eyes towards her perfectly arched eyebrows. "You actually begrudge me my little friend, my poetic companion? Why, one would almost think you were jealous! Pemberton will be so amused when I tell him! I simply had to include him. He would be heartbroken to be excluded, and you know full well, he shares with me certain interests without which my soul would simply shrivel and die, like a tender shoot uncurling too early and being blasted by the winter's frosts."

Joconda made a tsking noise with her tongue against her teeth.

"Think what a triumph it would be," related Mrs. Fluster dreamily, "if you were to steal Mr. Sheridan right from under Constance Holly's eyes. That would certainly put Lady Holly's nose out of joint! Think of it, Joconda! An aesthetic wedding, what I have always wanted for you! Bridesmaids in seraphic robes with wreaths of lilies on their heads, chanting a solemn, medieval chant as they proceed towards the altar, the ushers in lace-trimmed velvet doublets with daffodils in their hands, the church itself decorated with flowers, and the only light, candles, hundreds of candles flickering in the draughts like souls swaying to and fro in purgatory. Musicians playing hautboys and harps—why you might even persuade me to perform my harp sonata, except, of course, I must be greeting the guests. I shall have to teach someone else how to play it, but who could do it, I wonder, with the same sensitivity, the same delicate appreciation of its subtleties—"

Joconda shuddered. "It sounds frightfully expensive and uncomfortable to me," she declared.

It was Mrs. Fluster's turn to shudder. "How very, very practical you are, Joconda," she said disparagingly. "It's enough to make me wonder whether you are a changeling and not my real child. Alas!" She placed her ivory brow in her cupped hand.

Joconda who had often wondered the same thing, did not bother to reflect upon it. "Here, Mother," she said, holding out some rolled up pieces of parchment. "These are the menus."

Mrs. Fluster studied one and frowned. "Do you really think this is enough, Joconda?" she asked sharply. "You know, in America I'm told they consume whole sides of beef at a dinner as a matter of course."

"Mother, even supposing such was the case, which I doubt—I assume that the stories one hears about Americans are simply part and parcel of the unfortunate American tendency toward exaggeration—even supposing, as I have said, that such was the case, it would be impossible on our income to provide a similar quantity of edibles. I fear we must, to some extent, present ourselves exactly as we are. I confess, Mother, that I agree with dear Papa. To pretend to Miss Flutterby that we are a family with limitless capital is utterly unethical."

"That, my dear, is unimportant," said her mother tartly. "We are, with the sole exception of that terribly sordid commodity, money, one of the finest families in London Society, and if Miss Flutterby is fortunate enough to gain an entrée into our refined circle, she is a fortunate young woman indeed, especially for an American. Now Joconda, there are only a few hours before the guests arrive, and I know you must have a prodigious quantity of things to prepare, not forgetting for a moment yourself, my dear, so I will leave you to go up and begin my toilette."

Joconda, an extremely organized young woman, had no need of the hours her mother so graciously granted in order to complete her preparations. She needed only to inform the nursery governess and the housemaid of the roles they must play in the evening's entertainment, and accordingly, she mounted the stairs to the nursery to find Nessie, who should have been cleaning the plate for dinner, perched instead on the arm of a chair, rattling away to Cecily about the innumerable merits of Alf.

"Nessie," said Joconda sternly, stepping briskly into the room, "I thought you would be in the pantry."

"Coo! It completely slipped my mind," Nessie declared, pursing up her pretty lips. "I'll go right away, Miss Joconda."

"No need," replied Joconda, "for I have come to inform you that it will be your duty to watch over Baby tonight during the dinner, and you might as well begin now."

"I daresay you've forgotten, Miss Joconda," replied Nessie indignantly, "that I was hired pacifically as a housemaid, and a housemaid, I am, not a nursery maid."

"And as a housemaid you should be cleaning the plate, not loitering in the nursery," was Joconda's reprimand.

"Well, what do we have a nursery governess for, if not to watch Baby?" Nessie wanted to know.

"Miss Hawthorne is going to be required to wait upon table tonight."

Cecily looked up in astonishment. "Oh, I couldn't, I don't think," she said with amazement. "I've never been taught to serve at a dinner. Why shouldn't Nessie do it as usual?"

Nessie pouted. "I said when I was hired that I don't answer the door and I don't wait on tables. Such things is not within the scope of my duties!"

Joconda ignored this pronouncement. "Nessie has not, regrettably, worked out in the past," she replied, addressing Cecily. "Not only does she neglect the guests and hand the wrong dishes around at the wrong times, but she is also prone to eyeing the male visitors."

Nessie's mouth dropped open. "Never say that lie, Miss Joconda!" she declared. "I would no sooner look above my station than murder my mother."

"That is quite enough, Nessie!" exclaimed Joconda. "If you have not good enough sense to accept this assignment as a reprieve, bearing in mind the fact that you have been dismissed from your last eleven positions and would find it difficult, if not impossible, to find another anywhere in this city, then you are not the shrewd young person I believe you to be!"

Nessie was effectually silenced.

"Miss Hawthorne, if you will don your plainest dark dress and meet me in the dining parlour in half an hour's time, I will endeavour to educate you in the practices common at festive dinners." She turned abruptly and departed, leaving an astonished pair of women in her wake.

"Oh, Nessie, this is terrible," Cecily wailed. "How will I ever manage? And Baby, no offense meant, is fretful when left in your care!"

Nessie winked broadly. "Much as I dislike this turn of events," she said, "I wonder that you protest for your lover, Mr. Sheridan, is one of the guests."

"I'm well aware of that fact," Cecily declared passionately. "What will he think of me when he sees me in an apron, handing around the vegetables?"

"He'll think you have a ravishing figure beneath your navy-silk gown," decided Nessie. "Can't you see, Cecily, this is your one golden opportunity! Not that you haven't seen him when you bring Baby down for the portrait sittings, and, if you've been following my advice, you've made a stunning impression upon his very heart."

Cecily secretly doubted this as she usually found an excuse to leave the room as soon as Baby had been settled onto her mother's lap, though Mr. Sheridan as frequently invented a reason for the nursery governess to remain.

"Now," continued Nessie, "you will be with him during the course of an entire dinner. He won't be able to forget you if you play your cards right. Go get into your gown, Cecily. I'll take Baby along with me. I'm going to fetch you my cologne, the one that drives Alf wild. See what it does for your artist."

Despite Nessie's cologne, despite her awareness of the attractiveness of her dark, snug gown and the frivolity of the white starched apron and cap she now donned, despite Joconda's repeated rehearsal of her simple duties, it was not without grave misgivings that Cecily took up her position at the sideboard as the dinner guests filed into the dining room, or refectory as Mrs. Fluster preferred to call it.

Mr. Fluster was first, his round, red face beaming with pleasure as he led in Miss Flutterby, looking singularly ludicrous with her plain face shining above and her plump body stuffed into a befrilled blue gown with an exaggerated bustle. Joconda and Mr. Fogwell marched in next, she refusing to allow him to guide her to her seat, followed by Cedric and Mrs. Flutterby, a grandiose matron in a spotted gown as unsuitable for the occasion as her daughter's. Bringing up the rear were Mr. Sheridan and Constance, he seemingly indifferent, she timid, and Mrs. Fluster, giggling and effervescent on the arm of Mr. Flutterby, a large and taciturn man in an ill-fitting tweed suit.

One by one they took up their seats at the sparkling table, laden with massive floral bouquets and studded with the red glass Venetian goblets which were Mrs. Fluster's pride and joy, with a minimum of conversation for there had been little enough in the drawing room before dinner. Cecily waited, quaking by the sideboard, but no one seemed to have paid her notice, any more than they acknowledged the looming presence of Athelbert who waited at his master's left hand to pass around the first course: macaroni soup, boiled turbot and lobster sauce, and salmon cutlets.

At an agreed-upon signal from the footman, who wore his most splendid livery, a saffron and turquoise plush uniform with gold tassels for trimming, Cecily removed the heavy soup tureen from the sideboard and, staggering under its weight, brought it to the head of the table. No one noticed her, no one even looked up, and she found, to her dismay, that rather than cringing under Mr. Sheridan's fervent gaze, she was desperately hoping he would glance her way. Instead, she saw him whisper something to Constance Holly who sat on his right, something which was obviously confidential because he laid his hand intimately on Miss Holly's hand to get her attention, and something amusing for she laughed and favoured him with an appreciative look from her soft brown eyes.

"Mr. Sheridan, you know," said Mrs. Fluster, drawing his attention away from his female companion, "Mr. Flutterby was just telling me of his interest in Art."

As Mr. Flutterby had been declaring his opinion that all the fashionable artists were mere nincompoops and unmitigated jackasses, he was somewhat taken aback by this remark.

Mr. Sheridan nodded in his direction and said, "With a wife and daughter who are living tributes to Beauty, his interest is understandable."

Mr. Flutterby scowled as if to indicate either his distaste for flattery or his doubt as to the truth of this statement. But his wife was not so sceptical.

"Oh, Mr. Sheridan!" she declared, "Mrs. Fluster tells me you are one of the most expensive...er...lauded portrait painters in London and that you have even done portraits for the Royal Family!"

"I am currently completing a portrait of Princess Louise for the occasion of her marriage in thirteen days," replied Mr. Sheridan modestly.

"Oh, it is just so quaint to know we are dining with someone who has the habit of hobnobbing with Royalty, not you realize, that we, as Americans, think your Monarch is any different from the common citizen, Heaven forbid! I would be the last to say so. Yet the very excesses to which your, ahem, system of government lends itself, also contribute an aura of mystery and romance, don't you find it so? Why, Mr. Flutterby and I dined only last month with Mrs. Rutherford B. Hayes, our First Lady, and it was considered not at all remarkable, whereas your Queen! You know we have been contributing hundreds of pounds to this Duke's charity and that Earl's pet project, all in the hopes that one of them will come through for us and arrange to have Vera presented to the Queen at one of her drawing rooms!"

The always composed Mrs. Fluster dropped her spoon into the macaroni soup.

"Wasn't it five hundred pounds that we gave to the Duke of Tarpaper, my dear, for the construction of a model village on his property in Gloucestershire, George?"

George grunted his assent. Cedric's monocle slipped from his eye and plunged into his lobster sauce.

"Five hundred pounds!" he breathed, gaining a new respect for the guests.

"Oh, yes," went on Mrs. Flutterby, conscious that she had made a hit, "the Duke, he asked us to call him Choppers, it seems that's an old nickname from his Army days, wants to reproduce the village as he remembers it from his boyhood days—a millpond, the miller, simple peasants tending flocks of sheep. Isn't that quaint? We thought of doing the same thing at our castle in Ireland."

"A castle in Ireland?" gasped Mrs. Fluster, struggling to recover her equanimity. Her smile was slipping to one side.

"Oh, dear me, yes!" explained Mrs. Flutterby, looking about her with startled eyes as if surprised that anyone would be interested in such trivial matters. "We just purchased this mouldering old heap, at an extremely reasonable price, from the Marquis of Dower. Thirty bedrooms, two ballrooms, that sort of thing, very primitive, mind you, we had to hire a whole army of workmen to come out and install indoor plumbing and heating. A truly picturesque ruin, walls covered with ivy, a moat full of swans, old gardeners puttering about saying, 'Good day, Milady,'" she said, giggling, "and a dairy with dairy maids who produce really the freshest, richest butter you should ever wish to taste! We think of it as a summer place, you know, though we do have the mansion on the Hudson (that's in New York, you know) and a villa in Naples. Perhaps we shall have to give it to Vera for her own little parties. She was quite taken with it. In fact, I doubt we would have taken it if it hadn't been for her."

"Musty old heap!" declared George. "Full of mice!"

"It was Vera's idea to install a host of cats," announced Mrs. Flutterby proudly. "We had to engage a housekeeper, three maids and a cook just to care for the cats, you know."

"I like cats. They're much nicer than people," said Vera suddenly from the opposite end of the table.

"So you do, darling, so you do," said her mother, finishing off the last of the salmon cutlets.

An amazed silence fell over the assembled company, and only the sounds of the three Flutterbys munching contentedly could be heard. Cedric sat, mouth agape, barely able to comprehend the sort of wealth which could pass off a castle as a sort of dollhouse for a daughter. Mrs. Fluster attempted to paste her smile back into its usual position.

It was time for Cecily to remove the dishes and she went about the table, extremely conscious of her inexperience, repeating to herself Joconda's injunctions, "Walk silently." "Always remove and serve from the left. "Be sure your gloves are spotless; best to bring an extra pair in case some of the sauce or gravy should stain the first pair." As she took up Constance Holly's empty plate, she overheard a comment from the artist to Miss Holly, something to the effect that the artlessness and innocence of the English garden rose was much preferable to the American hot-house variety. Constance blushed red and so did Cecily, but the former was overcome with pleasure, the latter quivering with rage.

While the entrées were being brought in, with a bit more clatter and force than necessary by Cecily, Mrs. Flutterby, conscious of her enraptured audience, began again.

"Vera is so fond of animals, you know," she announced spearing a larded fillet of rabbit. "What began as a simple hobby—we do encourage children to adopt their own particular hobby in America, we believe it is good for the formation of individuality and character—has become a veritable obsession with her." No one noticed the pun, or if they did, politely declined to respond. Undaunted, Mrs. Flutterby repeated it. "A veritable obsession."

Mrs. Fluster nodded her head coldly in acknowledgement.

"The giraffe, alas, nearly died of the cold. We had to have it shipped to Italy where it is doing fine in a pen off the villa terrace—"

"How wonderful," murmured Mrs. Fluster conventionally.

"But we had to purchase a thoroughbred farm down in Kentucky, that is where all our fine racehorses come from in America, just to maintain Vera's menagerie of horses. She has a complete string of polo ponies, and several racing animals, as well as the very first little pony we gave her when she was only six years old. She never forgets the poor little waifs and strays that capture her first interest."

"A thring of polo ponies, you thay?" repeated Cedric dazed. "Dem, I thould like to see that."

"You must come to visit us in New York," said Mrs. Flutterby pleasantly, "and Vera can introduce you to all her little friends. We know the cream of New York society, and Vera and her chums often organize impromptu polo matches on the lawn of our home on Long Island. Do you play, Mr. Fluster?"

"No, but I dare thay it would come naturally to me," Cedric replied nonchalantly. "Thuch things do."

"Cedric is a poet," proclaimed his doting Mama, determined to bring him to the attention of their guests. "He requires a great deal of solitude and a certain delicacy of setting in order to create, an isolated way of life which, alas, precludes the rougher sports so often favoured by young men. I have always believed, and I am sure Cedric, as another artist, would concur, that too much exposure to the elements, to the World at large, to the coarse individuals which so often make up the masses of Mankind, dulls the artist's perception and renders him an empty vessel unable to cut through the veils of illusion which Art exists to explode."

"Demmit, Mother," contradicted Cedric, "polo ith not just any sport. Now polo theems just the sort of thing for me!"

"I think you could be a wonderful polo player," said Vera Flutterby, as if her word alone decided the matter. "You have the physique for it!"

"Now, Vera, I warned you!" said her mother crossly. "The English don't like to hear about such corporeal matters. Though we, in America, have long known the benefits of physical health and athletics, the English prefer the more sedentary pursuits of the mind."

"Cedric certainly does," interjected his mother.

"Egad, I wouldn't go tho far, Mother," replied the son. "I follow the affairs of the turf with great interest and at one time wath quite skilled in the use of the Indian clubs."

As no one could see any evidence of this manly sport in Cedric's frail build and hunched shoulders, which he had poured, for the occasion, into a tight black velvet jacket with lilac-satin revers, another silence fell upon the table.

"The table certainly appears festive, so very colourful," murmured Constance, trying desperately to think of some uncontroversial topic.

"As lovely as the ladies that grace it with their presence," seconded Mr. Fogwell gallantly. He sat on the other side of Constance from Mr. Sheridan, and was quite enchanted, as he had been on their first meeting, with her quiet dignity. A born womanizer, he found the existence of a shy woman a challenge to his very livelihood. Mrs.

Fluster was already his conquest, Mrs. Flutterby was evidently impervious to anything but monetary considerations and Mr. Fogwell never mentioned anything as crass as money, Joconda was not worth the waste of his considerable talents, and Miss Flutterby's candidness gave him the shudders. But Constance Holly, here was a woman elegant yet unaware of her own beauty, obviously of superior intelligence but too timid to open her mouth. She had all the hallmarks of one of Mr. Fogwell's most suitable subjects, and he could not resist the temptation.

"Your gown, for instance, Miss Holly," he said smoothly, "is so harmonious. You quite clearly have the instincts of an artist. On any other woman that particular shade of mauve might be too insipid or render the complexion sallow by comparison. But on you it is *ravissante.* One can imagine stumbling upon you, a rare orchid trembling with beauty in some unearthly jungle far from the haunts of man."

Constance smiled with amusement. "A fanciful image, Mr. Fogwell," she replied. "Shall you describe the other ladies for us in the same terms?" It was always her manner to turn the subject away from herself.

"Let me see," mused Mr. Fogwell, setting down his fork and resting his chin upon his elegant, white hands. "Mrs. Fluster is, of course, a lily, pure and cool and spiritual, shining in an alabaster vase somewhere. Mrs. Flutterby, if I may be permitted, my good Madam, is a spotted fritillary, as fresh and jaunty as the first harbingers of spring. Joconda is a daisy, simple and unassuming, in the window box of a cottage, and Miss Flutterby, a sunflower, bold and unaffected, twining along the fence near a meadow. And, over by the sideboard, waiting to remove our plates, I see a chrysanthemum, gloriously radiant, vibrant with life and strength."

All eyes turned toward Cecily, who tried to ascertain the proper composure for a servant in such a situation by watching Joconda. She assumed from Joconda's tight-lipped nod that she should remain silent, and, accordingly, bobbed her head slightly and began to perform her assigned duties. She was aware that Devin had noticed her at last, she was conscious of his dark eyes lingering upon her as she went in and out of the pantry with the dishes and then brought in the second course, but if she thought he would acknowledge her presence in any special way, if she thought he might favour her with a friendly smile or a kind word, she was mistaken.

"Damn the man," she thought, with a constriction in her throat as the diners fell upon the roast fowls and the stewed rump of beef *a la jardinière.* "He treats me like a servant simply because I have the misfortune to be one. I won't ever think of him with any warm-hearted feelings again. I shall exorcise his image from my soul, and good riddance!"

Mrs. Flutterby had not liked the turn of the conversation and was not certain whether or not she liked being a fritillary besides. She returned once more to her favoured topic.

"I know you are quite fond of Art, my dear Mrs. Fluster," she said, "and I think you will be interested to know that George and I are endowing a Museum in New York. Actually, to be quite frank, we are constructing it ourselves, to house our own collection since we could find no institution suitable in which to place our treasures. It is our intention to display the very finest works of every living artist, both on the Continent and at home. We have commissioned works from many of your contemporaries, Mr. Sheridan. Mr. Landseer has promised to do a portrait of Vera's favourite lap dog, and Mr. Frith is going to paint an historical picture depicting George, as the Architect of American Industrialism, surrounded by his factories and machinery, you know. It would be our fondest wish, as you are so well-known for your portraits, if you would do a portrait of Vera on her wedding day, with her intended, whoever he might be, at her side."

"What a wonderful thought!" declared Mrs. Fluster, giving Cedric a meaningful look. "You must have in mind some young man who is extraordinarily handsome, talented and fashionable besides."

"I don't know," replied the American matron. "It's really up to Vera to decide. We had hoped for the Earl of Corrough's son, but Vera will have none of him, and even, I must be honest, of the Duke of Drumland, though Vera insists he's too old—but his first wife died quite young and he really is, you know, entirely eligible, and we so hoped for a coronet for our little girl. Think of it Lady Vera!"

"Mama, don't be such a snob!" reprimanded the daughter, launching into her slice of boiled ham with gusto. "I have told you repeatedly that I shall choose my husband on the basis of my feelings and my assessment of the moldability of his character. I certainly am resigned by now to the fact that the man of my dreams does not exist in any shape or age or suitable prosperity anywhere on several continents. So I have considered the matter carefully and concluded that I must shape him myself, and where better to start than with someone completely compliant, adaptable, in short, unformed and immature. Then, and only then, can I be sure I have exactly what I want."

Cedric was not deaf to this request, nor did he have the character to feel insulted by Miss Flutterby's description. "I have always felt myself to be a veritable *tabula rasa*," he chimed in quickly, "awaiting the beneficial influences of whatever breeze might blow my way."

"I know," replied Miss Flutterby with a tender look, and a mouth full of cabbage.

Mrs. Fluster was not quite so certain that she liked this definition of Cedric's personality, but she thought of the castle in Ireland, the villa in Italy, the Museum, the polo ponies, and stifled her protests. "Cedric has always been a most amenable, obedient, even docile boy," she offered brightly.

Mrs. Flutterby, on the other hand, was quite clear about Cedric's suitability for her daughter. "Of course, you know," she said firmly, "we absolutely won't go below the rank of a Baronet for a husband for dear Vera. No, darling," intercepting her daughter's fierce glance, "there can be no discussion on this subject. Your papa and I are quite decided, aren't we, George?"

George grunted his agreement and signalled to Cecily to bring him some more of the stewed rump of beef.

Mrs. Flutterby had accepted the Fluster invitation only because she thought them to be a particularly good example of English "quaintness," but she had entertained no notions of allowing Cedric Fluster to present himself as a suitor for her daughter's hand and fortune. Now that the danger was apparent and hemmed her in from all sides, she was anxious to remove Vera from its noxious influences as swiftly as possible. Accordingly, she ate her way through the rhubarb tart *á la* Turner with as much speed as she could muster, declined the desserts and ices for both herself and her family, and departed abruptly, George in tow, and Vera propelled, complaining, before her.

Mrs. Fluster was distraught and retired to the drawing room, calling for smelling salts and a stiff cordial to revive her, remedies which had to be clumsily applied by Mr. Fluster. Strangely, Mr. Fogwell had absented himself; he had found the opportunity, in the general rout, to pull Constance aside and solicit her impressions of the dinner party, impressions that he found, to his delight, were sharp, telling and not altogether kind. This freed Mr. Sheridan to seek out Cecily, who was busily engaged in clearing the table and transporting the dishes to the pantry.

"Hello, there!" he said brightly. "What a pleasure it was to be able to feast my eyes upon you while I feasted upon the Fluster's spread."

Cecily made no response.

"I say, that's not very friendly," Devin pressed his point, "considering how long we have known each other and under what circumstances."

"Circumstances have changed," responded Cecily primly. She stormed past him with an armful of dishes and silver, and he detained her with his hand upon her arm.

"What circumstances?" he demanded. "Don't tell me you've gone and tied the knot with that blithering fool, Thrash, Thrust, whatever his name was who came to call upon you at Swan Walk.".

Cecily shook his hand free. "His name is Chester Thrush, Mr. Chester Thrush," she replied with dignity, "and I mean that precisely. We are engaged to be married, and the sooner the better as far as I'm concerned." She stalked into the pantry, striving to maintain her composure and neglecting completely to take note of the extraordinary expression on the face of Joconda Fluster, who stood in the doorway, mouth agape, having just come in from the kitchen.

Chapter Thirteen

In Which Mr. Thrush Considers Becoming a Mormon

"I HAD NO IDEA YOU were engaged, Mr. Thrush!" said Joconda sternly to that gentleman when he presented himself the following morning to inquire after the success of the dinner. "And to our nursery governess, Miss Hawthorne. Congratulations are in order, I guess, all around." She bent over her books, while he sat floundering on the cast-iron sofa, searching for words to express his amazement.

"M–m–miss Joconda," he stammered at last, "it is t–t–true that I have offered for Miss Hawthorne, b–but—"

"Explanations are not necessary to me," she answered coldly. "Though I have not known myself the joys of romantic affection, though I have long resigned myself to a life of solitary and un-appreciated endeavour, I can still sympathize, I hope, with the feelings of those who choose different paths."

"H–how did you learn of this?" Chester asked, his sandy hair standing on end as he struggled with the emotions which twisted in his chest.

"Do you really require all the sordid details, Mr. Thrush?" asked Joconda contemptuously. "If you insist, the young lady did not inform us of her immediate intentions for matrimony upon taking on this position. If she had, I assure you, I would not have hired her. Nor would I have permitted you to waste the few precious moments you have to spend with her assisting me with my household duties instead. I don't know from what misguided sense of loyalties you operated, Mr. Thrush. I do know I overheard Miss Hawthorne informing another individual of her upcoming nuptials with you only last night. I was, to put it mildly, shocked."

"You must b–b–believe me, Miss Joconda," began Chester.

"Miss Fluster," she said coolly.

"M–m–miss Fluster," he struggled with the words, "that it was s–simply my pleasure to assist you when I could, and not from any other motive that I acted."

"Very well, Mr. Thrush, if you insist," she replied without conviction. "And now, Mr. Thrush, I have a great many things to do. If you wish to see Miss Hawthorne, she is upstairs, second floor, second door to your right. Good day."

Chester arose and stood in the doorway, turning his hat in his hands. "And the d–dinner?" he asked. "How was it?"

"A disaster! A complete and total disaster!" she said sharply, not bothering to look up. "Good day, Mr. Thrush."

But was it the fact that the dinner had gone off so badly that caused her to lay down her head upon her menus and sob violently once the door had closed behind Mr. Thrush?

Unaware of Joconda's grief, Chester timidly ascended the stairs and stumbled into the nursery to find Cecily on her knees, a very fetching sight, growling and worrying at Baby who squealed with pleasure from her refuge under a table.

"M–m–miss Hawthorne!" exclaimed Chester, overcome by this sight.

Cecily leaped to her feet with eyes wide with amazement. "Chester!" she declared. "How did you come here? What do you want with me?"

He advanced into the room deliberately and laid down his hat with great precision upon a table.

"I have come to see my fiancée," he said simply. "Miss Joconda has been the one to tell me that you have, at last, accepted my proposal."

"Good Lord!" groaned Cecily. She brushed off her skirts briskly. "Joconda? You mean, Miss Fluster? How did she know of our engagement?"

"Then, I may be permitted to c–congratulate myself!" exclaimed Chester, stepping forward with his arms extended. "C–come into my embrace, my l–little wife! And give your Chester a big k–kiss!"

Cecily neatly sidestepped her approaching admirer. "Just a minute, Mr. Thrush," she said with a wrinkle in her brow. "Miss Fluster must have heard me speaking to Mr. Sher…um…last night, yes, I do recall she was just coming out of the kitchen. But why would she disclose that to you?"

"I called upon Joconda…er…Miss Fluster, introducing myself as an acquaintance of yours," explained Chester, making another sweep to encompass Cecily. "Sh–she was rather s–surprised that you would have taken on this position here if you intended to be m–m–married shortly. Indeed, she was annoyed!" Chester thought it best not to mention that many weeks had elapsed since the time he first met Joconda and the occasion on which she had divulged the news about the engagement. "Have all your little f–f–fears and trepidations now been vanquished, m–my poppet, and c–can you give your proud husband some token of your affection?"

Cecily snatched up Baby and held her firmly as a shield against Chester's amorous intentions.

"Mr. Thrush," she said firmly, "it distresses me to have to say this, but a dreadful error has occurred, and I can explain it to you. Just grant me a second to organize my thoughts."

"No explanation is required, m–my little wife," said Chester indulgently. "You found, in my absence, that you regretted your f–former hasty rejection of my proposal, you determined to accept my offer at our next m–meeting. Perhaps you anticipated a little. I w–wouldn't be one to hold such an error in judgement against you!"

"But, Mr. Thrush," Cecily protested, "that's not the truth. It's much more disagreeable, I'm afraid. You see, I was—well there was a gentleman who was—actually he was annoying me with his intentions—"

"The c–cad!" declared Chester, through clenched teeth.

"And I wished to discourage him, and, in the heat of the moment, I'm afraid I lashed out with the first words that came to my head. He had made a faulty assumption, and I merely assented to it."

Chester was magnanimous. "Believe me, my poppet," he said benevolently, "I understand the circumstances entirely. In your desire to rid yourself of this fellow (and if you choose to name him, m–my dove, I will personally inform him of how deeply his behaviour is unacceptable to your adoring h–husband) and, not having the opportunity to c–consult with me in advance, you w–went ahead anyway and divulged our betrothal. I s–see no reason to f–find fault with you for such a happy m–mistake."

"Mr. Thrush!" Cecily said annoyed. "You haven't listened to me. I confess—"

"Never mind, m–my precious w–wife. Do not torment yourself about past mistakes, m–my angel! I freely forgive you. In truth, I have a confession to impart myself! In the interim, between the last occasion on w–which we s–spoke and today's f–felicitous news—" Chester's posturing was as tortured as his words as he strove to divest himself of his confession "—I have m–met another w–woman to whom I w–would have gladly given my h–heart were it not, of c–course, already bestowed."

"But—" began Cecily.

"I c–comprehend how painful such a disclosure must be to you, my own h–heart, and believe me, I would not willingly subject you to such an unpleasant topic, w–were it not that I feel strongly that there c–can be no secrets between two who will share the greatest adventure of a lifetime together."

"Mr. Thrush, I can't permit you to—"

"Don't say it, my pretty pigeon. You m–must not denigrate yourself so—"

"What did you think I intended to say?" demanded Cecily indignantly.

"You were going to release me from my bondage—"

"Bondage!"

"But it is a bondage of devotion. Even were it true that my s–sentiments for this other w–woman were stronger than those I cherish towards you, m–my dear poppet, I shall always bear in m–

mind that you came first c–c–chronologically. Perhaps we could settle the issue if we all moved to Utah."

"To Utah?" Cecily cried in perplexity.

"W–w–where the Mormons l–live," Chester replied beaming. "You know they're permitted to have more than one w–wife."

Cecily was speechless.

"Nevertheless, I assure you," Chester offered some consolation, "you w–would be my number one w–wife."

"What amazing effrontery!" said Cecily passionately.

"Such a confession m–must, I assume," said Chester gallantly, "render you s–something less than ecstatic. It is always a blow to l–learn that we are required to sh–share the affections of our chosen mate with another. I m–might add that I will not press you for a k–kiss to seal our s–solemn c–covenant at this time. I w–will grant you an interval to h–habituate yourself to the notion. Meanwhile, I have a most important and s–sacred duty I m–must perform alone. Mind you, I appreciate your k–kind offer of help, but I respectfully m–must decline it. The glad tidings must be broken very carefully to M–mother Thrush. She has a tendency to become overexcited, but, have no f–fears, m–my little w–wife, she will treasure you as much as I, once she gets to know you, and there will be ample opportunity for that as she will, naturally, be residing with us."

Baby slipped from Cecily's arms as she listened in consternation to this recitation.

"You l–look very f–fetching with a ch–child in your arms, m–my own one," said Chester, blushing red as he did so. "I h–hope it will not be too long before you w–will be tending Chester, Jr. Good afternoon, my dear deer. I sh–shall return to s–settle the final details—the date, the attendants, et cetera—with you shortly."

Once he had exited, humming a happy tune, Cecily sank down to the floor and placed her arms about Baby, clutching the little girl closely, uncertain whether or not to laugh or cry.

Chapter Fourteen

Some April Foolishness

MARCH CAME IN LIKE a lion but did not go out like a lamb. On the contrary, the bitter cold and freakish storms continued and each household in London, shivering under the unseasonable spring weather, met the challenges in its own particular manner.

In the snug two-pair front occupied by Chester Thrush and his mother, a different sort of storm held the occupants in thrall. Mrs. Thrush, incensed that the scheming vixen of a nursery governess had gotten her hooks into Chester despite her most concerted efforts, was not speaking to her darling boy. Whenever he approached her and humbly craved an audience, she spurned his peace offerings and laid siege to his peace of mind by sniffling constantly into a lace-trimmed handkerchief, refusing to order the delicacies he craved for supper and forgetting to lay a fresh fire. In the interests of her noble cause, she suffered all sorts of personal deprivations and each of these—her chilblains, her constant shivering, her emaciated condition—was laid at his door. Chester, waging this domestic battle, found little time to press his advances upon his unwilling fiancée, and she was humbly grateful for this unexpected reprieve.

In the rented house on Bruton Street, another sort of conflict raged, but this one was within the breast of Miss Constance Holly.

Misgivings about her feelings for Mr. Sheridan (and his for her) riddled her heart, yet under the constant barrage of criticism from her family, she pretended a gay indifference. Lady Holly pressed for details of the assumedly flourishing romance; Constance merely smiled. Even when her desperate sisters were enlisted in her mother's behalf and begged her with tears in their eyes to make a rapid settlement of her claims on the territory known as Mr. Sheridan, she merely replied she would see what she could do. And, feeling like a spy behind enemy lines, she sallied forth for another round of parties with Mr. Sheridan, grateful for his easy-going friendship but sorely puzzled as to his amorous intentions.

There was little opportunity for such outings, for Mr. Sheridan had lately become somewhat of a recluse holed up in his studio at Number Seven Swan Walk. Immersed in his work to a greater degree than ever before, Mr. Sheridan was finishing the portrait of Princess Louise, finishing the portrait of Mrs. Fluster, painting in the background for Lady Throttle's picture and working like a madman on his submission to the Royal Academy show. Consequently he neglected the welfare of his subordinates and morale was low. Willett was often found muttering to himself in his pantry, while Chlorrie's croissants grew leaden and rubbery from lack of application to her duties. Even the redoubtable Charlie was disheartened and Betty driven to despair by his neglect.

All of these separate skirmishes were as nothing when compared to the clash of wills exhibited daily in the Fluster's camp. Mr. Fluster was aggrieved with his uncooperative son, and Cedric, who for the first time in his life was actively pursuing a goal, was finding himself strangely rebuffed by the capricious Miss Flutterby, who herself was up in arms against her parents' insistence on tuft-hunting. Father was divided against son, and mother against daughter, for Mrs. Fluster held Joconda solely responsible for the rout of the dinner party. She was unable to take consolation, as formerly, in the soothing presence of Mr. Fogwell, for he was oddly withdrawn, and even that notorious pair of love-birds, Nessie and her Alf, had taken up arms and their hostilities were endless.

Cecily, who was not in the best of spirits, found herself playing the role of confidante to the injured party, Nessie, and sat patiently through endless conferences on strategy, offering advice that was not taken and suggesting tactics which were not deployed.

"How do they do it in those books you're always reading?" she asked, on the first day in April, a day which promised no relief from the miseries of March for it was cold and icy with a heartless wind.

Nessie, who sat in the only armchair and spread her skirts before the meagre fire (for coal was now strictly rationed at Fluster Fancy) pondered this question.

"Well," she said, at last, "the heroine usually pretends an interest in another gentleman. That always brings the hero round to his senses again."

Cecily shrugged her shoulders and read another line from the primer which she was using to entertain Baby,

> "A is for Adam who ate the apple.
> B is for Baby who drank some broth.
> C is for Cat who slept on the cot.
> D is for Dog who dug in the dirt."

"How the devil can I flirt with anyone else?" wailed Nessie, twisting her golden curls around her finger. "Not Mr. Fluster, he wouldn't be a party to it, and besides Alf would never believe it. And Mr. Fogwell never shows the slightest attention to me. I might as well be a doorknob as far as he's concerned. Then there's Cedric, mind you, I set my cap for him when I first came here, but then his nose is too far in the air, for him to notice a housemaid." She bit her lower lip wistfully. "I have it! I shall flirt with Mr. Sheridan!" Cecily looked taken aback. "Don't look so startled, Cecily," Nessie proclaimed. "You've told me over and over again, so often I believe you, that you have no interest in him at all."

"I doubt that he'll respond, Nessie," Cecily responded sternly. "He obviously considers servants completely dispensable for I have apparently become invisible to him."

"And it's no wonder," Nessie declared, "when you're always parading about in those drab brown and grey gowns with the mended aprons and your hair all fastened back as if you were a scullery maid, running in and out of rooms like a frightened rabbit. No, you destroyed your chances there, long ago, after that night you waited on table, and now you act as if you begrudge me a little amusement!"

"E is for Egg, a symbol of Easter.
F is for Fire which is a fuel."

Cecily continued, deciding to ignore this comment. "Not that we see very much of it," she told Baby, "not with Nessie pretending to be a fire screen."

"I think," announced Nessie, rising with dignity and shaking out her crumpled gown, "I'll go and put on my best dress, for Mr. Sheridan's coming today to unveil the portrait of the Missus, and I'm sure I'll be able to find a convenient excuse to be hovering about the drawing room. I'll wager he'll like my cologne, even though Alf turns up his nose at it now."

Cecily went on with her reading.

"G is for Girl who is very Good,
and H is for Horse who—"

She broke off as Nessie slammed the door behind her, and putting Baby off her lap, doubled over and gave way to the tears that had been pent up throughout the past month. It was true that Mr. Sheridan paid her no more mind than he did the sofas in the drawing room, and it was true that even Chester, unacceptable an alternative as he might be, had abandoned her altogether to a loveless fate. Except for the unshrinking adoration of Baby, who stood by her side, her tiny face contorted into a mighty howl as she watched her beloved governess sob uncontrollably, Cecily had no one who cared about her very existence. The betrayal of Nessie, whom she counted as her friend despite her treacherousness and unreliability, had been the final straw.

But Cecily was not the sort to indulge herself in senseless despair, and her infant charge clearly required her courage and calmness. With Cecily, careful performance of her duties was an anchor of significance in the midst of raging chaos. She dried her eyes carefully upon her apron, and swinging Baby up into her arms, carried her off into the bedroom to brush the little girl's thick curls and array her in her freshest frock for the ceremony of the unveiling which Cecily assumed would require Baby's presence.

Several hours later she and Baby were still waiting. The upper floor of Fluster Fancy was completely deserted; Cecily could only guess that Nessie was below stairs trying her hand at Mr. Sheridan. No summons had arrived for Baby, and no one answered the nursery bell when Cecily rang it. Cecily was in the process of re-reading the primer for the eleventh time when she flung it to the floor and said defiantly, "Damn it! I won't have the child left out when it is as much her honour as it is her mother's. Come along, Amaryllis, we're going downstairs to see Mama!"

"Mama! Mama!" repeated Baby as she lagged behind Cecily, for she adored her pretty Mama despite the neglect she suffered at her hands.

There were no signs of life anywhere as Cecily and Baby descended the stairs, and only as they approached the Early Italian Drawing Room were they able to discern the muffled shouts of laughter and clink of crystal. Cecily quivered with rage. The party had evidently been going on for quite some time and yet no one had bothered to inquire after her and Amaryllis. She pushed aside the turquoise curtain which hung across the door and, hoisting Baby into her arms, swept into the room.

The first sight which met her eyes was not one to lighten her spirits. Constance Holly, who had often accompanied Devin when he came for the portrait sittings of late, was hanging upon the artist's arm, laughing at something he said and turning to relate it to Mr. Fogwell who hovered close beside her. At one end of the crowded room, beneath the Fluster family banner, sat an easel bearing a large, shrouded picture. Mrs. Fluster waited before it with bated breath, while her son lounged beside her, puffing upon a vile-smelling cigar. Mr. Fluster and Joconda at the other side of the chamber were absorbed in a chess game.

"Why, here she is," declared Devin, detaching Constance from his arm and moving forward to greet Cecily. "We have been waiting for you these past two hours. Nessie keeps going up to the nursery and finding it empty."

Nessie, who was handing around the drinks, smiled at Cecily uncertainly and winked broadly to indicate the reasons for her deception.

"Well, now that Baby is here," announced the artist, "it is time for the unveiling. Mrs. Fluster, if you will be so good as to stand over here." He ushered her to a position beside the easel and placed a golden cord in her hand. "Ladies and gentlemen, I present, 'A Symphony in Blue and Green.'" The cord was pulled, the velvet shroud fell away, and the picture was revealed. There was a long period of silence.

"Why, you cannot see my face at all," complained Mrs. Fluster, staring at the canvas which showed a woman attired in a filmy peacock-blue gown bending over a little child in a green dress whose hair shone like the sun.

"That's your gown, Mother," pointed out Joconda looking up briefly from her chess game.

"Of course it's my gown," snapped Mrs. Fluster, "but my hair is obscuring my face. No one would know it was me!"

"It's a good likeness of Baby, dear," put in Mr. Fluster timidly.

"But what about me?" Mrs. Fluster wanted to know. "I think this is shocking, Mr. Sheridan! What can I tell my friends?"

"You must understand," he replied, not without entirely concealing the amusement in his voice, "the artistic principles behind this particular portrait."

"I see no artistic principles, merely an awkward inability to handle paints altogether," she retorted waspishly.

"I wished to show," Mr. Sheridan continued, "the similarity between mother and daughter, but rather than doing something so crude and obvious as to paint two similar faces side by side, I painted only the child's face, leaving the viewer to imagine the loveliness of the mother which must be magnified tenfold."

Mrs. Fluster was unconvinced.

"Pemberton!" she shrieked. "Come over here and give me your opinion." Mr. Fogwell removed himself, with some reluctance, from Constance Holly's side and coming closer surveyed the picture solemnly.

"A fascinating conception, Sophronia," he said at last. "You will be the talk of all London."

"I know that myself, Pemberton," she retorted, "but will it be because I have been made an April's fool?"

"Think of it, Mrs. Fluster," put in Constance coming forward, "how very few women can boast that they have had their portraits painted by Devin Sheridan. That is a great privilege, not a cause for dismay." She smiled at Devin in soft appreciation as she said these words, and he, in turn, took her hand and pressed it firmly.

"Baby, Baby!" called out Baby, pointing at the baby in the picture.

"Yes, that's a baby. That's Baby Amaryllis," instructed Cecily.

"And have you no opinion of the picture, Miss Hawthorne?" asked Devin mischievously.

"The brushwork is facile, the colours bold and the composition facetious," she responded coolly.

"Miss Hawthorne should have been an art critic, I fear," said Mr. Fogwell adroitly. "Despite the brevity of her remarks, that's a review with quite a punch to it."

"I have some background in Art," Cecily replied pointedly.

"You should paint a portrait of her, Mr. Sheridan," Mr. Fogwell suggested, "our lovely chrysanthemum."

Constance opened her mouth to speak, but shut it suddenly again. She had never mustered the courage to ask Devin why this young woman, who had been breakfasting with him so intimately only two months before, should now be ensconced in the bosom of a well-known family as a nursery governess, and fearing the answer and what it might do to her peace of mind, she resolved not to voice her unspoken questions.

"An excellent suggestion, Mr. Fogwell," replied Devin gallantly, "but I should hate to deprive Mrs. Fluster and Baby of Miss Hawthorne's excellent services."

"Then mind you don't!" declared Mrs. Fluster sharply. "Such an arrangement is completely out of the question. In fact, Miss Hawthorne, I hardly consider the Early Italian Drawing Room to be the proper place for a child of Amaryllis's tender years at this time of the day. Kindly take her up to the nursery and see that she is more presentable the next time you bring her down before company."

Cecily could not trust herself to respond to this command and, with a shake of her skirts which substituted for a curtsey, she clutched the child firmly and stormed out of the room, colliding violently with a table full of china roosters, some of which tumbled to the floor.

As she applied herself to their retrieval, she heard a light footstep proceeding up the hall, and, assuming that Nessie had come to offer some explanation for her treachery, said sharply, without looking up.

"Don't think you can butter me up, Nessie, with any of your ludicrous tales about romantic novels for I'm not in the mind for—"

"Then, perhaps, you are in the mind for this," said a determined male voice, and the next moment she was swept into Devin's embrace, as he pressed a kiss upon her trembling lips.

"Unhand me, sir!" she declared, struggling to free herself from his arms, but succeeding only in enmeshing herself further into his caress.

"How I have been craving this ever since the first day I saw you!" murmured Devin, brushing her neck and shoulders with his lips. "How extraordinarily sweet you taste!"

Baby clung to Cecily's skirts, looking on in wonderment but not, to Cecily's surprise, engaging in her usual displays of temper.

"Mr. Sheridan—" breathed Cecily.

"Call me Devin," he instructed softly.

"You will be missed," she protested. "Your fiancée, certainly, will be wondering where you are."

"Fiancée?" Devin stopped, loosened his hold, frowned down upon her. Cecily, oddly enough, did not retreat from his grasp. "Do you mean Constance Holly? Ha, ha! That's rich!" He threw back his head in a throaty chuckle. "Constance Holly is not engaged to me. Must I remind you, to the contrary, that you are the one who is engaged?"

"Oh, that!" Cecily dismissed Chester Thrush with a wave of her hands. "That was pure fabrication!"

Devin took hold of her shoulders with a remorseless grip and stared into her eyes intently. "Do you mean to tell me that I have been torturing myself for the past month with thoughts of you and that stuttering imbecile together, and it's all been a mistake?"

Cecily nodded happily.

"You little witch!" declared the artist. "I should punish you for that! Instead, I shall do this—" And he bent his head to place another kiss upon her lips. This time, whether it was because she was weary of a pretence of indifference or whether it was because she considered surrender nobler than defeat, Cecily did not resist. Her arms were intertwined about his neck, her fingers interlaced in his hair, and her heart inflamed with desire. She responded to him with all the pent-up ardour of her affectionate character, and it was he who first came up for breath.

"My lovely Cecily," he intoned with tenderness. "You must come back and sit for your portrait again."

"Oh, I couldn't do that!" she said quickly. "You heard Mrs. Fluster. She would never permit it."

"Well then, resign your position."

Cecily smiled mischievously. "Why, I wouldn't consider it! Some persons might accuse me of running away from my problems, abandoning projects to which my presence is vital." She fondled Baby's flaxen head.

"But your presence is vital to me also," the artist pleaded. Cecily found she derived enormous pleasure from seeing him beg. "The studio has been so barren without your sunny presence. Old Harry is in a decline."

"I'm needed here," said Cecily simply.

"Can you deny this need?" he asked, gathering her into his arms for another kiss.

Cecily was falling and she knew it, but all the familiar handholds were sliding by her and she did not have the energy to reach out and grasp one. Her mind was blank, or rather, filled with a warm unthinking darkness; her body was alive with an urgent vitality; her knees were growing weak and threatening to betray her susceptibility.

At that moment, Constance Holly stepped softly into the hallway, wondering at Devin's long absence and thinking she would fetch him back to the drawing room before his absence was noted. She stopped in amazement at the sight of the pair embracing passionately in the hall, china roosters littered about their feet, and a golden-haired child watching contentedly, her thumb in her mouth. As she stood there, hoping she could retreat as noiselessly as she came, Devin mumbled softly, but not so softly that Constance couldn't hear him.

"Do you mean to tell me that all this time you've been treating me so coldly because you believed me to be engaged to Constance Holly? What an absolutely ludicrous thought! Constance doesn't inspire me with the slightest desire to do this, my love!" And he embarked on another round of kisses and caresses to Cecily's gratification.

But not to the gratification of Constance, who turned, with tears in her eyes, and stumbled down the hallway in the opposite direction. Mr. Fogwell found her, half an hour later, still sobbing violently in the deserted dining room, her head pillowed on the gleaming oak table. She seemed a small girl adrift in the expanse of the stately formal room, dwarfed by the grandeur of the silver epergne and chafing dishes which thronged the table.

"My dear Miss Holly," he said, touching her arm tentatively. "Can I be of some comfort to you?"

"Oh, Mr. Fogwell, please leave me quite alone," she begged, averting her head to hide her wan face. "I cannot bear to be seen when I'm crying."

"But, my exquisite orchid," he responded with concern evident in his voice, "you are very lovely, pale and vulnerable, in your sorrow."

"Flattery will not comfort me, Mr. Fogwell," she said coldly. Her voice echoed in the empty room.

"Ah, but I do not flatter you," he replied, pulling out a chair and sitting down beside her. "That is the truth. You are as lovely, at this moment, as at any moment, at least in my eyes."

"Mr. Fogwell, I don't think it is appropriate for you to make such comments to me," she said with dignity.

"Any more than it is appropriate for Mr. Sheridan to trifle with the nursery governess?"

"Oh!" Constance gasped. She turned to face him, her tender eyes dark with pain.

"I saw them, as you must have, in the hallway," he explained with a little shrug of his shoulders. "Was it such a blow to you, then? I thought there was little between you but friendship."

Constance reflected on this statement for a time, tracing the pattern of the grain in the table with one forefinger. "It certainly seemed that there was little between us but friendship," she said at last, speaking slowly and choosing her words with great care. "He has never indicated otherwise by any little attention or action or even word. But Mama told me he planned to marry me within the year, and, how humiliating it is to learn that he has made me his April fool, so he can continue his philandering without fear of exposure!"

"He made an offer for you to your mother, but never mentioned his matrimonial plans to you?" Mr. Fogwell was frankly incredulous.

"It does sound improbable," Constance admitted ruefully. "Indeed it sounds more like one of Mama's schemes than anything else. Oh, how could I be so taken in, first by Mr. Sheridan and then my own mother? I really am just a silly, thoughtless, thick-headed old April fool!" She began crying again, pathetically, without trying to conceal her tears, her small white fists clenching and unclenching on the table top.

"You're not an April fool, my dear Constance," replied Mr. Fogwell soothingly, taking her into his arms and stroking her hair gently. "You are a tender, compassionate, sincerely sympathetic young woman, capable of an extraordinary depth of feeling and deep, abiding loyalties."

"How peculiar of you to say that, Mr. Fogwell," she said, sniffling. "No one has ever said that of me before. Why, I'm told that I'm cold, unfeeling, heartless —"

"Hush, my angel," he said, holding her more closely. "Hush, my love. No one has ever seen past the shy barrier you have constructed to shield your susceptible heart from the cruel world until I came along."

She cried a little longer, her hands placed confidingly on his chest, her head nestled upon his shoulder. If the truth were to be told, she no longer felt humiliated and rejected, but was savouring the unusual experience of being held in the arms of a man, of being cherished and treasured if only for a moment.

"You have been most kind," she said, breaking away at last and dabbing at her eyes with the handkerchief he offered. "I truly appreciate the consideration you've shown to one who was suddenly humbled. It is certainly an elegant sense of manners."

"My dear Miss Holly," he declared affronted, "I am not offering you my modest consolation because of good manners. I am truly concerned with every aspect of your well-being."

Constance was confused. "I wonder where my mantle has gotten to?" she asked nervously, pressing the handkerchief back into his hand. "I must really be going. Would you—I hate to request another favour—but could you be so good as to call a cab for me?"

"I am leaving myself," he said, holding out a hand to help her rise, "and my mind would be very much relieved if you will permit me to see you to your door personally."

"I couldn't expect it of you," she said hastily, bustling by him and pausing on the threshold. "It would be so inconvenient and totally unnecessary."

"Your expectations are far too low, Miss Holly," he answered, ushering her out of the room with a hand placed firmly upon her waist. "Your encounters with the stronger sex, I am afraid, have been disappointing, but that only makes it all the easier for me to try to compensate, and I shall do everything in my power to accomplish that end."

Chapter Fifteen

Offers More Insight into the Course of True Love

"I TOLD YOU HE WAS in love with you reportedly," Nessie declared.

"Repeatedly," corrected Cecily with a little smile upon her lips, as she closed the door to the nursery in which Baby was taking her nap.

"Reportedly," said Nessie stubbornly.

"I suppose that's why you were making eyes at him on Tuesday, and pretending that I could not be found," remarked Cecily complacently. Nothing, not Nessie's incessant cross-examination, nor the disagreeable weather, nor the increasingly meagre amounts of food being sent up for the nursery suppers, could disturb Cecily's self-composure since her delightful interlude with Mr. Sheridan. He had come twice during the four succeeding days, waiting humbly in the servant's hall like any other caller for one of the domestics, taking her and Baby for long rambling jaunts in his luxurious carriage, expeditions full of reminiscences, improbable speculations on the future, gifts of trinkets and flowers, and a few stolen kisses. The more he pleaded with her to resume sitting for the portrait, the more she insisted that she must persevere in her present duties, a plan of action she felt guaranteed further blandishments and briberies.

She fingered the gold chain about her neck with a wistful look in her eyes.

"Fancy this, the besotted simpleton thinks I were trying to snatch away her man!" proclaimed Nessie, following Cecily into her bedchamber off the nursery, where chrysanthemums bloomed in abundance in various plain crockery pots. "You really mean to tell me you didn't guess the nature of my artful plan?"

"What artful plan?" asked Cecily, aimlessly rearranging her flowers. "I wonder where he gets chrysanthemums at this time of the year."

"Coo! You certainly are slow-witted when it comes to romance," said Nessie stoutly. "I was attempting to make you jealous."

"Oh, were you?" responded Cecily, absentmindedly.

"Indeed, I was," the housemaid said with a shake of her curls and a wag of her finger. "And I succeeded like a trump!"

"A trump?" Cecily did not understand the application of the word.

"Yes, you have me to thank," Nessie announced with satisfaction, "for Mr. Sheridan's renewed ardour. And small thanks I've had for any of that."

"Thank you, Nessie," Cecily replied, turning to her friend and engulfing her in a warm and fervent hug. "I don't know how you did it, or what you did, but I thank you just the same!"

Nessie was beaming. "Now I expect you to do the same for me!"

"I, do the same for you?" Cecily asked uncertainly.

"Yes, you must go below stairs and flirt with Alf," Nessie declared with a great smile. "You may borrow some of my perfume for the purpose."

"Alf will think me ridiculous," protested Cecily. "Besides, it's not the same circumstances at all. Mr. Sheridan and I were estranged because of well, really, because of a little untruth that I let slip once when I was jealous."

"Jealousy! That is the divine clockwork which makes all romances run smoothly!" said Nessie knowingly. "Never mind how it is done. Only do this one thing for me, Cecily, and I shall be your slave forever!"

"Nessie, don't talk so!" Cecily protested. "I tell you I haven't the slightest hint as to how to begin to flirt with Alf."

"Well, imprevaricate!"

"Improvise," suggested Cecily.

"That's it," Nessie agreed, tugging at her friend's arm. "I'll outline the plot I have in mind for you as we go downstairs."

Cecily was never quite certain about the many variations and subtleties involved in Nessie's outlandish scheme, but she reluctantly agreed to do her best, aware that Nessie would be listening to every carefully coached word from her place of concealment in the broom closet.

"Good afternoon, Alf," she said cheerfully, straining her neck to look up at him. "Who do you think will win today?" It was the occasion of the Oxford/Cambridge boat race, and the house was deserted, the family having gone to watch the event.

"I have my money on the Blue, Miss Cecily," he said pleasantly. "I have very good information as to the likelihood of their victory."

"Oh!" was Cecily's response. She heard Nessie hissing at her from her hiding place and struggled to speak her rehearsed line.

"Do you ever think fondly of me, Alf?" she asked, placing her hand gingerly on his velvet-coated arm.

The footman peered down at her in evident amazement. "Not that I can think of, Miss Cecily," he replied politely. "You know as me and Nessie is walking out together. I've only room in my heart for one lady."

Cecily breathed a sigh of relief, her ridiculous role in this ridiculous charade could be abandoned. But Nessie made no move to emerge from the hall closet.

"Then why have you been treating her so coolly of late?" asked Cecily, heedless of Nessie's muttered rejoinders at her back to continue with the rehearsed speech.

"Jealousy, Miss Cecily, is the clockwork which makes romances run smoothly," he explained solemnly.

"The divine clockwork," murmured Cecily.

"Yes, the divine clockwork," Alf agreed. "You must have read the same novel which Nessie read to me. You see in this book, the hero and heroine were going along smoothly, but the hero realized that the course of true love never should run smoothly, so he pretended an interest in another woman, shunning his sweetheart, and she, driven to despair by his coldness, ran off and drowned herself in the river."

Cecily looked aghast. "What a horrible ending!" she said with amazement. "How can that be considered a romance?"

Alf scratched his head and pondered the question. "I'm not sure I understand myself, Miss Cecily, but then Nessie often tells me I have not a romantic bone in my body. I'm certain she would know the answer to your question. My guess would be that the tragic end was the moral to the story, warning all lovers in similar predicaments, that if the one suspects the other of some misunderstanding, some little omission or neglect, the offended party should come out into the open, not fearing a rejection where rejection there could be none, and find solace in the arms of their true love."

Suiting her actions to these words, Nessie tumbled out of the closet, curls askew, ribbons fluttering, and threw herself into Alf's arms. "Oh, Alfred, that was so romantic," she cried. "I'll never doubt your affections again forevermore."

Cecily, seeing that her role had been played and the drama satisfactorily concluded, withdrew to allow the reunited lovers a few minutes of intimacy. As she did so, there was a double knock upon the door, and Alf, in a voice muffled by Nessie's embraces, asked if Cecily would be good enough to answer it.

Though she knew it unlikely, suspecting that he would be also observing the boat race with the crowds of other Londoners, perhaps even with Constance Holly, Cecily dared to hope the unexpected visitor was Mr. Sheridan and threw open the door with a bright smile. The smile died upon her lips, for upon the threshold, turning his bowler nervously in his bony hands, stood Mr. Chester Thrush, with his pale lips bared in a terrifying grin.

"M–my little w–wife," he said, "it was your l–lovely face which I was musing upon in my thoughts. How s–simply stupendous to f–find it in the f–flesh!" His pale-lashed eyelids blinked rapidly and his pale tongue flickered out to wet his dry lips, for this pretty compliment was completely fabricated; he had been thinking of Joconda and had, in fact, come to bid her a lachrymose farewell.

"Do step in, Mr. Thrush," said Cecily ungraciously, for the bitter wind was howling through the open door, setting the tapestries flapping and the armour of the silent knight was clanging violently.

"M–my pleasure, m–my own poppet," he replied with an affected jauntiness. He attempted to twirl his hat upon his finger like a man about town but succeeded only in sending it careening into a table of painted china candlesticks. Cecily retrieved it and while returning it to its owner, her fingers brushed his. She withdrew from the moist, rubbery feel of his hands as if she had unexpectedly touched a toad. Chester, however, behaved as if he had been galvanized, twitching and jerking about with his eyes rolling back in his head.

"M–my own little w–wife!" he declared wildly. "Your tender touch quite unmans me!"

Nessie and Alf emerged from the shadows where they had been effecting their reunion, and watched with friendly interest.

"Coo! Cecily!" cried Nessie, from within the shelter of Alf's capacious embrace. "You are a deeper one than I gave you credit for! All this time, you had me thinking your heart belonged to another, and now I finds that you has a previous attachment. Why have you been holding out on your bosom friend, the sepulchre of all your hopes and wishes?"

Cecily did not bother to correct Nessie's vocabulary. "I didn't know of him myself until just recently," she snapped. "There's been a dreadful misunderstanding, but I'm certain it will all be cleared up shortly. May I have a little privacy?"

"Lawd, listen to her!" said Nessie, mimicking a fine lady with her nose in the air. "Come along, Alf." She dragged the lanky footman down the hall, he winking madly at Cecily (she assumed in celebration of his success with his lady love) as he disappeared down the corridor.

"Come in here, Mr. Thrush," said Cecily briskly, holding aside the curtain which cloaked the entrance to the drawing room. With a humble bow, he stumbled across the threshold and stood just inside the chamber looking about him in mingled horror and confusion. By the dim light which filtered through the heavy mustard-coloured velvet draperies at the window, the curio-loaded tables, the Fluster family banner, Mrs. Fluster's gilded harp and the spidery ferns waving their fronds from porcelain receptacles everywhere, seemed like the monstrous undergrowth of some Aesthetic jungle. Cecily, quite inured to the peculiarities of Fluster Fancy, took up a seat on one of the satin-covered sofas, spreading her sage-green skirts about her complacently, preparing herself for the ordeal of disillusioning Mr. Thrush. To her horror, he threw himself down upon the carpet at her feet and buried his head in her lap.

"M–my own little wife," he mumbled incoherently. "All of the h–hindrances in our path, all of the obstacles in our way, all of the m–myriad objections of m–meddling others have been at last swept aside. I h–have c–come to tell you that my h–heart is entirely yours to do with as you please. I have resolved to banish the other woman from my thoughts. Never again shall her name pass my lips, or her f–face enter my dreams. To you alone, I dedicate this h–humble body, this modest mind, these eager h–hands." So saying he grasped her hands with his own with such vehemence that his bones cracked loudly. Cecily tried to extricate herself as neatly as possible, but a move to one side would have imperilled a table loaded with china while a dash to the opposite direction would have enmeshed her in the strings of Mrs. Fluster's harp. She considered pushing Chester backward (to the imminent danger of an antique chamber pot full of aspidistras which sat on the floor behind him) but resolved instead to discourage his attentions with words.

"Mr. Thrush," she said firmly, "I have told you before how deeply sensible I am of the honour you do me in offering me your name in the bonds of matrimony —"

"M–my precious little w–wife," he muttered.

"But must confess to you that there is another man in my life. Of late, I have come to the realization that I can, in no way, render you or any other person my affections with a full heart, for they have already been granted freely to another."

Chester looked up, his mouth set in a pout. "And has this rogue, this s–swindler had the audacity to s–solicit the h–hand of my affianced w–wife?" he asked sulkily. "And h–have you had the temerity to give your w–word when it was already given to m–me?"

"No, of course not," snapped Cecily. "He has not spoken of marriage nor would I have thought to embark on a discussion of such a change of state without first clarifying my situation to you."

"And well you might!" declared Chester, raining wet kisses upon her cool hands. "There can be no turning back, not for either of us, no matter with w–whatever sense of deficiency my w–wife! I shall guide you gently and tenderly in the ways in which you may s–serve me, your l–lord and m–master. Your m–maidenly fears, your ch–chaste reservations are precious to me, and I am deeply conscious that the overwhelming sensations of inadequacy with which you face our impending nuptials might well lead to the invention of an imaginary l–lover whose m–mention might deter me from the too s–sudden c–completion of my h–hopes."

"That's not the case, at all!" proclaimed Cecily indignantly. "This gentleman is as real as you or I!"

"S–so it would seem to you, m–my trembling m–mouse," Chester replied fondly. "M–mother said it is often so with young brides. Illusions! Delusions! All m–manner of f–figments! Your protests do you c–credit, m–my dove."

"These are not figments!" declared Cecily. "The gentleman's name is Mr. Sheridan, and he is an artist!"

Chester was only momentarily taken aback. "Ah!" he grinned, "I grant you that! The fellow is, unfortunately, all too real! But your assumption of the serious intent of his s–statements, therein lies the delusion! Joconda—ahem! Miss Fluster has told me all about him. She says he preys upon unsuspecting females whose vanity is their greatest w–weakness, females such as her m–mother, pretending to care for them and f–flattering them, merely because he desires to paint their portraits for his greater glory."

Cecily was silent. It was true that Mr. Sheridan's conversations with Mrs. Fluster had been full of foolishnesses and high-sounding phrases employed merely to ensure her compliance with his own schemes. Perhaps the fine compliments, the little presents, even the kisses, were merely bribes to ensure the renewed services of a superior model.

"Besides," Chester went on fondly, "Joconda—ahem! M–miss Fluster tells me that he is certainly engaged to a young lady named M–miss Holly—"

"No! That's untrue!" declared Cecily.

"And my devoted m–mother, quite independently, has related the same information to me," Chester continued, "for she has done some alterations for Lady Holly and M–miss Holly, and she says the engagement is all the talk of the h–household. They expect the w–wedding to take place w–within the year. So you see, m–my sweetheart, you c–cannot expect me to take seriously your sweet assertions. I, your devoted and adoring h–husband, can see through your ch–charming deceptions."

"The cad!" breathed Cecily, clenching her fists, heedless of the fact that Chester's fingers were still intertwined with her own.

"Ouch!" he protested. "M–my angel, I had no notion of your s–strength. Can you f–favour your l–little dove with an embrace delivered with the same delightful f–fervour?"

He scrambled up to sit beside her on the sofa and placed his head upon her shoulder, one clammy hand reaching around and pressing her waist.

Cecily made herself as small as possible, but her thoughts were in such turmoil she did not resist as much as formerly.

"Together we shall banish the images of the other l–loves that have subsequently entered our l–lives. Together we shall sh–shun the temptations that lead us from a life of bliss, as one," he announced, gazing dreamily at the Fluster family banner as he spoke. "You m–must exorcise your imagined s–suitor, just as I have successfully l–laid to rest my aspirations towards an admirable young w–woman, whose s–station in life is f–far above my own. I have f–faced reality. I have confronted the grim f–facts that no m–matter what the tender feelings and throbbing yearnings which may or may not—I choose not to say which—exist between myself and this young w–woman—who shall forever go unnamed—it would be unthinkable for m–me to ask her to sh–share m–my humble life and equally impossible for me, thereby, to ever broach the subject in her m–magnificent presence." He sighed. "I m–make such a noble sacrifice as to c–continue with my w–wedding plans with you, not even m–mentioning this other woman, to indicate my firm sense of h–honour and obligation to a previous commitment."

The sound of voices, the slam of a door, the clatter of various footsteps were heard in the hallway, and Cecily struggled to rise to her feet despite the determined hold of her ardent admirer. She did not succeed before the curtain had been pushed aside and several of the race-goers—Cedric and Miss Flutterby, Mrs. Fluster and Mr. Fogwell and Joconda—had entered the room.

"Who is this?" asked Mrs. Fluster in tones of horror. "How is it that such a shabby looking, unaesthetic individual is soiling the purity of my Early Italian Drawing Room? Joconda, did you give the nursery governess permission to entertain gentlemen callers in my boudoir, my little sanctuary of Culture in an earthly world?"

For answer Joconda burst into tears and went flying out of the room, her skirts flapping.

"How very peculiar!" said Mrs. Fluster calmly. "I've never seen Joconda so emotional! She's been unlike herself for a month now. One would think, if one didn't know better, that she was in love! But that's clearly impossible! No man would ever favour her with his attentions, for no man could be attracted to someone so unconcerned with appearance, so graceless and tasteless—"

"My good woman!" declared Chester, stiffening, so that even his hair stood on end. "I presume I address the mistress of this house and the fortunate mother of an exceptional daughter?"

"Who is this creature?" cried Mrs. Fluster aghast. "Remove him, Pemberton!"

"Not until I have told you what I think of your neglect, yes, neglect and shameful abuse of one of the rarest treasures of womanhood I have ever had the good fortune to meet, a young woman whose domestic accomplishments alone transfigure her character with all the beauty of femininity, if such a transfiguration were necessary, as it isn't since Joconda…er…Miss Fluster is endowed with all the charms of any of the fairest of her sex!" Chester had completely lost his habitual stutter in his enthusiasm for his cause.

"Pemberton, what is he saying? Why do you allow him to continue?" cried Mrs. Fluster. "Oh, the shame of it, in my own little retreat, that a stranger should upbraid me about my own child who

I should be considered to know better than anyone else. I am, only, her mother!"

"Yes, it is a shame!" Chester continued as Mr. Fogwell on one hand and Cecily, crimson with embarrassment on the other hand, propelled him from the room. "A shame that a mother could be so wrapped up in herself, so oblivious to the concerns of her children, that she should overlook the jewel in the bosom of her family, a daughter who—"

The curtain flapping over his mouth cut short his last words and Mr. Fogwell, brushing off his hands, surveyed him with distaste.

"I'll show him to the door, I promise you, Mr. Fogwell," said Cecily hastily. "Oh, please, don't worry yourself further. I assure you this is entirely my responsibility and I do recognize my duties and my faults in this unfortunate situation. Just be so kind as to offer my apologies to Mrs. Fluster."

Mr. Fogwell nodded, with a dubious look in his dark eyes, and returned to the scene of the crime.

"Oh, Mr. Thrush, what have you done?" wailed Cecily, pushing him towards the door. "You have probably cost me my situation and what can you have been thinking of to defend Miss Fluster so and to her mother who everyone knows despises her—" She broke off, her eyes widening and her hand flying to her mouth as she absorbed the implications of the scene which had just occurred. "It's Joconda, isn't it?" she asked amazed. "Joconda is the other woman, isn't she?"

"And I shall allow no one, not even her thoughtless parent, to speak poorly of her in my presence," said her champion proudly. "No matter that I shall never be able to confess my feelings to her, no matter that I shall tie myself in matrimony to another, no matter that I cannot ask her to share my humble life, I shall not—"

"You feel that she is too far above you?" asked Cecily breathlessly. "You fear that she is too accustomed to living in...er...opulence and splendour to agree to become your wife and live on your...ahem..."

"Meagre income," suggested Chester.

"Yes, meagre income," agreed Cecily. "Oh, Mr. Thrush, you must not trouble yourself with that thought—"

"Never shall I reduce my splendid Joconda to poverty!" he declared, puffing out his chest, threatening to burst open the purple pheasants upon his waistcoat. "Never shall. I detach her from the comforts to which she is accustomed!"

"But she's not!" announced Cecily. "Oh, Mr. Thrush, she's not!"

"What?" demanded Chester.

"They're terribly, terribly poor," Cecily explained earnestly. Her hazel eyes were alight with enthusiasm; she gestured wildly. "Granted, they keep up appearances. If they didn't all the vultures of London would be down upon them in an instant. But there are bailiffs hovering about the door even now. The merchants no longer extend credit. The servants haven't been paid for nearly a year. They stay because they have nowhere else to go; that's why the service is so poor."

"Is this the truth? Do you swear to these allegations?" demanded Chester, taking her by the shoulders and shaking her soundly in his excitement.

"Oh, yes!" Cecily said, wide-eyed. "You have only to ask Mr. Fluster or Joconda. They would tell you the truth. It is only Mrs. Fluster who refuses to see the inevitable downfall, the impending bankruptcy. Why, a humble cottage shared with you and your mother, living on your salary as a clerk, that would be Heaven for Joconda after the humiliations under which she suffers here, the endless struggle to balance the books and still put food on the table and maintain the household—"

"Enough! Cecily, you are an angel! You have saved me from a lifetime of misery and unhappiness, being linked indissolubly to the wrong woman when the one I love is suffering all of the wrongs which should never afflict the gentler sex. Show me to Mr. Fluster!" He donned his hat in his enthusiasm.

"Mr. Fluster?"

"Yes, I wish to offer for his daughter's hand in matrimony! Don't just stand there like a gawking yokel, Miss Hawthorne. If you will not indicate the direction of Joconda's father's study, I shall open every door in this house myself until I find him."

Cecily shrugged her shoulders. "This way, Mr. Thrush!" she said demurely, ushering him through a labyrinth of corridors, around peacocks and through mazes of china-laden tables, until they reached the open door to the study in which Mr. Fluster could be seen, his spectacles perched upon his nose as he pored over his books.

"Mr. Fluster, may I present Mr. Thrush, Mr. Chester Thrush," said Cecily, withdrawing peremptorily.

"Yes, Mr. Thrush, what can I do for you?" inquired Mr. Fluster looking up and scratching his bald pate absently. He was surrounded by ledger books and a smudge of ink on his white shirt front spoke of the desperation of his struggle to make sense of his circumstances.

"You can permit me to solicit the hand of your fair daughter, the marvel of her sex, the finest of women in the world, in matrimony, sir!" said Chester, holding his head high.

"Do you mean Joconda?" asked Mr. Fluster in amazement. He narrowed his eyes and peered at his unexpected visitor suspiciously.

"I prefer to call her Jane, sir," replied Chester, "as that is the name she prefers."

"Well, yes, I call her my sweet Jane when we are alone together," said the confused father. He chewed on his lower lip thoughtfully. "Is she aware of your feelings, young man?"

Chester seated himself in a chair facing the desk and leaned forward eagerly. "Sir, I am aware that some individuals in this modern world might think to engage the daughter's affections before her father had given his approval. I am not so heedless of the proprieties. I would not think of encouraging Jane to form an attachment which might be frowned upon by her family until I ascertained the chances of our gaining parental approval."

"Admirable, though a trifle old-fashioned," observed Mr. Fluster. "Still, I think I can manage the proper questions. What are your qualifications, Mr...ahem...Thrash?"

"Mr. Thrush, chief clerk of Davenport and Cole Limited. Wages of one hundred twenty-five pounds per annum. Devoted and only son of Mrs. Isabella Thrush of Islington, the widow of the late Mr. Sanders Thrush, a merchant dealing in second-hand wearing apparel who succumbed of apoplexy some ten years ago, from which time I have supported myself and my frail mother on my income, supplemented, I might add, by certain small jobs of alterations which my fond mother undertakes but which I have repeatedly asked her to desist from as I feel such a connexion places us in a somewhat servile light to certain noble families. I can assure you that once she has grandchildren to occupy her, she will remain at home and devote herself entirely to the greater domestic felicitations of myself and my wife."

"Hmm," said Mr. Fluster, shrugging his shoulders. "Not perhaps the match I would have chosen for Jane, but really it is her decision to make, and if she is fond of you, young man, I see nothing in that biography to discourage the match. I might as well be frank with you and admit that despite our somewhat desperate attempt to keep up appearances, it seems likely that my business, which is presently in the completely incapable hands of a nincompoop named Muddle, Jr., the son of my late partner, will fail utterly, whereupon, even if you were an old-clothes dealer yourself, I should welcome the opportunity for Jane to free herself from the pressing worries which daily occupy her here."

"A most distressing circumstance, Mr. Fluster," said Chester familiarly, knitting his large hands together. "May I, as your future son, be permitted to inquire into the details of the business problems?"

Mr. Fluster sighed. He drummed his stubby fingers on the top of a thick ledger book. "Incompetence. Complete and utter income-petence," he said. "Muddle, Jr., is a thoroughly modern young man with no understanding of accounting, nor customer relations nor the proper conduct of dealings with merchants who used to buy from us. In a few short years he has brought a mighty firm to its knees. And I, alas, am prevented by certain provisions made when I retired, from stepping in and correcting the problems. It might be expected—I take it that you know of the existence of my son, Cedric—it might, I repeat, be expected that Cedric would be able to come to my assistance, but regrettably he has much the same distaste for business exhibited by Muddle, Jr. My sweet Jane could run the firm single-handedly, I believe, but Cedric would spend all the profits on his gaming, his club dues and his tailor, I fear. It's perhaps a matter of thanks that he has resisted all my efforts to interest him in Fluster and Muddle."

Chester pondered this for a moment, rubbing his chin with his bony fingers.

"Perhaps I can be of some assistance," he said at last. "I have been for some time considering resigning my position with Davenport and Cole because of certain—well—lack of appreciation they exhibit for my rather remarkable if humble talents. Would it be possible for me to enter your employ, Mr. Fluster, as a condition in my courtship of your daughter, and, if everything proceeds satisfactorily, carry out your wishes in as unobtrusive but firm manner as possible?"

"A godsend! You're a godsend, young man!" declared Mr. Fluster, bouncing round from behind his desk to pump Chester's hand heartily. "Yes, I see it, you could bring me the books, I could work on them here, dictate some correspondence, contact some of our old customers myself, send you back to be sure the orders were carried out smoothly! Why, we might be able to pull ourselves out of this yet! My sweet Jane has done me a great service in bringing you to our aid. Let me send for her. I'm sure you'd like to have a little time to reveal your hopes for the future to her."

He pulled on his bell pull several times but when no one came to answer his summons, sighed, murmured something about the quality of service in the house, and went off himself to fetch his daughter. Chester wandered about the study restlessly, now pulling his gold watch out of his pocket and letting it dangle by his side, then replacing it and pulling out a handkerchief to wipe his perspiring brow. There was a soft step in the hallway, a timid knock upon the door, and then Joconda had stepped into the room.

Rather than her usual dark, plain gowns, she wore a delicate yellow-printed cotton costume, traced with a subtle floral pattern and ornamented with pale lilac ruffles. Her hair, normally pulled back tight against her skull, had been dressed more softly, swirling in rich waves upon the back of her head with tendrils framing her glowing face. Her lips were full and soft, her eyes brilliant.

"Mr. Thrush," she said timidly.

"My darling Jane," he cried, rushing forward to take her into his arms.

Chapter Sixteen

*Depicts the Artist in a Garden
of Spring Blossoms*

"MAMA," SAID CONSTANCE TIMIDLY, as she stood in the centre of the drawing room table while Isabella Thrush, her mouth full of pins, trotted round about her studying the hem of a soft yellow-silk gown which she had just finished retrimming with purple and green braiding for Constance's Easter gown. "Mama, what if I were in love with someone other than Mr. Sheridan? Would you still wish me to accept his proposal, that is, if he does propose?"

"Nonsense, Constance," replied her mother who was gorging herself upon buttered toast and jam tarts at a small table along the side of the chamber. "Who else could you be in love with? You see no one but Mr. Sheridan!"

"Sometimes it seems to be, Mama," said Constance dreamily, "that Mr. Sheridan takes me about so much and introduces me to such a variety of other people because he expects me to meet someone who will be more suitable for me. You know, and he does too, I'm sure, that I know very little about Art and even feel intimidated by some of his more clever and...well...talented friends."

"Nonsense!" snapped Lady Holly. "If you continue to use the clever epigraphs I invent for your purposes, if you read the Art reviews studiously and con lines from them for later expression in his presence, if you endeavour to memorize the quotations from the classics I press upon you daily, you shall have no trouble holding your own in a conversation with Mr. Sheridan. And you shall have no trouble in winding the soft noose of your charms around his very neck."

Constance wrinkled up her nose at this metaphor. "How horrid!" she said passionately. "As if he were a rabbit and I some sort of hound pursuing him."

"Exactly the state of affairs," said her mother complacently. "Such is the nature of all intercourse between men and women. The men, foolish beasts thinking they require freedom and frivolities, ever flee from the women who know best that a man must be kept encaged in a web of sweet deceits and subtle snares. Before marriage, it is flatteries, exclamations of amazement at his wit, soft demurrers to his compliments, and that wisest of all weapons, tears. After marriage, it is of course, children, which makes the whole difficult procedure much easier indeed. You have only to admit him to your bedchamber now and then—I consider you at thirty-two, my pet, old enough to discuss these very problematic issues—and as soon as you discover yourself to be in an interesting condition, you may treat him howsoever you please. No man will be able to escape then. Of course, he may occasionally develop a passion for some opera dancer or actress, or even, in Mr. Sheridan's case, a model, but you may ignore that. After all, it does allow you to escape any unwelcome attentions he may wish to press upon you."

"Hop down, my dear," said Isabella Thrush. "You look as pretty as a picture, I declare."

Constance stepped lightly down upon a chair and from that perch to the floor. "Mother," she said, as Mrs. Thrush hopped up upon the chair to pull the gown from over her head, "that seems so—so disheartening somehow. Why would anyone marry?"

"How can you ask that, Constance!" shrieked her aggrieved mother. "You must marry so that your sisters can marry. That is the heart of the matter. Would you wish to spend the rest of your years as an old maid, growing old and feeble and doddering about in this rented house with me and your five sisters?"

"No, Mama," answered Constance honestly.

"Then you must marry."

Constance shivered in her petticoats, folding her arms over her bare shoulders and bare bosom while Mrs. Thrush fetched the threadbare blue dress she had discarded for the fitting. 'But then I may marry anyone. It isn't necessary that it be Mr. Sheridan," she pointed out. "I could marry the butcher—"

"Oh, Constance!" said Lady Holly shuddering.

"Or the butler."

Lady Holly paused in the act of inserting another slice of toast into her already stuffed mouth. "Really, Constance, are you trying to make me nauseous?" she asked sternly. "Of course you cannot marry the butler. What would people think? You must marry a man of good family, with a nice income, someone who moves in the best circles."

"Then any man who meets those qualifications," persisted Constance, "would be suitable in your eyes."

Mrs. Thrush bounded up on to the chair again and dropped the faded gown over the girl's head, while Lady Holly chewed her toast solemnly and considered this statement.

"It would depend entirely," she decided at last, "on how good his family, how nice his income, and the quality of his acquaintances."

"Suppose," said Constance, struggling to emerge from her blue cocoon, "just for the sake of speculation, he was of somewhat mysterious origin but accepted widely by the cream of Society and always presented himself with faultless manners?"

Lady Holly scrunched up her mouth expressively.

"And suppose," Constance went on heedlessly, allowing Mrs. Thrush to pull her arms through the sleeves as if she were a doll, "he had no ascertainable source of income but was always attired in the most impeccable taste, including excellent and elegant jewellery, and drove a most luxurious carriage drawn by a beautiful pair of matched greys?"

Lady Holly choked on her toast and had to take a hasty sip from her glass of Madeira.

"And suppose he was made welcome by such families, as for example, the Flusters?" concluded Constance breathlessly. Mrs.

Thrush was doing up her buttons. "Supposing there was a gentleman who could be described thusly, would he be suitable in your eyes?"

"Sounds like a parasite and gigolo to me," announced Lady Holly contemptuously. "Sounds like that scurrilous snake, what is his name, Fogwell, who's always toadying about Sophronia Fluster!"

"Oh, no!" protested Constance, as Mrs. Thrush tugged at her waist to fasten it with a hook and eye. "I wasn't thinking of anyone in particular. Heavens! I don't believe I've ever spoken to Mr. Fogwell, though I have naturally seen him about town. He was at the Opera with the Tremblechins last week when I went with Mr. Sheridan and his party."

"Well, I can answer categorically, without a moment's hesitation, that I would not permit you even to sit beside that dangerous bounder Fogwell at a dinner," said her mother stoutly. "He's far too handsome for his own good, and knows it, what's more. I think, though, you can exempt yourself from the circle of his victims, for he prefers married women, I'm told. Not!" she declared, noticing Constance's stricken look, "that I have ever encouraged his blandishments, nor, in truth, has he ever foisted his unwelcome flatteries upon me, doubtless realizing that I, unlike Sophronia Fluster, am a woman of good sense and dignity."

Constance fought down an impulse towards tears. "May I be dismissed, Mama?" she asked plaintively.

"Shouldn't you be writing a little note to Mr. Sheridan?" suggested her mother archly. Lady Holly had coached her daughter into mounting a campaign of three-cornered notes on scented pink paper which had been rained upon the Sheridan establishment like so much pastel snow. Lady Holly was the proud author of most of these billets-doux and was always the final arbiter of their acceptability.

"Go to your desk, my dear," she prompted, "and scribble off some little request. Perhaps it would be expedient for you to ask him to meet you; we haven't used that ploy on your fiancé in quite some time!"

"Mama, how many times must I remind you that Mr. Sheridan does not consider himself engaged to me," mourned Constance, "and I doubt he ever will. In fact, I'm not sure that I care for him at all. He's far too—too—well—thoughtless and preoccupied."

"Constance! Constance!" Lady Holly shook her massive head ponderously. "You shall never be a married woman if you retreat from the battlefield at the first signs of conflict, if you belittle your own not inconsiderable accomplishments, and ignore the expert advice of an old campaigner like myself. You overheard a careless remark, to a servant no less, and you construe it to mean the war has been lost. Now, no more of these niggling doubts! Off with you, and use the lavender-coloured ink this time. It's so much more feminine!"

Constance withdrew in some confusion, and mounting the stairs to her chamber, which she shared with two of her sisters, searched her mind for some pleasant nothing or general remark she would not be embarrassed to direct to Mr. Sheridan. But her thoughts were crowded with images of Mr. Fogwell, his burning dark eyes, his broad shoulders, his pretty compliments, the firm grasp of his hands. He had been so comforting the evening of her great disillusionment, he had been so concerned with her welfare in the carriage on the way home, he had been so attentive at the Opera and she was aware, everywhere she went lately, of his dark eyes following her. It evoked a strange feeling in her own breast, a feeling she had never known before, a soft fluttering, a gentle trembling, a smug, proud, confused, thrilling, womanly sentiment, a feeling which for want of a better term she named love. Alas! Given her mother's disparagement and downright stricture, there was little likelihood of her experiencing anything more than this rudimentary stirring of her heart. If only, she thought helplessly, as she sat down at her desk and faced her pink stationery which bore the imprint of Mr. Fogwell's graceful figure to her besotted eyes, if only there were someone whose help she could enlist in her quest to explore the inclinations of her spirit.

The answer was right before her eyes. She would write Mr. Sheridan and ask him to meet her somewhere, perhaps at the Flusters under the patronage of Joconda who in the past fortnight had become an altogether different woman, a soft, compassionate, glowing being who had extended a gracious and tentative friendship toward

Constance Holly. Yes, Joconda would help her, and maybe, Mr. Sheridan.

She sent off the little message, after it had passed her mother's grudging approval, and waited anxiously for the reply, which arrived shortly, entrusted to a little messenger with as many buttons upon his suit as freckles on his face. Constance pressed a shining copper coin into his hand as she took her answer, and the boy, with a gallant bow, flipped it into the air, caught it in his hat, which he placed back upon his head, and went whistling off down the wet streets.

It had been raining all morning and was likely to begin again shortly, and Constance feared that the inclemency of the weather would have encouraged Mr. Sheridan to put off the conference she had urged. But no, he would be glad to meet her at Fluster Fancy in an hour's time. There were a few more amusing lines about the likelihood of his being treated as a *persona non grata* by Mrs. Fluster after the disappointment of her portrait and other diverting non-sense, but Constance was conscious only of the affirmative reply. She flew to her wardrobe to choose her warmest and most fetching bonnet and coat, and well before the hour of their appointment, was ensconced in Joconda's snug little parlour sipping a cup of tea and chatting away brightly about the shockingly icy condition of the streets and the accident to a pedestrian who had slipped in front of an oncoming carriage on her way to South Kensington.

"What a charming picture!" said Devin Sheridan, coming in quite a bit later, clapping his hands together and blowing on them to warm them. "How fortunate I am to share such a cosy retreat with two blossoms that flourish despite the bitter cold of this spring."

Though it was an over-used metaphor, there was really no other expression quite so apt for both Joconda and Constance were radiant with the first burgeoning of love, a love which both had thought they would live and die without. Joconda was attired in a buttercup-yellow gown, trimmed with rosettes of green and red crape, her dark hair braided elaborately on either side of her pale face, and her spectacles lying unused in her desk drawer. Constance shone in a lavender suit, trimmed with artificial violets and white lace, and complemented by a fetching little bonnet which framed her glowing eyes. They both laughed softly at Mr. Sheridan's remark.

"You must allow me to excuse myself," Joconda said, rising with a smile. "I fear my head would be turned if I stopped to hear any more of these wicked compliments. Besides, I must go in and help Chester and Father with the books for the Firm. If you require anything, Constance, just summon one of the servants, and hope that they come!" As she whisked out of the room, she left a faint scent of rosewater in the air.

Devin watched her go puzzled. "What a transformation," he said. "I should like to know what is responsible for that."

Constance smiled. "Would you think me a sentimental fool," she asked, "if I said love?"

Devin shrugged his shoulders inelegantly. "The poets have always agreed," he said, "but I find it difficult myself to believe that love can have such an effect. Money, yes. I have seen money transform people so, and fame, certainly, fame—"

Constance put down her teacup abruptly. It rang against the china of the saucer. "I fear I have called you here for nothing," she said, "for I wished to speak about, well about," she lifted her troubled eyes to his, "about love."

Devin shifted uncomfortably on the cast-iron sofa upon which he lounged. "Miss Holly," he began, "I am inclined to chastise myself for not being more open with you previously. My feelings towards you are respectful, admiring—"

She laughed merrily. "Oh, dear!" she declared. "I know you are not in love with me. Oh, goodness, no! I didn't mean to speak about that. Why, everything is quite understood between us. We are merely good friends, is that right?"

"Yes!" Devin smiled with delight. "You are a young woman of great good sense," he said proudly. "Very good friends, indeed, I hope, for to be able to count you as one of my friends would be a privilege most deeply appreciated."

"Well consider it so," she replied. "It is precisely because I do think you are genuinely concerned with my well-being and have, without a doubt, a greater understanding of the ways of the world and the behaviour of people in it, which is why I wished to ask your advice on a most delicate subject."

"Hmmm, pass me the teapot," he replied carelessly. "Well, I am your willing subject, divulge!"

"Recently," related Constance, pouring him a cup of steaming tea, "a certain gentleman has seemed to favour me with very particular attentions. I fear, I may be exaggerating the degree of his interest. I fear, even, that he may be trifling with me, as reputedly he trifles with others. He hasn't yet approached me with any direct declaration at all, though, he hasn't had the opportunity. His name is often linked with that of a married woman whom he—" Her voice faltered and a tear rolled down her cheek and fell with a plop into her teacup.

"My dear Miss Holly," said Devin, springing to his feet, and pressing a hand clumsily upon her shoulder. "Pray don't cry. I cannot bear tears in females!"

"Oh, Mr. Sheridan," she sobbed, pressing her wet face against his coat, "please forgive me. I'm being an utter fool! It's all so hopeless! I must put this all out of my mind. Swear to me that you'll never give this another moment's thought!"

"No, no, Miss Holly," Devin said, kneeling down beside her chair and resting his hands on its arm. "I cannot think of anyone who answers to that description. Of course, there's Fogwell, but you couldn't be thinking of—Devil take it! I've done it again!" he moaned as she dissolved into wracking sobs.

"I'll stop in a moment," she murmured brokenly. "I know it's unthinkable! It's absolutely impossible. I'm such a goose!"

Devin narrowed his eyes. "That's why he came over to our box the other night at the Opera," he said. "It was to talk with you. And that evening at Lord Corrough's ball, you danced with him several times. Why, I paid it no mind. You mean to say he's been bothering you—"

Constance wailed again.

"I mean flirting with you," Devin said hastily, "for some time now. And what has he said?"

"He understands me as no one has ever done before," sobbed Constance. "He tells me I am beautiful and warm and womanly. He says that he has never felt the same about any other woman—"

"Of course, he would say that," pointed out Devin.

"But what could he want with me?" asked Constance, becoming indignant at the unspoken criticism of her lover. "I mean, people say he only likes married women because he doesn't wish to be tied down, and they say he likes wealthy women because they can support him, but I am neither married nor wealthy. Surely if he were the sort of man he is rumoured to be, he wouldn't pay me the slightest heed."

"Well, it is hard to determine his game," Mr. Sheridan said with a frown. "Perhaps he has some misconceptions about the amount of your fortune."

"No, that's not it!" Constance shook her head stubbornly.

"He took me home one evening in his carriage and he saw the shabby little house we've rented for this Season and he knows about the smelly old hack Mama rents from the livery stable because once I met him in it—"

"You've been granting him secret meetings?" asked Mr. Sheridan aghast.

"And he knows all about my five sisters and my stodgy old brother," Constance went on, with two red spots of colour glowing in her cheeks. "He says it doesn't matter. He says our love will flower as in a desert. He says we can live happily in a little cottage with honeysuckle blooming on the fence and only our love to keep us warm against the storms."

Mr. Sheridan groaned.

"Well, of course it sounds silly to you!" said Constance sharply. "You're not in love, as we are."

"Even if I were in love, I hope I wouldn't be quite so impractical."

"Impracticality is the essence of love," replied Constance with dignity. She smoothed out her bunched gloves which she had been using to dry her tears. "Oh, dear, I see you feel the same way about him as Mama. I shall have to make a decision without—"

"Now, now, not so hasty, my dear Miss Holly," said Devin as she rose to leave the room. "I will endeavour to do all in my power to assist you. Perhaps I could speak personally to Fogwell, you know, man to man, to elicit from him how he feels about you, that sort of thing."

Constance regarded him steadily and reproachfully. "I could never sanction the use of subterfuge and double-dealing regarding such an important matter," she said calmly. "No, I see I must confront him myself and ask him to explain his intentions."

Inclining her head gracefully, she moved out of the room, Devin grabbing up his jacket and hurrying down the hall after her. He did not see Cecily who was tumbling down the stairs in her eagerness to see him. Nessie, who had admitted him to the house, had come up to the nursery under the mistaken belief that Mr. Sheridan had come to call upon the nursery governess, and Cecily's shock was great when she saw him overtake Constance Holly and take both her hands in his own. She paused on the landing, hands over her heart to still its restless movements.

She was at such a distance from the couple that she could not hear Mr. Sheridan as he murmured to Constance, "You can count on me, as your devoted friend, to respect your confidence and to approach Mr. Fogwell with the same sort of frank assumption of his better nature as you do yourself. Let me do you this simple favour, Constance, as a token of our friendship and as a small way to thank you for your constant good humour and companionship. Will you trust me?"

Cecily could see Constance nod her head mutely, with the sweet hesitancy of a woman in love, and she also saw Mr. Sheridan plant a tender kiss upon her forehead. She waited to see no more, but whirled about and scrambled back upstairs to the sanctuary of the nursery, where the conflicts of romantic Love did not yet rage.

Chapter Seventeen

In Which Miss Flutterby Makes an Offer

MR. FLUSTER HAD RECOVERED the bounce in his step. Mr. Fluster had rekindled the twinkle in his blue eyes. Mr. Fluster had redoubled his appetite, and his paunch was growing daily. But most importantly, Mr. Fluster had reasserted himself as the master of his household, and this entailed many unpleasant encounters for the helpmeet of his soul, the companion of his life, the partaker of his board, the intrepid Mrs. Fluster.

"The harp must go, my dear," he said firmly, motioning to Alf to place the instrument on a heap of other rejected items, which Mrs. Fluster referred to as "the pyre of her dreams and yearnings."

"No! No!" she shrieked, throwing herself before it in an attitude of supplication. "Not the harp! Oh, Arthur, what will I be without my harp, what shall we all be? A house without music is a house without a soul, a house stricken of any transcendence or any refinement!"

"We shall retain the piano," he said helpfully.

"The piano! The piano is a common instrument," scoffed Mrs. Fluster. "Everyone has a piano."

"Well, then we shall be just like everyone, my dear. And very much more comfortable besides," he replied, as Alf firmly wrested the harp from Mrs. Fluster's grasp and bore it away.

"What next?" asked Mrs. Fluster wildly, looking about her Early Italian Drawing Room which was almost completely denuded of its contents. "What next shall be the object of your fiendish quest? What other tortures have you devised to reduce me to a poor, paltry thing, a thing even Lady Holly can look at with scorn and contempt?"

"Sophronia, my dear," responded her long-suffering husband agreeably, "I have explained to you that we must begin to live within our means. Now that this thoughtful young man has been so good as to assist me with the Firm—"

"Oh, don't speak to me of him!" cried Mrs. Fluster, threatening to tear her hair out in her distraction. She had taken to her bed for several days after hearing that her daughter had promised to marry a mere clerk, and still refused to meet him. "Don't speak to me about that Philistine, that vulgar, nondescript bourgeois. Even his name is enough to rack me with grief."

"Thank goodness the wallpaper has been preserved behind those dreadful, flapping tapestries," observed Mr. Fluster jauntily. "We won't have to repaper the room."

Mrs. Fluster scanned the walls now covered with mustard-coloured paper emblazoned with a small brown geometric print. With an unearthly shriek, she searched for a chair upon which to fall dramatically, but unfortunately all of the furniture had been removed and replaced with cast-iron pieces of Mr. Fluster's manufacture. Choosing to remain standing rather than recline upon one of these, Mrs. Fluster said, "I hope you will be satisfied if I waste away and expire now, Mr. Fluster, now that you have divested me of all the things which made my poor life bearable, the refinements, the luxuries which raise Man above the beasts. Why, I have nothing to do with myself, no volumes of poetry to mull over, no portfolios to fill with drawings, no instruments on which to make celestial music—I never learned to play the piano, thank God! I cannot attend my meetings in the simple garments you have permitted me to retain after stripping my closets of all my verdure and my bureau of all my jewellery."

"For a beginning, you may take over the care of Baby," suggested her husband helpfully. "The nursery governess shall have to go, once we are able to provide her with the wages we owe for her present and past services. And then, you may study to undertake Joconda's tasks as she will soon be leaving us, and someone must order the food and superintend the servants. I think we will be able to retain the rest, and Joconda…er…Jane feels Nessie and Alf will both settle down considerably once they are married."

"Oh, this is too, too utterly revolting!" wailed Mrs. Fluster. "None of this would have happened were it not for that odious, sandy-haired, goggle-eyed Thrash creature! I should like to thrash him within an inch of his life!"

"Thrush, my dear. You must endeavour to remember his name as our sweet Jane will soon be Mrs. Thrush. We owe many thanks to that young man. If it were not for him, we would have been bankrupt before long, and then there would be no question of keeping the house or any of our possessions. Now our only remaining problem is Cedric."

"Oh, how, you heartless monster," Mrs. Fluster wanted to know, "can you call your only son, the heir to your name, a problem?"

"Well, he is, my dear, and no getting round it. I think we shall have to buy him a commission in the Army as soon as we have managed to save a little."

"The Army! How plebeian! How gruesome!" cried Mrs. Fluster, gritting her perfect teeth.

"My dear, we simply cannot continue to support his considerable gaming debts, his tailor, his club dues, his tickets for plays. In short, we cannot keep him in the style to which he is accustomed. I fear we simply have no other alternatives."

But there was another alternative and it breezed into the room in the person of Vera Flutterby who was dressed in an outlandish costume consisting of voluminous navy breeches that ballooned out from her waist and fastened tightly at her ankles, a plain white blouse fastened with a tie, and a stark, mannish navy jacket. Her wispy light brown hair was brushed back and fastened with a navy-coloured ribbon. She looked considerably more at ease than in her Parisian dresses and not altogether unattractive.

Mrs. Fluster stared at her costume in horror. "Bloomers!" she ejaculated, and was rendered speechless. Fortunately so, for she could have been quite a detriment during the conversation which ensued between Miss Flutterby and Mr. Fluster.

"Sit down, Mr. Fluster," said Miss Flutterby briskly, indicating one of the cast-iron chairs, now covered with plain serge pillows sewed by Joconda and Nessie. She seemed not to notice the drastic alterations in the room as she took up her own seat on a cast-iron bench before the fire. "Mr. Fluster, I must be quite frank with you. I have come here today without permission or sanction of any kind from my parents. Not that such permission is necessary. No, I do what I please. But I wish you to know my position quite clearly. I have come to make you an offer, and a very good offer, I feel. I hope you will give it your careful consideration because it concerns something most central to my happiness and your son's future."

Mrs. Fluster sighed and did fling herself upon one of the cast-iron sofas, thereby incurring a tremendous blow to the back of her perfect skull.

"You see, Mr. Fluster," explained Vera earnestly, "I have determined that in all of London there is not a man more suitable to be my husband than your son, Cedric."

Mrs. Fluster gasped. Mr. Fluster nodded in a puzzled manner.

"I have come," the American girl continued, "to ask you for the hand of your son in matrimony."

Mr. Fluster looked stunned. Mrs. Fluster fainted.

"Does Cedric know of this?" asked his father with a gulp.

"I think he knows such an arrangement might be forthcoming. I've spoken to him about it at some length during the races. But I warned him that I had not yet made my final decision, that he was only one of many candidates I was considering. I have since recognized that only Cedric is as perfectly moldable, as absolutely unformed a personality as I require. What do you think?"

"Well, I—" Mr. Fluster attempted to speak and found his tongue failed him.

"Oh, how stupid of me!" declared Vera. "I've forgotten to outline the conditions I have in mind. Once we have been formally betrothed, I would advance you and your family the sum of five hundred pounds as a token of my good will. After the marriage ceremony, another five hundred pounds would be forthcoming. From then on annually, I would provide you with the sum of two hundred and fifty pounds per annum as long as everything remained satisfactory between Cedric and myself. In return, I would expect him to adopt the name of Flutterby. Cedric Flutterby has a nice ring to it, don't you think? I would take him with me to New York. In fact, I believe the wedding will have to take place in New York, for it will be necessary to introduce him to all of Daddy's business friends and our relations. He would live with me in the house in New York throughout the winter, and in the summers we would come abroad, to stay in the castle in Ireland or perhaps we'll buy a house in London, I've seen one I like overlooking the Park. He'll take a hand, once he has been groomed for it, in Daddy's business, probably as the Vice President and will become the President upon Daddy's demise. Let me see, is there anything else? Oh, I shall, of course, give him an allowance. I'd like to discuss that with you more thoroughly for I wish it to be enough for him to live comfortably but not so much that he can squander it on useless luxuries."

"Oh, Governor, I say," drawled Cedric, strolling into the room. "I require some funds so as to enable me to pay my dues at the Young Aesthetes Club." He stopped short as he spied, Miss Flutterby in her outlandish attire and staggered back at the sight of his mother lying unconscious upon her cast-iron bier.

"I say, what's wrong with Mother?" he asked.

"This young woman, this audacious, impertinent minx!" cried Mrs. Fluster reviving suddenly. "My darling boy, she considers you a business proposition. Oh, don't be tempted by her fortune! Don't desert your poor mother now when all the glories of her life have been taken from her!"

She reached out for her darling boy, her perfect white fingers entangling in the scarf he wore loosely about his neck. But her devoted son paid her no heed. He stared at Miss Flutterby with amazement and asked, "Do you mean to tell me, Vera, that you've chosen me?"

She turned a bright pink, gave him a wistful smile and said softly in a voice quite unlike that in which she had spoken to Mr. Fluster, "Yes, Cedric."

"Darling!" he cried, rushing to her side and kneeling before her chair. He left his scarf dangling in his mother's fingers. "You shall not regret this, I swear to you, Vera. We shall be the happiest couple in New York, no, in all of the United States. I will do whatever you say. I shall be your devoted slave! I shall do everything you require for your happiness!"

Vera bent and brushed a kiss upon the top of his fair head.

"It seems that Cedric has made up his mind, my dear Miss Flutterby," said Mr. Fluster happily. "The arrangements you have outlined seem excessive. No matter! We shall go over them another time. I think, my dear Sophronia, that we should leave these two young lovers alone!" He held out his stout, pudgy hand for her perfect, slender one, and she unwound from the sofa like a smoke ring uncurling from a cigar, draping herself limply across his arm and suffering herself to be led from the room.

"Extraordinary!" Mr. Fluster chuckled as they marched out through the open door. "Within a fortnight I've accepted two proposals for the hands of my children. Extraordinary!"

Chapter Eighteen

Explores the Background of a Mysterious Gentleman

"THE FIRST FINE DAY IN SPRING, SIR," Willet announced cheerfully one morning, trotting into the breakfast room where Devin Sheridan sat glumly looking out the window at the fluffy clouds that filled the bright blue sky and the fresh, tender green leaves which clothed the old beech trees in the garden.

"So it is," replied Devin shortly, taking another sip of his coffee.

"Congratulations are in order, sir. Your painting has been accepted by the Committee, sir," Willet said, handing him an envelope which bore the imprint of the Royal Academy.

Devin snatched it away impatiently but it was still unopened. "How the devil did you know that without opening it, Willet?" he demanded.

"Ah!" replied his valet, "the word has been out for hours. I had it from Lord Muttonchop's butler who had it from the cook at Mrs. Captooth's who heard it from the boot-boy at Sir Frederic Leighton's, if you will, Mr. Sheridan."

Ignoring the details of this impressive communications network, Devin tore open the envelope and read therein exactly the same news that Willet had just imparted to him. He tossed the letter aside restlessly and ran his fingers through his hair.

"Absolutely uncanny how you learn these things, Willet," he said. "I've been trying to run to ground some facts about the background and occupation of a certain gentleman, a Mr. Fogwell, for some weeks now with absolutely no success whatsoever. I wish I had your—"

"The Mr. Fogwell whose name has been linked with Mrs. Fluster, who drives a grey carriage with a pair of matched greys and employs Mr. Addams as his tailor, sir?" asked Willet obligingly.

Devin stared at him in some amazement. "How did you know all that?" he asked. "No one I've spoken to seems to know a thing about him!"

"These sorts of facts seem to stick to me, sir," replied Willet modestly. "Again, sir, I must call your attention to a letter from Lord Throttle regarding his wife's portrait."

"Deuce take him!" swore Mr. Sheridan, taking the letter and tearing it dramatically into little white bits which he threw into the air.

"Is that all, sir?" asked Willet disapprovingly.

"No, wait! I think you can be of some service to me, Willet!" said his master. "Would it be possible, do you suppose you could find out something more about this Mr. Fogwell, where he comes from, how he lives, where he lives, that sort of thing?"

"Sir," said Willet, with as deep a bow as he could manage with his rheumatism, "it would be my pleasure."

The next day proved to be as fair, and when Willet entered the breakfast room, he found Mr. Sheridan once again looking out gloomily upon the bright spring morning, absentmindedly stroking the fur of the lonely wombat as he pulled upon a cigarette. His breakfast had gone untouched.

"Another lovely day!" said Willet pleasantly, advancing into the room with a light step.

"For those who like it so!" snarled Mr. Sheridan. "I prefer the rain."

"Was the breakfast not to your liking, sir?" inquired Willet solicitously, taking up the dishes as he spoke.

"I'm never hungry in the mornings, Willet," Mr. Sheridan said sulkily. "I don't know why you have Chlorrie make such a quantity of food."

Willet did not contradict his employer, though he knew well that Mr. Sheridan usually consumed prodigious amounts of edibles for breakfast. He had grown used to the dramatic changes of mood through which the artist suffered.

"Sir," he said quietly, as he was about to withdraw, "I have some additional information regarding Mr. Pemberton Fogwell."

"Already, Willet?" asked Mr. Sheridan, his face brightening.

"I spent the greater part of my day yesterday pursuing various acquaintances who might be expected to have the pertinent facts," said Willet, with pride.

"Well, let's hear it!"

"Very well, sir. It seems that Mr. Pemberton Fogwell was born in 1849 in Gloucestershire to very respectable parents. His father was a cousin by marriage to the Duke of Marsh; his second wife, Mr. Fogwell's mother, was the only daughter of a family of local gentry, a Miss Emily Nettle, by name. She was a young woman when she married Mr. Fogwell, and rather fanciful, thus the names of her children, who were called, respectively, Algernon, Pemberton and Alphonse. Unfortunately she died young, when Pemberton was only five years old, and his father, grieving greatly at the premature loss of his pretty wife, became somewhat of a recluse. He died not too long thereafter, and his one son by his first marriage inherited what little fortune there was to be inherited. The younger Fogwells had to make their way in the world quite alone, and they did extremely well. The eldest, Algernon, is serving in the diplomatic service in Malta. It was he who enabled his younger brothers to attend Cambridge. At that time, Mr. Fogwell acquired his great interest in Art and after matriculating came down to London with the hopes of finding a position in a gallery or writing reviews for a paper. Alphonse, I regret to say, ran away with the daughter of a tavern keeper and is presently the father of twin boys and an infant daughter."

"Never mind about Alphonse," said Mr. Sheridan impatiently.

"I agree, sir," replied Willet. "He put himself quite outside the concerns of our story by his reckless and imprudent actions. Let me see, where was I? Ah, yes. Pemberton appeared in London, quite penniless and quite proud, having garnered many honours at the university, including prizes for his poetry, and found that his talents were not as much appreciated as he had thought. Not appreciated except by rich matrons with inclinations towards Culture. The first of these, a striking woman, a Mrs. Newcomb, the wife of an Army major-general, was quite generous to him and enabled him to take on an apartment at the Albany."

Mr. Sheridan lifted his eyebrows.

"Yes, sir, quite a nice address, and I'm told, it's decorated in the best of taste, very subtle but very luxurious. Unfortunately, Mr. Fogwell had some trouble with Major-General Newcomb, and, I understand, was less than pleased, anyway, with the incessant demands of Mrs. Newcomb, so he broke off the liaison, quite discreetly, and attached himself instead to Mrs. Fluster. Of course, it's well known that the Flusters are undergoing great financial difficulties—"

"It is?" asked Devin.

"Yes, it is," responded Willet, "and so there was no question of any real intimacy or economic reward from Mrs. Fluster. Rather, he saw her as an entrée to some of the best families in Society and, in turn, provided her, I understand, with an outlet for some of her aesthetic maunderings."

"Maunderings is a rather strong word, Willet," said Mr. Sheridan reprovingly.

"Maunderings, it is, sir," repeated Willet.

"Very good, then what?" asked the artist, fascinated by this tale.

"Now comes the strange part of my tale," related Willet with a frown. "No one is quite certain what has come over him, but it is reported that Mr. Fogwell has broken off his friendship with Mrs. Fluster and, it seems, has formed an attachment for a young lady of quite high standing though little wealth. She apparently favours his suit but her family does not, and he is suffering through, what would be termed in a female, a decline. He is on the verge of giving up his apartment and his carriage and his tailor, and taking on a position as a floor manager in an emporium on Bond Street. A strange comedown for one who has aspired so high! No word, as yet, on what the young lady will think of this, nor, odd to relate, on exactly who she may be! Though I think, Mr. Sheridan, that you perhaps know that better than I."

"Indeed I do," replied the artist, coming to his feet. "Willet, fetch me my coat. I'm going out. And give me the address at the Albany, if you please!"

It was not difficult for Mr. Sheridan, a few hours later, to locate Mr. Fogwell's chambers nor difficult for him to gain entry for the door stood open. The occupant was evidently on the verge of quitting the premises for the room was full of packing boxes, and only a few reproductions of famous paintings and a few well-thumbed volumes of poetry were left out.

"Hallo! Hallo there! Fogwell, are you in?" called out Devin stepping across the threshold.

Mr. Fogwell peered out suspiciously from the inner chamber. Several frilled linen shirts and brocade waistcoats were draped across his arm, and he was evidently about to insert them into a voluminous leather portmanteau which lay open upon the bed.

"Come in, come in," he said with a slight frown. "Sheridan, I believe. Don't know how you found me, old man, but if you've come to plead Sophronia's case, you might as well leave immediately. I won't go back there, no matter how she pleads. The woman doesn't know what a good thing she has in her husband, and when I think how I might have imperilled one of the few decent marriages in London—no!" He shook his head. "When she began to talk about leaving him, I made my farewells and glad to do it."

"It isn't Mrs. Fluster whose emissary I am," said Devin. "I'm here as a friend of Constance Holly."

"Constance!" breathed Mr. Fogwell, setting down his wardrobe and clasping his elegant hands together. "Constance!"

"Yes," said Devin sternly, "and as her friend I wanted to speak to you about your intentions regarding her."

"Intentions! Hah!" laughed Mr. Fogwell bitterly. "I have no intentions towards her. Intentions! That's a joke. How do you think she would like to be the wife of a haberdashery salesman? What do you suppose she would say to a miserable one room above a butcher shop? More to the point, what do you suppose Lady Holly would say? No, more than I regret anything, more than I regret Mrs. Newcomb—you don't know her, a memory, a distinctly bad memory from my past—more than I regret Mrs. Fluster, I regret what I have done to Constance. She deserves far better than I! She deserves a chance at a happy married life and children around her knee! Do you know there's not a woman in London better suited to be a mother than Constance Holly, no woman with as much patience or tenderness or sensibility, and instead she's fated to die an old maid or marry— Excuse me, I quite forget myself! Miss Holly is, can be, nothing to me."

"Quite to the contrary, Fogwell," said Mr. Sheridan calmly. "She is certainly not fated to marry me, if that was your thought. I didn't realize her mother still cherished that foolish notion, but it is quite out of the question. I have fish of my own to fry!" He took up a seat on the one armchair in the room and offered Mr. Fogwell a cigarette from his silver case. For a moment there was silence as the match was struck and both men drew upon their cigarettes. "You know, I quite agree with you about Miss Holly's virtues. In fact, it was my intent, when I began to squire her about town, to find a man for her who would be able to offer her the very things you named—a pleasant home, a solid marriage, children. I never, I must admit, considered you to be that man."

"Why should you?" asked Fogwell bitterly from beneath the cloud of smoke which enveloped him.

"But I consider myself a flexible, a tolerant man," said Devin slowly, "capable of evaluating the facts once they have changed and altering my opinion. Now I've been told that you've made quite a success out of a difficult life."

"A few prizes for poetry in college!" scoffed Mr. Fogwell. "What use are they to me now? I might just as well have married a tavern keeper's daughter!"

"I think, Mr. Fogwell," said Mr. Sheridan, reprovingly, "you give yourself too little credit. Talent is a gift which can never be taken away, no, matter how little it is appreciated. But we both know, as men of the world, that talent counts for little. Rather one must bank upon Lady Luck and contacts, which you have lacked up till now."

"You've said it there," agreed Fogwell.

"I said, till now, you notice," responded Devin patiently. "I think that I might be able to offer you some assistance. I understand you have quite a good knowledge of the Art world."

Behind the veil of smoke he could see Mr. Fogwell's dark eyes brighten.

"Some," he replied deprecatingly.

"Well, if it is only paltry, I fear I cannot be of help at all," said Devin, rising.

"Actually my knowledge is quite compendious," put in Mr. Fogwell cautiously. "I may seem deprecating to you, but it's just that I have found so little outlet for it, I tend to depreciate its worth even though I retain a great pleasure in my knowledge."

"Excellent! Capital!" said Devin beaming. "I know a man, a Mr. Monceau, he handles the sale of my etchings for me. He has a small gallery on Bond Street, and just last week when I was there, he informed me that he was looking for a capable and knowledgeable assistant. I told him then I knew of no such person. I could return to him today and introduce you as such a man. The salary is not grand, but Mr. Monceau is an elderly man and he longs, I know, for someone he can train in his business to take it over when he dies. There are lodgings in the back of the shop—he has his own home in Hampstead—and you would be handling the works of some of the better-known London artists, as well as historical prints of great interest."

"I am ready at a moment's notice," responded Mr. Fogwell, his voice vibrating with a vitality that had been lacking since Mr. Sheridan's entrance. "Lead me to him!"

It was a master stroke. Mr. Monceau declared himself eternally grateful to Mr. Sheridan for the presentation of the oh-so sympathetique young man! Mr. Fogwell informed Mr. Sheridan that he was forever obliged to him for this unbelievable opportunity. Constance called Devin her hero and kissed Mr. Monceau soundly upon his whiskered face. Alas! There was one party who was not delighted. There was one party who was not overwhelmed with gratitude. There was one party who denounced Mr. Fogwell as a rogue and scoundrel and declared Constance to be a foolish, simple-minded idiot!

That party was Lady Holly.

"I forbid it, Constance. I completely forbid it!" she declared to her wilful daughter, the afternoon after Mr. Fogwell had presented himself and humbly requested her laughter's hand, providing impeccable references and detailing the luxuries he would be able to offer her daughter.

"But, Mama!" cried Constance, biting her lower lip. "He is artistic! You wanted me to marry someone who moved in artistic circles! Why, with this new position he will be an intimate friend of some of the greatest English and French artists now living! And he's a literary man too! He sent me the most beautiful poem, half of it in French. I only wish I had studied my French harder when Mademoiselle Duclos taught us!"

"It is impossible, Constance," declared her mother, helping herself to another whole boiled chicken. They were at dinner. The five Holly sisters bore silent witness to Constance's battle. "He's a nobody. His father was a Nothing and his mother a Nonentity! You are the eldest. You must make a good match. Your sisters are depending upon it!"

"Mother, he loves me!" pleaded Constance. "You've told me repeatedly that I'll be an old maid. You wanted to marry me off to Mr. Sheridan, who is certainly a good friend, but who doesn't treat me like a woman in any of the important ways."

"I am most displeased with him" said Lady Holly, her mouth full of poultry. "He has meddled to a surprising degree in this whole unsavoury affair. I believe I shall cut him the next time I meet him in public."

"Mother, if you don't give your permission for this marriage," declared Constance, laying down her knife and fork with determination, "I shall elope!"

"Hah!" said her mother contemptuously. "You have no more courage than a lamb. You'd no sooner elope than I would eat this plate," she made fierce gestures with her knife at the china plate before her, "so let's hear no more of this foolishness! You shall be confined to the walls of this house until I hear no more of this Fogwell nonsense!"

But Lady Holly was doomed to hear a great more of the Fogwell nonsense, for on the following morning, once she had fought her way out of a troubled slumber full of half-done lamb cutlets and ominously large rumps of beef, she was informed by Alva that Constance had disappeared.

"Disappeared? What do you mean, disappeared?"

"She has run off, Mama," said Alva plaintively. "She left this note. She says when she next communicates with us it shall be as Mrs. Fogwell. Mama, now can I marry Johnny?"

It was nearly an hour before Lady Holly could be extricated from her bed. During that time it was discovered, through the constant scurrying about of servants and various messengers, that Constance and Mr. Fogwell had driven off in a grey carriage drawn by a matched pair of greys on the previous evening and no one knew their direction or their destination. Mrs. Thrush had been scheduled to come and fit Constance for what had been hoped-to-be her wedding gown, and when she arrived the household was in an uproar, with Holly daughters sobbing and whining and their mother, enthroned in a great armchair, feeding her sorrow with biscuits and wine and gnashing her teeth.

"My good Lady Holly," said Mrs. Thrush pleasantly, bounding into the room, all her curls ajiggle and her skirts swaying. "I have found the most precious Valenciennes lace for your daughter's wedding gown. It will complement the ivory satin exactly. Allow me to—"

"Argh!" wailed Lady Holly. "There will be no wedding gown. My simple-minded, deceived, imprudent daughter has had the temerity to elope! Oh, how shall I face the world? What can I say? Her name shall never be mentioned again in this house! She shall be as one who is dead to us, for dead to us she is indeed! She had no thought of filial duty, no sense of sisterly love! She thought only of her own selfish desires! I hope he makes her very miserable! A gigolo! A nobody from Gloucestershire! An impudent upstart! A sly, wheedling, cozening scoundrel!"

"Do you refer, my good Lady Holly, to Mr. Pemberton Fogwell, the new assistant to Mr. Monceau, the well-known art dealer on Bond Street?"

Lady Holly stared at her aghast.

"I know of such things through my beloved son, Chester," said Mrs. Thrush sweetly. "He hears them from his fiancée, that sweet young lady, Miss Jane Fluster. Can you believe that, my good lady? My humble son, a mere clerk, has solicited and won the hand of the daughter of one our city's most prominent merchants! A minor triumph for the Thrushes! Of course, in marrying my Chester she marries into a family also known for its mercantile abilities! Yet, still there is no getting round it! My Chester, who at one time considered marrying a servant, a mere nursery governess, is now engaged to this lovely and talented girl. It does make a mother proud!"

Lady Holly growled by way of response.

"Oh, I did forget your own unfortunate circumstances, my good Lady Holly," said Mrs. Thrush, bobbing her head and setting all the tassels of her gown aquiver. "You probably find it hard to listen to the ravings of a mother who takes such joy in her child's impending nuptials! You doubtlessly find it annoying to hear that someone has made a match so far above them and been quite pleased with the outcome! Did you know that Mr. Fluster is considering making Chester a full partner in the Firm? Now that Cedric—that's Mr. Fluster's son—has departed for New York with his American heiress, Mr. Fluster wishes someone of his family to be represented in the Firm, and who better than my clever boy, my own son, my sagacious Chester?"

"Mrs. Thrush," said Lady Holly with ponderous dignity, "we are no longer in need of your services. Kindly remove yourself from my premises, at once!"

"As you will! As you will, my dear Lady Holly," replied Isabella Thrush irrepressibly. "I no longer have need of these trifling pursuits anyway. My son has just purchased a lovely house on Robert Street, and I am expected to assist that wonderful young woman, Miss Jane Fluster, in setting it up for our occupation. I am planning to become a woman of leisure, my good Lady Holly, and my only task, so my Chester informs me, will be to dandle my grandbabies upon my knee. Good day to you and your daughters!"

Chapter Nineteen

Describes an Artistic Event of Great Moment

IT WAS THE FIRST OF MAY, and as if in deference to the new month, a promise of better things to come, the sun deigned to shine in the afternoon. The streets were still slick with rain from the morning downpour, the air was frosty and a new bank of clouds piled up across the river, yet for a space of hours, the sun shone and shone quite cheerfully. It came pouring through the dusty windows of the nursery, through the freshly starched white muslin curtains and danced about the room scattering a blithe-hearted light upon the two heads bent over a puzzle, setting Cecily's reddish-gold hair ablaze and transforming Baby's pale wispy locks into an ethereal halo.

The two were utterly absorbed in this task when suddenly there was a rustle of silk and Mrs. Fluster swept into the room holding her skirt (rose-coloured moiré with old lace insets and forest-green satin ruching) off the floor disdainfully. She paused to look about the room with a puzzled frown before saying abruptly, "I have come for my child!"

Cecily looked up in amazement. Never, in the several months she had been employed by the Flusters, had she seen Mrs. Fluster on the nursery floor, and there had been no warning that such a cataclysm was about to occur.

"What? Why is she wearing this common little cotton smock?" demanded Mrs. Fluster pulling at Baby's simple dress with her perfectly gloved hand. She had lost none of her pretensions since the change in circumstances; in truth, she required her illusions to live on, and Mr. Fluster, recognizing this fact and abetted by the generous donations of Miss Flutterby, had permitted his extravagant wife to keep many of the luxuries and refinements she considered indispensable.

"It's quite practical, Mrs. Fluster," replied Cecily honestly. "She often gets dusty while she's playing, and the cotton dresses are easier to launder."

"She shouldn't be engaging in any activities that might render her dusty!" declared Mrs. Fluster. "My precious treasure," she cooed to Baby, who was astonished but pleased at her mother's unexpected appearance. "Has that naughty nursery governess treated you like an ordinary child when you are instead my very own ineffable damozel?"

Baby squealed with pleasure at this remark.

"Miss Hawthorne," directed Mrs. Fluster, "go fetch Amaryllis her velvet frock and the little sable cloak and bonnet. We are expected at a most uplifting social event, I might say, the event of the season!"

"Very well, Mrs. Fluster," replied Cecily, going to do her bidding. She sighed as she removed the impractical dress from the wardrobe, but realizing that to comply with Mrs. Fluster's demands was her duty, she bundled the child into it despite Baby's earnest protests. Amaryllis was at the age during which every action which was forced upon her, whether it was brushing her hair or donning her shoes, was vehemently protested, and Mrs. Fluster watched with a curled lip as Baby fought Cecily's best efforts.

"It's obvious, Miss Hawthorne," she said at the end of the struggle, "that you have established a very poor precedent with this delicate and fragile being. My child would, of course, cry out against such rough handling as you have exhibited. She, no doubt, inherits her Mother's very sensitive feelings and rightfully resents having a common person paw at her. I shall be glad when the quarter is through and Mr. Fluster pays you off. Then I shall take over Baby's training and see that she is brought up as a proper lady."

"Not half so glad as I," said Cecily impertinently, though she knew she would miss Baby greatly. The challenge of transforming a frightened, sickly youngster into a sturdy, independent being had not been without its rewards, and the thought of finding a new situation and enmeshing herself again in all the intrigues and conflicts of a new family and its staff seemed incredibly dispiriting.

"My own little darling! Mama's precious girl!" cooed Mrs. Fluster, lifting up Baby who fretted and pulled at her fancy dress. "How can I have neglected you so?"

"Permit me to observe, Mrs. Fluster," said Cecily, who had no fear since she knew she would be dismissed shortly, "that if you had not been so preoccupied with your various meetings, artistic achievements and the flatteries of your friend, Mr. Fogwell—"

"Enough!" shrieked Mrs. Fluster. "I will not have that cad's name mentioned in my presence. Imagine, he actually married that insipid, commonplace, drab little female! They were carrying on an intrigue right under my nose! Well, he gets what he deserves! She'll bear him so many children he'll be eating, drinking and sleeping babies! A typically bourgeois habit!"

Cecily merely smiled. She knew that Mrs. Fluster was feeling bereft, so suddenly deprived of her two older children and her constant companion, and newly pressed by the reasserted demands of her husband.

"Perhaps there will soon be a young Fluster so this nursery will not seem quite so empty," she suggested.

Mrs. Fluster stared at her coldly. "Such matters are none of your business, Miss Hawthorne," she replied sharply. "If Arthur and I plan another addition to our family, we certainly will not review our plans with the nursery governess. Come along now, Amaryllis. Mama is taking you to a very special place where you will be much admired."

Mother and daughter departed, Mrs. Fluster with a parting sniff for Cecily and, Amaryllis with a timid farewell wave.

It was dreary in the empty chamber once the echo of their footsteps down the hall had faded. In all the time Cecily had been employed at the Fluster's, saving of course the times when Amaryllis was asleep, she had never been without the child's company. She felt oddly truncated, completely set adrift, as she wandered aimlessly about the room, picking up toys and restoring them to their places, straightening the coverlets on Amaryllis' bed and stoking up the fire.

When Nessie, a gown draped across her arm, entered the room some time later, Cecily was gazing absentmindedly at the glowing coals, her head resting on her hand.

"Egad!" exclaimed Nessie. "We've a lot of work to do if we're to have you ready in time."

"Ready in time for what?" asked Cecily, not without reason.

"Never you mind about that!" declared Nessie. "Thank God the gown's been provided. That 'un would never do." She shook out the garment which she was carrying and Cecily gawked at it like a rustic up from the country gapes at the lions in the Botanical Gardens.

"Oh, Nessie!" she breathed, "I hope you haven't gone and prigged that from Mrs. Fluster's wardrobe. You know what—"

"You are a dashed nuisance, Cecily," retorted Nessie, shoving her friend into the adjoining chamber. "As if any dress of Mrs. Fluster's would fit you. No, this is yours!"

Cecily was fingering the fabric lovingly.

"Good lord, this is tremendously costly, Nessie!" she declared.

"To some and not to others," remarked Nessie cryptically. "At any rate, it's yours, and the faster you get into, it the happier I'll be."

Cecily opened her mouth to protest and Nessie silenced her with a wave of her hand.

"Now, not another word," she said firmly. "It's a present, a token of appreciation for a job well performed, as is the rest of the entertainment we have planned for you this afternoon. You'll need help with the buttons and your hair. Here then, move over!"

Within the space of an hour and through the magic of Nessie's nimble fingers, Cecily had been transformed. Vanished was the drab nursery governess with her hair twisted into a utilitarian knot, her plain grey dress submerged beneath an apron of chaste whiteness. In her place stood a young lady of fashion, attired in a turquoise polonaise looped up at the sides with pale silk apple blossoms to reveal a deep green plush underskirt. Similar pink blossoms accentuated the low corsage and another was tucked into the gleaming masses of Cecily's braided and looped golden-red hair. A pair of gloves, stockings and slippers to match had materialized from nowhere, but Cecily's protests had been squashed by a fierce lecture from Nessie.

"Listen to me, Miss Know-it-all, and listen good!" Nessie had declared sharply. "You can ask as many questions as you please and I will answer as many as I please. Furthermore, if you annoy me sufficiently with your reservations and misgivings and protests and impretunities—"

"Importunities," suggested Cecily.

"Nonsense," snapped Nessie. "I know full well what word I wish to use. If you ask me one more question," she glowered at Cecily with all the quelling effect she could muster (very little), "I might just as easily answer you, and then what would you have accomplished? Lost a great deal of fun, spoiled a surprise that's been a long time in the making, deprived yourself of a chance to dress up and play Cinderella—well?" She shrugged her shoulders expressively. "I tell you if I was you, you foolish girl, I'd do exactly as I was told by one of my dearest and warmest friends who says right now. 'Hurry downstairs, Milady. Your carriage is waiting.'"

"A carriage?" asked Cecily, but Nessie's lowered eyebrows and crossed arms indicated she would be proof against any further interrogative assault. With a sigh, Cecily eyed herself once more in the dark, tiny mirror over her bureau and with Nessie bounding ahead of her, she picked up her velvety skirts and hurried down the stairs. Alf who thought her "getup was swell" gave her his arm and escorted her to a waiting hackney coach. Cecily saw him gesturing to the cabdriver and handing him a scrap of paper before the horses were whipped up and the coach started forward with a clatter.

It was a peculiar feeling, being transported through the gleaming streets of London all alone in a carriage. No matter that the straw on the floor was damp and muddy or that the windows were scratched and dim. Cecily pressed her face up against the pane like any schoolgirl, but drew back in dismay as the driver pulled up before Burlington House.

As she shrank back on to the leather bench, trying to gather up enough courage to meet the fashionably dressed crowds she had seen milling upon the steps, the door to the coach was swung open and the cabby's whiskered face appeared in the opening.

"Here we are then, Miss," he said cheerfully, setting her down on to the pavement and pressing a piece of pasteboard into her hand before she had a moment to think. "And have a lovely afternoon. They say the pictures is beautiful."

Cecily watched him go in some amazement. Never having seen a cabdriver so cheerful, she could only guess that he had been compensated generously for his services.

The card which lay in her palm was a ticket to a special showing of the Royal Academy's Annual Exhibition. Though she was sure the doorkeeper would look at her and refuse her admittance, she advanced boldly to present it and found herself within minutes inside the first room of the galleries.

She received a few peculiar glances but thinking it best to blend in with the crowd and thus escape undue notice, she brought her attention to bear on the picture closest at hand, which turned out to be the painting number 188, an offering from the President of the Royal Academy, Sir Frederick Leighton. Cecily studied it carefully, attempting, with little success, to understand why the angelic-looking creature, who seemed to have rubbed her wings up against a rainbow, was using her finger as a stopper to a green bottle, a question which was later to puzzle the reviewer for *Punch*. No answer offered itself immediately to her mind, and as she turned away in perplexity she was even more surprised to hear the sound of a familiar voice.

"Millais has a most fortunate subject here, does he not?"

"Mr. Thrush!" exclaimed Cecily, nearly colliding with that individual who was sporting a collar so high he was nearly strangling for lack of air, and was supporting on one hand the frail but irrepressible form of Mrs. Thrush while Joconda in a becoming garnet-coloured gown clung to his other arm.

"Miss Hawthorne!" he said in some astonishment "Fancy meeting you here!" He had not spoken to her since the afternoon on which he revealed his love for Joconda, but Cecily had been well aware, through the highly knowledgeable grapevine of Alf and Nessie, of the progress of his romance. "Mother, this is Miss Hawthorne."

"Ah yes, the nursery governess," said Mrs. Thrush with wicked smugness. "You must share, as we all do, in pleasure with Chester's good fortune."

Joconda blushed and lowered her eyes.

"I'm sure if I had chosen her myself," declared Mrs. Thrush, with a little stamp of her foot which set all her curls and fringes trembling, "I could not have found a sweeter or more suitable daughter-in-law. And it's so important we get along as together we are responsible for my bonny boy's every comfort."

"I certainly wish you the very best," said Cecily absently. She was aware that several gentlemen had stopped a few paces away and were staring at her quite fixedly.

"I have you to thank, Miss Hawthorne," Joconda put in softly and shyly, "for if it were not for Chester, I may call him Chester to one of his friends, coming by to check to see if we were a suitable family for you to be residing with, we never should have met. Such a good friend. If only more young girls had friends like him!"

"Indeed," replied Cecily. She was now the object of quite marked attention from the Art patrons. "If you will excuse me, I see some-one I must speak to," and she darted into the next gallery, hoping to find a quiet alcove where she could sit and collect her composure.

Unfortunately there was no such retreat. Instead, she was the object of even more marked attention. Women whispered to each other behind gloved hands, watching her the while with too bright eyes, and then giggled. Gentlemen surveyed her with a speculative and appreciative gaze. Cecily wondered if perhaps there was some-thing wrong with her dress, but a quick and unobtrusive check revealed nothing amiss. With cheeks flaming, she sailed forward into the next gallery there to find that her presence was met with a hush followed by a low buzz of conversation. Only one couple seemed oblivious to her presence and that was because of their absorption in each other. The woman was Constance Holly, her neat figure set off in a cream-coloured suit trimmed with scarlet piping; she was inclining her ear to the lips of a slim gentleman in a narrow black velvet coat and smiling in evident pleasure at his whispered words. For a moment Cecily's heart constricted for she thought Miss Holly's partner was Mr. Sheridan, but then as the gentleman crushed her in a quick but fervent embrace, she saw that it was Mr. Fogwell. No one at Fluster Fancy had known of the reason for his defection, though Nessie insisted he had foreseen the impending financial disaster and had jumped, like rats do, from a sinking ship.

"Why, it's Cecily!" Constance called out in a clear voice, as the crowds shifted and she and her escort were jostled closer to Cecily. "I may call you Cecily, mayn't I? We've known each other for ever such a long time, ever since that dreadful breakfast at Devin's house. I was so mortified!" She laughed gaily at the memory. "But that's ancient history now."

"Yes, it is, Miss Holly," murmured Cecily conventionally.

"Oh, but you don't know!" exclaimed Constance, a smile illuminating her face. "Allow me to introduce my husband, Pemberton Fogwell."

Cecily was so taken aback she nearly did not take the hand which Mr. Fogwell proffered for her to shake.

"Delighted," he said smoothly. "I hope you shall be as happy in your impending nuptials as we are," and he stooped to impress a kiss upon his wife's laughing lips.

"It is so ridiculously wonderful to be a married woman," confessed Constance, pressing Cecily's hand in her own. "You will enjoy it too, I'm certain, and, as Pemberton said, I hope you know even a small part of the pleasure I have known within the bonds of matrimony." She gazed up at her husband with adoration.

"But I have no plans to be married," confessed Cecily confused.

Constance smiled broadly. "Oh, Pemberton, how charming! She really has no notion! Well, far be it from me to spoil—oh, but there I almost ruined it!"

"You must," said Mr. Fogwell adroitly, "see the picture of the year. I believe it's in the last gallery."

"Of course," murmured Cecily uncertainly. The happy couple watched her with fatuous smiles as she drifted along with the flow of traffic.

"I shall never get married if it addles my brain as it clearly has theirs," thought Cecily, suspecting she had found the picture of the year by the large crowd gathered before a large painting of a lone soldier in rags and tatters journeying homeward. Cecily submerged herself in the crowd, admiring the painstaking attention to accuracy and the highly realistic representation of the artist, Lady Elizabeth Butler, but she could not understand why Mr. Fogwell would refer her to this particular work. As she stood before it, she heard snatches of conversation ranging from "The sole survivor of Jellalabad, you know" to "She actually interviewed the old fellow—" and gradually changing to "Oh, look, it's her, the one in the—"

"She certainly is a looker!" which latter comments Cecily slowly understood were being made about her.

Again with cheeks flaming she hastened into the next gallery, only to see before her Mrs. Fluster, with Baby by her side, regaling a host of friends and admirers in front of the large portrait Mr. Sheridan had painted of her and her daughter.

"Oh, yes, he's a most spiritual man!" she was saying to a thin, bony woman in a crimson-velvet dress. "So perceptively utter, if you know what I mean!"

"He has certainly captured the extraordinary ethereality obvious in both mother and child," said this crimson-clothed art critic.

"Oh, you think so!" shrieked Mrs. Fluster. "How clever of you to notice! Yes, dear Amaryllis is a most remarkable Baby. I have been superintending her daily instruction and she has shown a remarkable capacity for the Arts. I fear she will be just like her Mother!"

Cecily hurried past and might have gone unnoticed if it were not for Amaryllis who let go of her mother's skirt and fled to Cecily.

"Why, it's her!" exclaimed the woman in the crimson dress. She applied her *lorgnon* hastily to the bridge of her nose and looked Cecily up and down thoroughly. "Isn't that astounding? A bit more red in the hair perhaps and the eyes are not so light—"

Cecily began to feel that the whole world had gone mad. What on earth was the woman talking about? Mrs. Fluster's angry remarks as she wrested Baby away from Cecily were reassuring by their very normality.

"One never knows the sort of servants one gets these days. Actually sneaking around behind my back with that artist. Don't think that I don't know about it, Miss Hawthorne! I'm surprised you dare to show your face here!

Still it was not pleasant to have Mrs. Fluster's loud denunciations added to the unusual attention she was already receiving. No one in the gallery made any pretence of doing anything other than watching her with avid interest.

She turned and fled, hoping to find an exit through the next door. Instead she found a small chamber crowded with Art patrons who were grouped around a large painting in a gilt frame in a place of prominence on the end wall. Thinking she could escape notice (for some of the oglers from the other gallery had actually followed her), she plunged herself into this throng and soon was washed up directly before the picture.

To her amazement she saw that it was the portrait of herself as Pandora that Mr. Sheridan had begun while she was residing at Swan Walk. No wonder she had been the object of such interest for it was a wonderfully realistic representation.

Her golden-red hair fell about her shoulders with a thousand sparking highlights, her hazel eyes were wide with astonishment, her soft lips slightly parted, the amber gown clothing and yet not concealing her charms. Yet where there should have been a gold box and a cloud of spirits escaping, there were only her outstretched hands, reaching out as if to embrace the viewer and draw him into the frame. It was a startling concept, one that made every individual who saw it feel as if he or she had been drawn into a loving and affectionate embrace.

A large golden nameplate was affixed to the bottom of the frame, and Cecily bent to read it to learn if Devin had continued to call it "Pandora" despite the lack of props. The crowd parted before her, as if they were the Red Sea. Murmurs and whispers grew louder on each side as she, at length, was the only one before the painting, the cynosure of all eyes.

"Wonderful likeness!" said someone.

"A most beautiful young woman!" said a gentleman.

"He's a lucky dog, indeed," seconded another.

"Think of it! How romantic! An artist and his model," whispered a lady.

Cecily heard them not at all. For she was reading over and over again, with her heart beating madly, and one hand pressed against her lips, the inscription on the nameplate: "To the Wife of My Heart."

She turned, feeling a trifle unsteady, seeing the patrons of the show reeling about her on both sides, and caught the dark, mysterious eyes of Devin Sheridan who lurked on the other side of the room. He held out his arms and, with a little cry, she ran into them. The Royal Academy visitors applauded with vigour as his lips fastened hungrily upon hers, but neither of them was aware of anything outside the circle of their arms.

END

About the Author

NANCY FITZGERALD learned to write at about the same time she learned to type—at the age of eight. One saga, composed when she was twelve, grew to three hundred pages before she lost interest.

She wrote her first novel, *St. John's Wood*, while working at the Los Angeles Museum of Art, researching the book as she rode the bus, back and forth to work. She began teaching novel writing through the UCLA Writers Program, with her friend and colleague, Ellen Pall, shortly after her novel was published by Doubleday.

In 1980, she moved to Seattle with her young daughter, changed her name to Waverly and continued to teach writing, for the University of Washington and Seattle Central Community College.

After publishing three novels with Doubleday and one with Jove, she took a long break from novel writing, focusing instead on non-fiction writing about seasonal holidays and natural time. Her book, *Slow Time: Recovering the Natural Rhythm of Life*, was published in 2009.

When she began writing novels again, she took up the mystery novel. Waverly wrote one series featuring a female Seattle PI and then co-wrote a series of humorous mystery novels, featuring a talking Chihuahua, with her friend and colleague, Curt Colbert, under the name Waverly Curtis. The first book in that series is *Dial C for Chihuahua* and was published by Kensington in 2012.

She currently teaches online for *Creative Nonfiction* magazine and Hugo House, the literary arts center in Seattle. Her most recent novel, Queen of Shadows, is also set in Victorian London.

Learn more at http://www.waverlyfitzgerald.com.